MAN
Inn
TROUBLE

A French Country Inn Murder Mystery

A Novel by

CLYDE DEIGHTON

Clyde Deighton

Penny Loafer Press, L.L.C.

Published in the United States by Penny Loafer Press LLC.

Lake Geneva, Wisconsin.

www.pennyloaferpress.com

Book Cover Design by Holly Leiter

ISBN 978-0692-92128-9

Printed in the United States.

No beavers were harmed during the writing of this book.

Kathleen, Marie Charlotte, AJ, Justin
and the apples of my eye Dominic and Luca

AUTHOR'S NOTE

The French Country Inn really exists. Physical descriptions in this book are based on the actual inn.

Chapter One

CHICAGO, ILLINOIS

A roldis Gonzales Garcia sat in his favorite red leather chair and smoked a private-blend, "Double-G," hand-rolled Cuban cigar. The six-inch-long, four-millimeter-wide corona was made to exact specifications in a tobacco factory in El Vedado, not far from the barrio where he'd grown up as a tough muchacho in the streets of Havana.

Each of the cigars had been hand rolled on the inner thigh of a virgin Cuban mujer, exactly to his specifications, a feat not so easily achieved in the free-spirited modern Cuban culture. His power, wealth, and position of importance afforded him the ability to demand, purchase, or simply take, without fear of retribution, anything that he desired—and that included mere trifles such as a hand-rolled cigar, a beautiful woman, or more ominously, a human life.

He handled the cigar as if it were nothing more than a prop, rather than the personal indulgence that he enjoyed four times a day. He flicked the cigar between his thumb and forefinger as he sullenly listened to Santo Sotto, his childhood friend and now the second-in-command of Gonzales Garcia's Chicago empire.

"Everything is planned, Ari. Right down to the last, minute detail, I assure you. Just the way you asked," explained Sotto, or the General El Tercero, as his minions referred to him.

Only El Tercero and Aroldis's own mother called him—or were allowed to call him—by his childhood moniker, Ari. All others respectfully referred to him as Señor, Mister, or El Hombre.

Sotto and Gonzales Garcia had grown up together in the same Havana neighborhood. In their early days they had been equals, but as years passed, through toughness and a willingness to take risks, Gonzales Garcia had emerged as the leader of the two. As teenagers, they had arrived in Miami as part of the Mariel boatlift, and soon they made their way to Chicago. Before long, their tentacles had woven their way into every type of illicit activity, sucking money and power from less powerful men and street gangs.

As Aroldis Gonzales Garcia's strength grew, his conscience diminished. He had become the undisputed leader of crime in Chicago. The once-equal Santo Sotto was no longer a peer, and despite their longtime roots and familiarity, he feared the crime boss to the same degree that his own subordinates feared him as second-in-command. He was deeply aware that if he did not perform the deed in the manner delegated to him, his fate would be sealed.

"Are you sure, my friend? Is everything in motion, for all three?"

"Yes, Ari, as we agreed. Patrona will be the most difficult one, but if we are lucky, it will happen as I have planned."

"Lucky? I do not like that word. I prefer confidence and ability. One should never rely on luck to achieve one's goals."

"But Ari, your specifications were much too complicated. We could have ensured success if you had given us a simpler plan."

"Tell me all about it, my friend? What part of the plan do you see as the problem?" Ari asked of his second-in-command. From lack of effort the cigar no longer contained the bright ember, but it still remained in the boss's mouth. Almost inaudibly he asked exactly how and when his requested deeds would transpire.

"I do not think it wise for me to inform you of the time and details, Señor. You may need what our political friends like to call 'plausible deniability.' It is best you know nothing. But to answer your questions: When? Very soon. How? Up close, the way you demand. And very, very personal."

Chapter Two

CHICAGO, ILLINOIS

In a Greystone apartment on Chicago's West Side, a tall, thin, Black man dressed in a broad-pinstriped, poly-wool sport coat burst out of a back bedroom and announced that he was bored.

"I'm goin' out. I'm tired of sittin' in this rat trap with you two dicks. I'm goin' down to Boss Martin's and havin' a drink, either with you two or without," said Leon Du Perles as he adjusted the collar of his red silk shirt over the lapels of the sport jacket.

The "two dicks," as Leon referred to them, were two Chicago police officers named Mike Williams and Herman Durkin respectively. Their challenge was to keep Leon alive long enough for him to give testimony before a grand jury.

Leon's erratic behavior and devil-may-care lifestyle made their job more difficult. And now, after spending day and night with him, listening to his ignorant rants, political conspiracy theories, and impossible demands, the two officers began to secretly hope that Leon would meet a grisly demise. But their professionalism would not allow even a tinge of that desire to affect their behavior, or the mission.

Officer Williams pleaded his case: "You know going out on the town is a very bad idea, Leon. Rolling the dice in a fixed crap game is stupid, and you have a lot more to lose than money." Williams was a stocky, forty-something, wide-shouldered man, who had been playing a game of solitaire on the dining room table.

"There's no talking sense into this dumb Democrat. Call for the squad car," his partner responded. He was also in his forties, but much leaner and taller than his partner. Durkin, a longtime Chicago police officer, always referred to African Americans as "Democrats" because of the race's undying allegiance to the political party.

"He is who he is, and he is going to do what he does," Durkin continued. He turned to speak to Leon. "God gave you a lot of courage, but he sure shorted you on brains."

Never bothering, or perhaps not wanting to learn the names of the revolving corps of Chicago cops, Leon simply called each of them Mac.

"Hey Mac," said Leon, "I ain't gonna let no greasy Cuban spic run my life. If the City of Chicago and the State of Illinois wants my cooperation, then it has to be on my terms. I set the rules, I go where I want to go, see whatever sons of bitches I wants to see, and eat and drink whatever and whenever I wants to. You understand me, Mac?"

Leon looked at the other officer, Williams, the broad-shouldered one, hoping he had made his point and that there would not be another argument about his freedom to do anything he pleased and go anywhere he chose.

Leon's innate stupidity and arrogance were why he was here in his West Side apartment in the first place. The State's Attorney's Office and the Chicago Police Department had been entrusted with the protection of their primary witness, and they had originally wanted him to stay elsewhere. They'd intended to relocate him to a suburban safe house, a place known only to a select few. But Leon, a man who believed he was invincible, would not agree. He'd only agreed to the protective custody if he could stay in his own home. Freedom of movement throughout his neighborhood was also a stipulation.

When told of the protection order parameters that had been thrust upon them, Officer Williams had asked: "Why not also request that we set a table in the sight of his enemies?"

Williams was also an African American, and he despised every-thing that Leon Du Perles represented: ignorance, amorality, no respect for person or property of others. To him, Leon was simply a piece of Black trash whose blight shone badly on every hardworking, respect-able, and well-educated person of color like himself.

Despite his hatred of the man, the officer would do what he was paid to do: protect the life of Leon "The Black Pearl" Du Perles. He would protect this piece of dirt long enough for him to give tes-timony against one of Chicago's most notorious drug lords—Aroldis Gonzales Garcia.

The two officers checked their service revolvers and adjusted their Kevlar vests.

"Listen to me, Leon. Put this on. It's for your own good." Williams offered Leon a vest of his own, but he declined.

Durkin said, "Don't waste your breath. This cocky Democrat thinks he's bulletproof and believes the gods of good luck will keep him safe."

The three men exited the apartment just as the squad car pulled up to the building entrance. The officer on the passenger side carried a 12-gauge shotgun in his hands. His eyes darted east, then north. The driver had his service revolver readied at his right side. Tonight, Leon had decided to be chauffeured the two blocks to his favorite neighbor-hood bar; he and his bodyguards eased themselves into the backseat of the squad car, Leon strategically placed in the middle.

Boss Martin's, their destination on this particular night, was considered a classic drinking establishment and eatery in this old, near-West Side neighborhood that was quickly becoming gentrified by the influx of young, middle-class professionals. It served cold, tap-drawn PBR and the tastiest chicken wings and hamburgers in all of Chicago.

Leon had been a patron of the tavern ever since he, his Grand-mamma, and his seven siblings had moved to the neighborhood, long before anyone ever coined the term "gentrification" to describe the transformation of a blighted community. At that time, many years ago, the neighborhood had been filled with junkies, pimps, whores, and street toughs. Leon had cut his teeth on the cruel streets of this area and had lived there until this day. He would often say, even before he entered police protection, "I grew up here, and I'm gonna die here too. Maybe right here in front of Boss Martin's."

He had eaten so many orders of Boss's delicious, deep-fried-in-duck-fat chicken wings with a handsome side of French fries that no one would have been surprised if Leon had keeled over from a heart attack brought on by clogged arteries and a cholesterol count well over three hundred.

Tonight, however, Leon wasn't at Boss Martin's to eat or drink; he was at the tavern to prove that his life would not be dictated by fear. Not just any old common variety of fear, such as being afraid of spiders, or a phobia, like the fear of open or closed spaces. He had to prove that he feared no man, even if it was a man whose very name and reputation inspired hesitance in the bravest of men.

Leon had been the street enforcer for Gonzales Garcia's crime syndicate. He liked to brag, "I'm the Black Pearl and Chicago is my oyster." He'd started as a petty gofer and worked his way up from bag man for the pushers and pimps to liaison among Gonzales Garcia, and the other drug lords. In the Black community, Leon was feared by all, friends and foes alike.

Although the chronology didn't match, Leon had always claimed that, long before the Johnny Cash ballad was written, he had once "killed a man just to watch him die." But no one ever dared to question his wild boasts.

Relentlessly and with impunity, he meted out justice as directed by his bosses. He knew where the bodies were buried because he'd been the one who'd buried them there. This knowledge would make him incredibly valuable in the upcoming trial, and it was the reason the police department had so thoroughly acquiesced to his conditions for protective custody.

Before Leon could enter the bar, two of the police officers entered the premises and swept through the inside, checking the restrooms, broom closet, kitchen area, and main barroom. Fortunately, this evening the clientele was sparse, and the officers breathed a collective sigh of relief. One officer moved to bolt the rear door, and the other exited to inform his partners that it was safe to enter.

With the squad car parked in front of the building, two policemen standing sentry at the main entrance, the other two officers inside the bar itself, Leon felt invincible, and his words and swagger did not belie the fact. He bragged to the bar patrons, "I'm so important, and my ass so valuable that the government assigned four bodyguards to protect me. Ain't nobody going to mess with me."

He looked at Jeremiah Shane, perched upon his usual barstool near the front door, and said, "My posse could take you even on your best night."

Shane was Boss Martin's famed bouncer—225 pounds of pure muscle and hostility. If any type of fisticuffs broke out, Shane quickly put an end to it, usually with only a stare or a verbal threat. Back when the area was still mostly segregated, he would escort the occasional white patron to his vehicle to ensure that no neighborhood street thugs would treat one of Boss's guests with anything less than genuine hospitality. The police had run a background check on Shane, as they had on a number of the local high-profile individuals. Shane was clean: a former semi-pro football player, ex-military man. They were cautious around him, but they believed he would be no threat to Leon.

Leon Du Perles insisted that he would not testify against Aroldis Gonzales Garcia if it meant being holed up in a safe house, far from his beloved neighborhood, having no right to come and go as he pleased. He loved the West Side, its bars and stores and the barbershop where he had his "fro" straightened every two weeks. His modest apartment was his castle, even though his nefarious skills had afforded him the ability to live a better life in a fine condominium in a more upscale district. The West Side—at least the old one—defined Leon. He and the neighborhood were gritty, tough, and world-wise, even though the area itself was changing, and Leon had rarely left the confines of Chicago.

He downed his third brandy and seltzer water, removed his hand from the gelatinous rear end of Yolanda Payne, and announced that he wanted to return home. Leon grabbed a package filled with a dozen chicken drumettes from atop the bar. Duck fat penetrated through the brown paper bag, and Leon licked the thick suet off the tips of his fingers.

"Mmm," he said. "I can't wait to get home and eat these babies."

Despite his stated desire to get home in a hurry, Leon argued with the officers when they insisted that Leon return home in the squad car. The more they argued, the more Leon became entrenched in his desire to walk the two blocks to his apartment. The broad-shouldered officer wished he had insisted that Leon walk home; then, he would have been sure that the contrarian Leon would want to ride in the squad car.

The three men on foot, followed by the two officers in the squad, moved deliberately in the direction of Leon's apartment. Their collective eyes searched the doors and nooks and alleyways. Leon, by contrast, strutted as though he were on parade, in his finest suit with boutonnière, walking home after Easter services. They were only yards from their destination when Williams elbowed Durkin in the ribs.

"Is that someone over there?" He moved his head sideways to indicate the direction he wanted his partner to look.

"It's nothing, looks like a couple making out," Durkin said.

"I shouldda axed you guys if you wanted anything to eat when we were at Boss's," Leon lamented. "With the government paying, I wouldn't have cared what you had ordered, even if it was—"

Before Leon could finish his sentence, an unnoticed steel door opened quickly and snatched Leon from the phalanx of the two men who were on foot. Both were tased before they had a chance to lift their service revolvers from their sides. The heavy steel door was closed shut and double locked behind Leon. The two abductors quickly slit Leon's throat from ear to ear. Leon fell to the ground as blood oozed from his severed carotid artery, the same way the duck fat oozed out of the brown paper bag, which remained clutched in his left hand.

By the time the other officers had exited the squad car and blown the hinges off the strong steel door with the shotgun, Leon had already bled to death, and the two perpetrators had left the building, moving swiftly through a maze of hallways and out a rear service entrance into a waiting getaway car.

In his battle with Aroldis Gonzales Garcia, the cocky, arrogant, but likeable Leon Du Perles had lost. He would not testify against his former boss. He would not tell the grand jury how the money was laundered, the times he'd heard the Cuban order the killing of his enemies, and how the organization of drugs, prostitution, and illegal activities worked. He would not testify which politicians had been bribed and which police officials were on the payroll.

In a pool of blood and duck fat, the body of the "Black Pearl" lay on the pavement in the neighborhood that he called his oyster.

Once again, Aroldis Gonzales Garcia had triumphed over one who had betrayed him.

Chapter Three

Geneva, Wisconsin

It was a pleasant and calm morning up here in Walworth County, Wisconsin, just the way I liked it. If someone crawled inside of my head, they would probably say that I spend too much time daydreaming, but calling what I do daydreaming might be a bit of a misnomer. That word has a connotation similar to fantasizing, like maybe thinking about how I would spend 100 million dollars once I cashed in my winning Power Ball lottery ticket.

What I do falls more in the category of reminiscing. I think about the good old days, which usually, upon closer scrutiny, weren't really that good after all. My favorite recollections are about the years I spent in Catholic school, both elementary and secondary, and my years as an officer with the Chicago Police Department. Collectively, they were the best of times and the worst of times, but with a lot less Charles Dickens and far more Stephen King.

While I've recently been thinking a lot about my days as a Chicago cop, I am currently the Chief of Police in the town of Geneva, a rural hamlet in southeast Wisconsin about 90 miles northwest of the second-to-none Second City. It is a position I hope to remain in for years to come. I've lived here for several years now—I moved up here after finishing my time in the Chicago PD.

It was my quest for peace and solitude that propelled my decision to become a full-time resident of a town that I'd spent countless summers in as a youth. Chicago had become tiresome. It was too noisy and too corrupt, hectic and corrupt, crowded and... did I say corrupt?

Personally, the city makes me jittery and nervous. Rural Wisconsin is more my cup of chamomile tea. It soothes my soul and relaxes my bones. With the exception of last winter's murder at the French Country Inn, life has been calm, likewise my demeanor.

"The murder," as everyone refers to it, took place last January during a writers' workshop at the French Country Inn. The murderess, Greta Olsen, knocked off her best friend, Chandra Harper, tried to frame the dastardly deed on the head chef at Kirsch's Restaurant, and then, using her beguiling charm and my presumed naiveté, set me up as her alibi. Money was the motive; Chandra Harper had plenty of it, and Greta wanted it for her own. Her husband, Hector Harper, was Greta's pawn in the whole scheme.

The murder upset the town and the county, but normalcy has since returned to Geneva. By normalcy, I mean that there has not been another murder. I don't mean to imply or infer that my little berg is normal. There are simply too many odd fellows residing herein to say we are "normal" in the true sense of the word. I just mean to say it's normal because no one has been murdered recently. In fact, except for a couple of burglaries, nothing much has happened up here for the past several months.

And nothing happened last night either; now it is almost dawn. I've been killing the last vestiges of the night shift by thinking about a few of the guys I used to work with in the 18th district: Dave Tedeski, Theo Boycek, and Rory O'Quinn, just to name a few. Dave Tedeski has been dead and buried for nearly three years now, and I hadn't heard from any of the others for quite some time. I wondered what they were up to, and, divorces aside, if life has been good to them. They all occupied a special place in my heart, as I presumably did likewise in theirs. If a situation arose and I was in trouble, even though I hadn't seen them in years, I knew I could call on them and they would be available to do whatever I asked of them. I too could ask the same of any of them in return. We used to be as thick as thieves, which really wasn't the best metaphor to use when you were a member of the same law enforcement community.

Once upon a time, the meager budget for the town of Geneva did not afford the Chief of Police the luxury of not having to work an eight-hour patrol shift; it was necessary and mandatory to meet the bottom line. Now times have changed. I work a patrol shift out of habit and as an example to my officers, and I still work the night shift two times a month because I like the peace and quiet of the wee hours of the morn.

I had one cup of coffee left in my Thermos, and I poured it into my travel mug. It was still piping hot. From under the driver's seat I pulled out a small metal flask and dropped a few ounces of brandy into the mug. It was strictly a pick-me-up after the boredom of the long night. Even though I was the Chief of Police, I would occasionally have a drink while on duty. I knew I shouldn't, I wasn't proud of it, and I was fully aware of the consequences if my infraction were to come to light.

My reasoning was simple: if Winston Churchill could drink on the job—he reportedly drank a quart of Scotch each and every day— then who was to say I shouldn't have a nip or two after a long night? Churchill drank while Prime Minister of England and Minister of Defence during WWII, and his duties far outweighed mine. He did a fine job while downing a quart a day. Like Churchill, I am always on duty; therefore I figured I should be allowed to have a drink whenever and wherever I chose without the least worry of retribution.

I decided to place all comparison with the great Englishman aside while I sipped my coffee with brandy in anticipation of the great event that was about to unfold: the moment when night became day.

Ernest Hemingway described the morning sunrise as having "true light." It was the time of day when the light was the most accurate, a time when the morning sun made every detail more stunning, more exact; a time when even the shadows were well defined.

The great writer and outdoorsman was speaking in terms of hunting; the moment when the light was at its best for the hunter to view and stalk its prey. But for me, the true light of the morning was the best time to observe nature, and autumn was the truest season of the four.

A red-tailed hawk hovered high above the ground, perhaps searching for a field mouse to assuage its morning hunger. I wondered how much more acute the bird's eyesight was than my own. A much higher degree, I was sure, especially on those mornings when my eyes were dry and bloodshot from a night of drinking too much alcohol.

As quickly as night transcended into day, I became miffed with myself for allowing my bad habit to intrude upon a rare moment of tranquility and reflection on nature. How and why do I allow my mood to change so quickly? I asked myself. Why do I allow negative thoughts to cloud an otherwise beautiful time of clarity and introspection?

I wished that a few rays of Hemingway's "true light" would penetrate the dark, hidden recesses of my inscrutable brain and bring a waterfall of clarity to my thought process. I was sure that would not occur.

As I began to sink deeper into the waters of self-loathing, a life preserver in a form of a telephone call was tossed in my direction. It was Dorothy at the stationhouse.

"Mornin' Chief."

"Good morning, Dorothy," I droned.

"What's wrong, Chief? You sound down."

"Nothing's wrong. Simply tired from the long shift."

I wasn't really tired, and Dorothy had been correct when she recognized the subtlety in my three-word response. I pulled myself together and changed the tone in my voice.

"What's up, Dorothy? Nothing serious, I hope."

"Mrs. Martel called. She wants to talk to you. Says it's important, and asks that you call her at your earliest possible convenience."

"How long ago did she call?"

"I just hung up with her now." Her voice changed, and I knew she was about to deliver a choice piece of gossip. "Did you know Jonah Junior is about to—"

I cut her short. "Not now, Dot. Is it about Jonah Junior or Jonah Senior?"

"Not sure, Chief. She didn't say."

"Text me her number and I'll call her on my way back to the station."

I didn't phone Jerri Martel. I was only a couple of miles from the Martel farm and chose instead to pay her a personal visit rather than give her an impersonal phone call.

The Martel spread was almost one-hundred acres of prime Wisconsin land. Fifty acres or so were tillable, and a two-acre cranberry bog rested on the south end. The rest was timberlands and thicket. Northwick Creek weaved back and forth across the east acreage of the property like an imperfect seam on a pair of home-stitched trousers.

As I approached their house, I could see Jerri tending to her vegetable garden not more than a couple of dozen yards from her front porch. When she noticed me as I approached the garden, she said, "Dang it, Chief, you didn't have to drive all the way over here. I only asked Dorothy for you to telephone."

"I was nearby, just a couple of miles away, so I thought we could talk in person."

"That's mighty nice of you, Chief. Very thoughtful. It's Jonah that I want to talk to you about."

Jerri turned her back to me and picked up a hand sickle whose edge was stuck in a tree stump. She bent over, and with one quick swipe of the blade cut through an 18-inch high cluster of rhubarb, drove the edge of the instrument back into the tree stump, and gathered up the stalks into her arms, all with a single motion. With her faded, long skirt girded above the knees and a babushka holding back her hair, she resembled a peasant farm worker in tsarist Russia, one with a certain degree of agility and spryness.

"Looks like you've done that a few times before," I said. With the sickle only an arm's length away, I thought it best not to mention that she resembled a Russian peasant.

"Garden's my passion. Been doin' it for years."

Together we walked to the front porch and sat in a pair of weathered Adirondack rocking chairs. "Chief, I wonder if you would talk to Jonah about something that's botherin' him.

"Junior or senior?" I interrupted.

"Senior, of course. Junior never been a problem."

"That's because he's not a teenager yet." We both laughed.

"No, it's Senior. Please have a talk with him. Use some of that country reasonability you're so good with. I'm worried he's going to do something real stupid, and there might be some consequences."

"What kind of consequences you talking about, Jerri?"

She moved her jaw from side to side. If she were a man I would have expected a chaw of tobacco to come flying out.

"A killing," she said. "I'm worried about a killing."

Chapter Four

Chicago, Illinois

In Chicago's 33rd ward—which resembled the suburbs more than part of a large city—a man walked his two German Shepherd dogs across the street from a modest, bi-level, brick home. The Budlong Woods area was only five or six miles from Leon Du Perles's West Side neighborhood, but in appearance it was worlds apart. Broad lawns, well-kept homes, and clean streets defined Budlong Woods.

It was the longtime neighborhood of Celia Jaynes.

Celia Jaynes was skilled with numbers, adept at maintaining two complete sets of accounting ledgers and balance sheets, a master of disguising and transferring large amounts of cash, and the financial consort to Chicago's most notorious crime syndicate boss.

She was trustworthy and boundlessly loyal to the man who had made her rich beyond her dreams. But her loyalty had ended when the prosecutors at the Cook County State's Attorney's office threatened her with indictment on numerous racketeering charges, including money laundering. She agreed to become a witness for the prosecution, and was placed under house arrest. Like Leon Du Perles, she had placed a condition that custody would be at her Budlong Woods home, a home that she had transformed over the years into a virtual fortress, with reinforced doors, an alarm system, and an impenetrable panic room in the event of a home invasion.

In front of Celia's home stood two uniformed Chicago police officers, another two on duty at the rear entrance. A third detail in a squad car circled the block every several minutes and then returned to its position on the corner of Troy and Cullom Streets, with the front end of the vehicle facing the Jaynes residence. There were large signs on each end of the block of Cullum Street, declaring "Local Traffic Only." Sawhorses prevented pedestrian traffic from crossing in front and to the side of the well-guarded home.

Twice daily for the past several years, an old man walked his pet dogs Shemp and Moe to the neighborhood park. James Hoenig, a retired schoolteacher, wore a Cubs baseball cap and a White Sox windbreaker rain or shine; he was a rare Chicago fan who liked both major league baseball teams. He always took the same path to Wilton Park, which led him past Celia Jaynes' bi-level; that is, he had taken the same route until the police moved in and politely asked the old gentleman not to proceed directly in front of the house they were guarding.

Since then, to and from the park, Jacob walked the dogs on the opposite side of the street, always offering the officers a friendly wave and a tip of the brim of the Cubs hat. On his return home, he clutched a plastic bag filled with his dogs' business that he had scooped up from the grass. His background, as well as all of the residents' backgrounds in the surrounding vicinity of Celia Jaynes' home, had been vetted by the police department's advance team.

Even Shemp and Moe had been checked out: "Old and docile," read the reports.

This late afternoon, two unmarked black police vehicles pulled up to the side drive of the Jaynes house. The driver of the first pushed the remote control door opener and entered the two-car attached garage and then closed the door behind him. Chicago Police Detective Armand Depke left the vehicle with Celia Jaynes close behind. Once the pair was safely inside the home with the door securely latched, the detective turned the garage light off and on, signaling to the driver that it was all right for him to leave the premises.

Depke had a routine: Celia would remain on the first floor while the detective went upstairs. He would first check the two spare bedrooms, one of which had been converted to his sleeping quarters, and then he would inspect Celia's master suite. He drew open the window drapes and inspected the front yard, eyeballing first the officer, located at the front door, and then the police car, parked on the corner. If the squad car was circling the block, Depke would remain at the upstairs window and wait the few minutes until the vehicle returned.

On the return visit from Wilton Park, on this particular day, the old man with the two German Shepherd dogs approached the house, but was still a distance away from the structure. The squad car had left only seconds ago for its routine ride through the neighborhood. One of the two policemen near the front door held his left hand out to signal James Hoenig to halt.

"Mr. Hoenig, please move to the other side of the street and—"

Before the officer could finish his sentence, the old man flung the plastic bag, seemingly filled with dog droppings, at the feet of the two officers, who were now side by side. A cloud of smoke and caustic vapors filled the air, sending the duo to their knees in excruciating pain and temporary blindness.

The man—who clearly was not old, and clearly not James Hoenig—tossed a small explosive device in front of the home which, upon impact, shattered the large picture window. The first dog leapt through the window, and with precision, proceeded up the staircase to address Detective Depke, who had drawn his gun to no avail. Unlike the real Shemp and Moe, this dog was neither old nor docile; he clamped his fangs down around Depke's arm and then twisted his body, pulling the two-hundred-plus-pound officer off his feet and into a brutal fight with the canine. Seconds after the dog's entrance came the man, followed by the second dog at his heels.

Celia Jaynes screamed in terror. She was now face-to-face with a hired assassin, and she was looking death squarely in the eye. The withering sounds of pain from the two blinded officers in front and the growling dog entangled in a deadly dance with the detective were hardly noticeable to the middle-aged woman. With speed and agility, the killer flung open a finely-honed barber's razor and split Celia's throat wide open in a similar fashion to Leon Du Perles', only Celia's wound was deeper and more gruesome.

One of the dogs stood guard at the rear door, waiting for the two officers in the rear of the home to enter, but they never did. Upon hearing the cries of their fellow officers and the noise from the percussion bomb that shattered the front window, they broke rank and proceeded around the home to the front entrance. This breech of protection protocol allowed the killer's escape to go easier than planned. While the dog stood at attention, awaiting his unfulfilled assignment, the razor-wielding killer fled alone through the rear door, out across the back yard, and into the approaching nightfall.

The entire deadly attack had taken only seven short minutes, faster than most of the dress rehearsals and numerous training sessions that had been acted out in a vacant warehouse, where a scale-model facade of the Jaynes residence had been reproduced.

Alive, but bleeding badly, Detective Depke gathered his wits and wrapped his damaged arm in a kitchen towel. The substitute German Shepherds were shot dead, and Depke raced across the street to James Hoenig's home. With his recovered service revolver in his hand, he kicked open the front door, aiming his size-11 shoe squarely at the door handle. Inside was another gruesome discovery: while old man Hoenig was alive, his hogtied body lay next to the lifeless corpses of his beloved Shemp and Moe.

"Routine," El Tercero liked to say, "It is the road that leads to the end of those who follow its path." It was the seemingly banal routine of Jaynes and Depke that had allowed General El Tercero to plot the demise of the key informant in the manner his boss desired.

El Hombre wanted not only to kill his enemies, he wanted to make a statement in doing so. And indeed he had.

Chapter Five

Geneva, Wisconsin

It was 8:15 a.m., and the graveyard shift I'd just completed had caught up with me. I glanced over at the bundle of rhubarb Jerri had given me. Rhubarb, to me, fell in the same category as asparagus, beets, and green beans. It was a food I disliked as a young lad, but now I love to eat it. My mother often baked rhubarb pie when I was a kid, adding strawberries into the filling: I wouldn't touch them as a child; now I crave 'em.

My talk with Jerri Martel had been brief. She'd explained the situation that had gotten her husband into such a snit that she was worried he'd commit a felony over it. She pleaded with me, asking that I take a look at the problem and intervene, more as a friend than an officer of the law. Even though I was getting tired, I agreed to drive down to the opposite end of the farm to see for myself. Situations such as these didn't arise every day, especially in Geneva.

Following her directions, I drove east and then north up a narrow dirt and gravel road that funneled down into more of a broad pathway than a road. It was bumpy, overgrown, and rutted, and made the Jeep feel as if it were lacking shock absorbers. I wouldn't dare maneuver this pathway in anything less than an SUV. According to his wife, Jonah usually took his ATV when he went up to this part of the farm.

I had driven for what seemed like miles, and was concerned that I might no longer be on Martel property, but I thought the ruggedness of the property had perhaps given me a false sense of distance.

The road narrowed even more, and I considered parking the vehicle and traveling on foot, but then, in the distance, I could see a clearing and a wider path. I was now in the glen that Jerri had described.

To the north lay a groomed farm tract owned by gentleman farmer named Jason Orleans. A white equine fence separated his farm from the Martel spread. Beyond was a pumpkin patch, perhaps three acres or so. The acreage around the patch was manicured and well groomed, unlike the rest of the property I had just navigated, which was raw and in a state of overgrown vegetation. Northwick Creek meandered through the Martel property here, then abruptly cut east and circled north into the neighbor's spread. It disappeared far in the distance, over and through a ravine.

I looked at what I thought was the boundary line between the two properties and saw the problem just as Jerri had described it to me. Along a crescent-shaped parcel formed by the arcing Northwick Creek, a beaver had built a dam, flooding the road that lead to the western portion of Jonah Martel's property. The water was too deep to drive a vehicle through and too wide to build a bridge across without great expense. The western parcel of Jonah's land was now rendered useless by the beaver, and inaccessible, except by canoe or other watercraft. On the other side of the beaver-made pond, there was a small cabin that couldn't be more than twelve feet long by twelve feet wide. Beyond the cabin, not more than ten yards away from the side entrance, was an outhouse, replete with the mandatory quarter-moon-shaped slot in the door.

Jerri Martel had told me the little spot was Jonah's retreat house, a quiet place where her husband could visit nature when he needed to get away from civilization. It had a wood stove, water from an old-fashioned hand pump, and all the comforts of a pioneer log cabin. Most of all, it had no modern conveniences. When the mood hit him, Jonah often holed up there for days on end, fishing and game hunting. Now, because of a damn beaver dam, he'd been denied easy access to his spot of tranquility.

I walked up and down the creek and perused the beaver dam. I was at a loss for ideas, and the tiredness from the all-night shift drifted over me like a shadow of doom. I took a folding chair from the back of the Jeep and positioned it on a mound that allowed me a view of the surrounding landscape. I zipped my jacket to the neck to ward off the morning chill.

To my right was the gentleman farmer's pumpkin patch and gentle rolling hillsides; to my left spread the natural, rustic beauty of Jonah and Jerri's farm. Straight ahead lay the deep pond formed by the beaver's handiwork. It was as if I were seated in a Norman Rockwell painting, if, of course, the great artist had painted landscapes instead of the pastoral vignettes of small town people. I thought I saw a beaver poke his head above the water just as my eyes closed and I drifted asleep.

Minutes later I was awakened by a swarm of gnats that flickered about my face—or perhaps it was the annoying sound of sloshing water I could hear in the distance. Thirty yards or more from my prone vantage point I could see a figure—who was not Jonah Junior or Senior—traipsing up the middle of Northwick Creek. The water rose from shin bone deep to above his thigh the closer he got to the beaver dam.

Realizing the water was growing deeper, the man exited the stream and walked alongside the bank; he then became startled by my presence in the folding chair.

"How are you?" he asked.

"Just fine," I answered.

"You the county sheriff?"

"No, the town's chief of police."

"What brings you over here?" he asked.

"Simply enjoying a moment of solitude after working the graveyard shift," I said. I hated answering questions about my behavior, and usually I simply ignored the request, but for some reason I answered before I could muster up a satirical retort.

"How about you? What are you doin' up here?" I asked.

"I'm sorry. Let me introduce myself. I'm Harland Bevis. I'm with the Wisconsin DNR, the Department of Natural Resources." He held out the official-looking state ID from the lanyard that hung around his neck.

I decided not to mention that, around here, because of their unreasonable intrusion on property rights, most people claimed DNR stood for "Damn Near Russia."

He asked, "Are you here about the problem created by the beaver dam?"

"No, I'm just visiting," I lied. "What about the beaver? What are you talking about?"

Field Administrator Harland Bevis proceeded to explain in bureaucratic bleepspeak the details surrounding the conflict involving Jonah Martel, the gentleman farmer neighbor to the north, and the beaver. Just as he had begun to describe the part about the threats made by the "owner of the property of parcel A," as if on cue by a predetermined script, Jonah himself arrived, brandishing a 12-gauge shotgun. He had the look of an angry man, and foolishly I leapt from my chair and placed myself in harm's way, directly between Bevis and the fast-approaching Jonah Martel.

I grabbed Jonah by his arm and steered him away from the DNR Administrator, removed the shotgun from his grip, and leaned it against the crotch of a small river birch tree. Jonah was compliant, but a look of anger distorted his face. I wasn't sure if Jonah brandished the gun out of a desire to shoot the beaver or the nerdy bureaucrat.

"How much tax does that beaver pay?" Jonah yelled at Bevis. "Is it the beaver's tax dollars that pay your salary, or are they mine?

"Section 5B of the Wisconsin ordinance code states that no habitat of an animal, fowl or mammal, shall be tampered with in a way that may result in harm to said animal, fowl or mammal. Nor shall there be any harassment to protected wildlife. If you touch that beaver's lodge, I can have you arrested right here on the spot. Isn't that true, Officer…"

He looked at the name tag on my chest, but before he had a chance to invoke my name, he was interrupted again by Jonah yelling about the lack of tax dollars the beaver had paid. He sounded similar to the many politicians who have made a career for themselves by railing against the rich for their failure to pay their fair share of taxes. I guess Jonah was convinced the beaver in question was not only squatting illegally on his homestead, but had the gall not to pay his fair share of property taxes to boot.

I led Jonah away from the riverbank toward his ATV and asked about his intentions. His gaunt face was animated as he explained that his only intentions were to "muss up" the beaver den by pulling it apart using a rope and grappling hook. He nodded to the equipment in a rear basket to his vehicle.

"Why the rifle?" I asked.

He ignored my question and went on to explain that many years ago his father had faced a similar confrontation with an unwanted beaver, and he and his dad had ripped the den and dam apart using a grappling hook tied to his pickup. It had taken several attempts, but finally the unharmed, but surely frustrated, beaver moved his residence a half mile or so upstream, where it did not intrude on the surrounding landscape.

Trying to discourage the pickup approach indirectly, I said, "Look, this situation is a trifle at best. I suggest you two simply back off and let me find a solution. Give me a week or two to do so. I have a couple ideas already." I really didn't, but I figured I would be able to think of one... eventually.

Administrator Bevis said that he would take no action at this time, but would monitor the beaver's residence through onsite inspection and by aerial surveillance. For a single beaver. Do these agencies have too big of a budget at hand? I wondered but didn't share my musings aloud. Bevis was the consummate bureaucrat. He was such a tight ass I was sure he'd had hemorrhoids while he was still in diapers.

Jonah reluctantly said he would take no action against the beaver, but then he muttered some words under his breath that sounded menacing. After the bureaucrat disappeared upstream, I was able to speak with Martel at greater length. He repeated that he wouldn't do anything, but not because of my words or the administrator agreeing to hold off until I could find a solution.

Instead, he told me he and Jeri were heading out of town in the morning. They were visiting Jerri's sister in North Dakota, where the women would quilt and the men grouse hunt. He would be gone for two weeks. Upon his return he would take all necessary action to once again make his property useful.

I asked him if I could have access to his property during his absence, if I could find a solution.

"Come and go as often as you please, Chief," he said. "Spend the night if you want; just don't burn the place down."

The whole situation was ridiculous. I wouldn't have been surprised if later in the week I would get a call from Judge Goggin telling me to serve the beaver with a cease and desist order. Bevis, of course, would file an amicus brief on behalf of the beaver.

My trip back to the station house was filled with thoughts of incredulity. My late-night, relaxing shift that had ended peacefully and included a magnificent sunrise now had me embroiled in a standoff between a farmer, a beaver, and a strictly by-the-book bureaucrat.

To me, Jonah Martel was the consummate good old country boy. He loved to hunt, fish, hike, and camp in the woods, and most of all he loved the creatures of the forest and its plants and trees. He respected the streams and the rivers and the lakes. This might seem an anomaly to city folk—someone being a hunter and yet still respectful of the animal kingdom. Whatever he hunted and fished, Jonah kept for food. He wasn't the type to kill a moose just for sport and then stuff the animal's head and place it above his fireplace mantle.

When I thought about Jonah refusing to answer my inquiry about the purpose of the rifle, I instinctively knew the answer.

He would not harm the beaver; it was the bureaucrat who should be worried.

Chapter Six

Chicago, Illinois

At 7:00 p.m. that same evening, veteran detective Theo Boycek made a call on his untraceable burner cell phone and learned that Leon Du Perles and Celia Jaynes were both dead. Their throats had been slit wide open. It was the signature trademark for those marked for death due to the disfavor of Aroldis Gonzales Garcia.

A short time ago, a team of El Tercero's men had been shot dead in a failed attempt on the life of Lieza Patrona, Gonzales Garcia's ex-girlfriend, and the government's third key witness against her former lover. The four would-be assassins had overpowered their way into a suite at the Palmer House Hotel, just blocks from Lake Michigan, where they believed she was being held in protective custody.

Theo had been aware that Lieza was not at the Palmer House. He had concocted the ruse himself, using a female Chicago police officer as a body double for Lieza Patrona. He'd placed the team at the hotel in the Loop, informed them how an attempt on the witness' life might come down, and the time he believed an attempt would take place.

In his almost twenty years on the police force, Theo had begun to understand the fine line between crook and cop, the difference between the good, honest cop, and the dishonest ones who would sell their own souls for a fistful of cash. He'd learned to trust only himself and his own instincts. He suspected someone on the police force was cooperating with Gonzales Garcia and his cadre of thugs.

Theo knew, for now, that Lieza was safe. While he had spoken on the phone with his partner, she had been napping in the adjacent bedroom of the three-room suite he had rented under a fictitious name at the Algonquin Hotel. To the best of his knowledge, only he and Lieza knew their location, but he was still concerned. Jaynes and Du Perles were dead, and Theo thought it best that they not remain at the Algonquin. He decided it was time to make a bold move.

Chapter Seven

CHICAGO, ILLINOIS

Despite the cool autumn evening air, Santo Sotto was sweating like it was a hot summer night. His nerves caused his hands to shake, but he hid the fact by coupling them behind his back. He hoped his boss would be grateful that two of the three witnesses had been eliminated exactly in the manner that had been dictated.

But the tall Cuban knew better; Ari would not be impressed by a two for three. That would be an excellent showing at the plate in a baseball game, but in matters of great importance such as this, nothing less than 100% would suffice.

"What happened, my friend? Where did you go wrong?" said the man as he fiddled with one of his ever-present Double-G cigars.

"Leon and Celia are gone, sir, just the way you wanted. Leon was arrogant and boastful, and did not take precautions to adequately protect himself. He was easy. But Celia was a different story. It was difficult to get close to her. I had wanted to use a sniper, from a long distance, but you insisted upon an almost-impossible task, with the difficult caveat that no police officers would be killed during the execution."

"But yet you have failed. One of the traitors is still alive."

Ari's voice was calm and deliberate. This made El Tercero even more nervous. It was when his boss was soft spoken and unanimated that he was most dangerous. The expression of anger, with a contorted face and loud, belittling words, scared many in Gonzales Garcia's coterie of underlings, but El Tercero knew that many of his boss's histrionics were mere gestures used to scare and motivate his men. Nothing was more powerful than fear, and he ruled through fear and a high degree of intimidation.

Ari pointed the tip of his cigar at his second-in-command and asked, "If three men are sent to kill you, and you kill only two of them, are you now safe? If someone throws three grenades at you and two of them are duds, does not the third still possess the capability of killing you?"

"Yes, of course, Ari." Santo used his childhood friend's nickname, hoping to remind his boss of the lifetime bond between the two men.

"Tell me what went wrong, my friend. Why is that miserable bitch still alive, alive to torment my very existence? Tell me."

"The information we obtained was incorrect. Our contacts let us down. We sent a highly trained team into a suite at the Palmer House Hotel. We were told there were only three officers guarding Lieza in room 1327. We hit them with a concussion grenade and tear gas, but it was as if they were aware of our plan: when we were coming, what our approach was, and all about our execution," El Tercero explained.

The man was now less nervous than before, believing that by enumerating the many extenuating circumstances he had successfully removed the blame from himself and placed it upon others. Then he pulled his trump card.

"Ari, I believe we may have a traitor right here in our midst. I could not say for sure, but I think the police may have been tipped off before our arrival at the hotel. Lieza, I am now told by our police contact, was not even at that location. She has disappeared from sight, and no one knows where she is hidden. Perhaps she is even out of the country."

The Cuban crime boss would have none of his underling's excuses, however.

"Why do you use the word 'we'? Is it not you who planned the killings? You who hired the assassins? You who will reap the reward when the job is completed to my satisfaction and is it not you…" he hesitated for a moment, only long enough to take a puff from the cigar, "who will pay the ultimate price if you are not successful?"

The two men had been friends from childhood. Together they had built an empire of crime. But at times Sotto harbored fears that loyalty between the men was only singular. Noble, educated English kings had committed fratricide and even patricide. Why would homicide against an old friend be out of the question?

Each man remained in his position: El Tercero standing, El Hombre seated. Then the crime boss spoke again.

"One does not simply disappear. And how could she be out of the country when in several days she appears before the special prosecutor and gives testimony to the grand jury? She must be here in Chicago, or the suburbs. Maybe close by, over the border in Indiana, Michigan, or Wisconsin. She may be at a motel, someone's house, a farm, or in a boat out in Lake Michigan. You must find her and you must do it quickly."

He put his cigar into a cut glass ashtray and reached down to pick up a leather briefcase that was beside his chair. He handed the leather case to his minion and instructed him to open it. El Tercero's eyes widened like a teenage boy who had just seen a naked woman. The case was filled with bundles of cash, stacks of hundred dollar bills banded together in little packages of $1,000.

"There is one hundred and fifty thousand dollars in the case, my friend. Spread the money far and wide, but spread it wisely. Tell all of our friends that the one who reveals the whereabouts of Lieza Patrona will earn not only my undying gratitude , but will be given enough money so that they never need to worry about anything, for as long as they live."

Chapter Eight

Geneva, Wisconsin

The brief nap I'd taken on the Martel farm—before I'd been awakened by the sloshing boots of DNR Administrator Harland Bevis traipsing up Northwick Creek—had reinvigorated my spirit. While on my second attempt to get back to the station house, and then eventually home and into my own bed, I decided to take a side trip. A small panhandle slice of Geneva Township juts across Highway 50 and invades the expensive real estate of the more desirable Geneva Lake, where an additional twenty-six lakefront homes and nearly 4,000 linear feet of lake frontage are in my jurisdiction. The high real estate tax levied by the town on one of these McMansions is sufficient to pay my salary for an entire year, if not longer.

Located here were two homes that had been burglarized three weeks ago. The cases remained unsolved and had become a deep source of irritation to me. These were the only cases of any importance that my office was working on, yet after continued scrutiny, I had no good clues or even a good hunch to follow. It was obvious the burglar had been smart enough to choose a lakefront mansion containing objects of wealth, but in doing so, he'd exposed himself to greater risk. Most of these homes had security alarm systems, often the high-end, sophisticated systems that could only be disarmed by a professional. Some had estate managers who lived on the property. Although the homes had wide lot lines along the lakefront, they often had other smaller homes nestled up behind them. Those more affordable lake-access homes often had full-time residents living in them, which increased the possibility of being seen.

I was heading over to patrol the area, hoping I would learn or see something new that would set me off on a fresh line of inquiry, when I received a call from my Deputy Chief Bert Burr. He was at the French Country Inn and asked me to stop there, "immediately." He emphasized the "immediately." Before I had the opportunity to ask him the reason why, he disconnected the call. Since I was only a few minutes away from the Inn, I didn't bother to call him back. Besides, anytime I was in the vicinity of the French Country Inn, I usually took a side trip just for the simple delight of viewing the little gem.

Besides the timeless beauty of the old buildings, the historic oak staircase, and the inlaid wooden floor in the lobby, it is the Inn's location on the shores of Lake Como I love the best. Especially at sunset.

As I reached the stop sign at the bottom of Red Chimney Road, I saw Deputy Bert Burr talking to the innkeeper, Jocelyn Hayes, near the entrance of the building called L'Auberge. Even from a distance, I could see that the innkeeper was upset. Usually a model of composure, Jocelyn was flailing her arms about as she paced in hurry toward the hotel's main lobby, Deputy Burr in tow.

I pulled my Jeep around to the main building and exited the vehicle at the precise moment the two of them reached the same spot.

"Jocelyn, what's wrong?" I asked.

Deputy Burr started to say something, but before he could, Jocelyn said, "He's going to kill us; he's going to kill us all. But most of all, he is going to kill me... kill me first."

Bert started to tell me what she was upset about, but before he could, Jocelyn cut him off.

"Shuddup Bert," she yelled. "I'll tell the chief what's wrong."

We were both taken aback by Jocelyn's behavior. I couldn't imagine she had ever told a barking dog to shut up. If any other person had told Deputy Burr to shut up the way Jocelyn did, they would be handcuffed and on their way to the station house.

"Calm down, Jocelyn," I said. "Tell me, what's wrong? Who's going to kill you, and why?"

"The boss. That's who. Tony's going to kill us all, but especially me."

Bert's eyes and mine met, tacitly acknowledging that she was referring to Tony Navilio, the owner of the French Country Inn and Jocelyn's boss. Smiling at my deputy, I asked the hysterical woman, "Why would he kill you? What did you do, forget to make him coffee and lay out his morning newspaper?"

"It's his car. It's missing."

"The Audi?" I asked.

"No, you idiots. It's the other car. That's the one that's been stolen. The Bugs Moran car is gone. Someone stole the Bugs Moran car... either last night or early this morning. You need to find it right now before he gets back up here next week."

It was no wonder she was so upset. Jocelyn was referring to Navilio's newly-acquired prized possession: a 1929 black Packard 8 Phaeton that was reputed to have once been owned by George "Bugs" Moran, the famous Chicago gangster, racketeer, bootlegger and one-time nemesis of Al "Scarface" Capone. It was Bugs Moran who had been the intended victim of the killings that took place at a building located at 2232 North Clark, in Chicago, Illinois, on February 14, 1929—better known as the infamous St. Valentine's Day Massacre.

The vehicle had been purchased by Moran as a gift to his wife, Lucille, but she never received the automobile because she filed for divorce from old Bugs. She fled up here to the Lake Como Hotel almost before the ink was dry on the divorce papers. The Lake Como Hotel was the forerunner to the Red Chimney Inn, which was the predecessor to The French Country Inn.

For many years, Lucille and Bugs Moran had vacationed at the hotel. They'd become friends with its owners Hobart Hermansen and brothers Inar and Harry. Tired of being on the lam after the massacre, Lucille Moran returned to the Lake Como resort and worked as a co-manager for Hobart. She ran gambling operations and the bootleg speakeasy in The Sewer, which was located in the basement of the hotel. After Lucille divorced Bugs, she quickly became the new Mrs. Hobart Hermansen. Oddly enough, the trio—Hobe, Lucille, and Bugs—remained friends even after the divorce and subsequent remarriage.

Thrilled by the gangster history of the property, the current owner, Tony Navilio, had purchased the vintage automobile when it had come up for sale at the annual antique car and boat auction that took place here in Lake Geneva every autumn.

Navilio had only owned the car for a matter of weeks, and now, according to the innkeeper, the vehicle had gone missing.

"What makes you think the car has been stolen?" I asked Jocelyn. "Maybe Navilio took it back home or lent it to someone. Maybe Kirsch has it."

I was referring to Jim Kirchschlager, the owner of the restaurant at the French Country Inn and Navilio's good friend.

"No, no," said Jocelyn. "Tony emailed me this morning to remind me to call Ryan to come over and pick up the car to work on the engine. I called him this morning to ask him how he had taken the car to his shop in the bay, since the keys were in the office. But he didn't take the car because he didn't have the keys to it. I'm telling you, Chief, it's been stolen!"

"C'mon, Jocelyn. We haven't had an actual car theft here in the township for ages. There has to be some other explanation."

I used the word "actual" because real car thefts—someone intentionally taking someone else's vehicle with no intention of ever returning it to the rightful owner—were almost a nonoccurrence. But we did have a large amount of "borrowings:" someone taking a friend's car with the intention of telling the owner about the "borrowing" when the time was appropriate, or at least when there was some sobering up of the parties involved.

I believe the scarcity of thefts is due to the fact that everyone around here knows who drives which vehicle. They may not know the person's spouse, where they live, or what they do for a living, but surely they know their car's make, model color, and year.

Some of these guys couldn't pick their own child out of crowd at ten paces, but they could recognize someone else's pickup truck traveling seventy miles an hour down a gravel road on a moonless night.

License plates, especially the vanity variety, were also memorable around here: BLU BY U was Kirsch's Beemer, Ron Frankel's Escape was FRIO, Navilio's cars were FCI 1 and FCI 2; FCI was an abbreviation for the French Country Inn. The plate on my personal vehicle was, what else: "PCW CHIEF."

"You awake, Chief?" Jocelyn asked.

"Yeah, I'm just thinking. Besides an outright vehicular theft, what could have happened to the car?"

"It's a classic car," said Jocelyn. "Why can't you accept that it may have been stolen?"

"For one, it's too recognizable. Two, it can't be sold at auction or online, because it's one of a kind. Eventually, its origin would be traced back to the auction and Navilio's purchase. Though I guess some sorry SOB might buy it and keep it in his garage, sort of like a museum piece."

I added, "I'll make some inquiries."

"Well, you had better make it quick, before Tony gets up here," said Jocelyn.

I had no intentions of making any inquiries, at least for now. Except for the burglaries at the lakefront homes, there wasn't anything more important to do. It was simple: I believed the car would show up on its own. Not necessarily today or tomorrow, but certainly soon, and I didn't want to waste any amount of time looking for a vehicle that I believed was missing but not stolen.

Deputy Bert Burr pulled me aside away from the prying Jocelyn and said, "Chief, this auto theft has to be related to the cat burglaries. We should look at them not separately but as a whole."

"What do you mean, 'cat burglaries,' Bert?" I said derisively. "You mean the Geneva Lake break-ins? They're burglaries, just plain old burglaries. There is no such thing as cat burglaries, except in the movies. Besides, the car will show up in a day or two, trust me on that."

"Whatever you say, Chief."

"I'm going home, Bert, and I want to be left alone for the rest of the day. Tell Dorothy too."

On my way home, I ran into mi mujer, the lovely Annie Madden. She didn't really like the pet name mi mujer, the Spanish word for woman. Every time I used it, she would complain, "It makes me sound like a sweater made out of farm animal." So I used the nickname sparingly.

Annie Madden was a former underling at my office at the Town of Geneva. She was technically still an underling, in a more pleasurable way, so to speak, but she was no longer an employee. Shortly after the murder of Chandra Harper at the French Country Inn had been solved, she'd taken a more prestigious job in a neighboring city. That had worked out well for both of us. Annie had received a bump in pay, and I didn't have to grapple with dating someone in my office, which was a clear violation of company policy. Not to mention it was a violation of my own code of ethics as well: Don't dip your pen in the company inkwell.

"Hey, Chief! Working hard or hardly working?" she asked from her car; we'd both pulled up to the same stop sign.

"That's original," I answered. "I haven't heard that one in a long time."

"Okay, I know it's lame, but don't be sarcastic. It's an oldie, but goodie. I'm glad I ran into you. I want to tell you about a new position."

I interrupted her before she could continue. "Don't tell me about it. You can show it to me. I'm on my way home right now. Follow me and we can have some fun with this 'new position.'"

"Don't be crass. It's not that type of position. It's the possibility of a new job."

"What is it?" I was feigning interest. I was really much more interested in the other type of position.

"I can't talk now, I'm late for a deposition at the DA's office. I'll call you afterwards."

"Okay, see you later." I couldn't resist the temptation and added, "Alligator."

Once at Casa Blanca, as I referred to my little hacienda, I poured myself a vodka rocks. When we were growing up together in Chicago, my late best friend and fellow cop Dave Tedeski, for obvious reasons, always called our family home Casa Blanca—and not just because it was painted white. I'd kind of forgotten about it until recently and so named my current home for the same obvious reason.

I thought about today's events: Jonah Martel and the beaver, the trip to the burgled homes, and finally the missing Bugs Moran car. Then the vodka set in and made me mellow, and I thought about how wonderful, weather wise, the month had been. Summer had come and gone, and my favorite time of the year, autumn, had now arrived. The humidity and oppressive heat of summer had dissipated along with the demanding tourists. Greenery had changed its coat to soft, colorful reds and glowing ambers, and I looked forward to a quiet and uneventful fall that would eventually drift into a quiet and uneventful winter.

The murder that had occurred last winter at the French Country Inn would be fodder for the gossiping crowd for years to come. But for me it would remain a distant memory—with the exception being the murderess Greta Olsen's shrill tirade when I arrested her for the murder of Chandra Harper.

Even though I seldom succeeded, I tried not to dwell on the negativity of the past, but preferred instead to keep my focus on more recent events—like Officer Bert Burr's latest crime theories, the burgled lakefront homes, or the progress of a close friend who had been on the wagon for almost six months now.

I had a simple, sort of neutral, approach to law enforcement, similar to the physician's Hippocratic Oath: First do no harm. There was never any sense in making matters worse. Both here in Wisconsin and back when I was with the Chicago police force, I watched many a cop take a minor incident and escalate it into a major event. And it was not just the rookie cops; some of the seasoned veterans did the same as well.

I preferred to keep things calm, perhaps have individuals shake hands and part ways, or when warranted, forsake a ticket for a warning citation. My approach kept my paperwork to a minimum and alleviated the courtroom backlog. I'd been called Barney Fife far too many times, but I thought of myself more as the common-sense, Andy Taylor type, without the southern brogue and twangy guitar. Around here, though, I am simply "Chief," friendly, helpful, and not the enemy of the people.

Chapter Nine

CHICAGO, ILLINOIS

The business offices of Aroldis Gonzales Garcia were located on Bonfield Boulevard, on the South Side of Chicago. The top floor of the largest building in the compound contained the personal living quarters of the notorious crime lord. The apartment contained a nine-room suite: living and dining areas, restaurant-quality kitchen, a workout room, and two dens, one private and one for the bodyguards. There were also three bedrooms, one for each of his favorite women. Lieza had the largest of the trio, the one adjoining Ari's quarters, with a private entrance door leading into his room.

Lieza had been complacent with the arrangement of the nearby rooms and the other women. She knew that her Cuban lover had a penchant for new, young girls. She saw others come and go, sometimes after only a week or two, but she did not care about the other mistresses. She only disliked the other women when she was summoned to participate in a session with one or both. Still, she never refused her lover's demands, no matter how much she disliked them or how cheap and used it made her feel. Lieza did not enjoy performing with the other women, but she never spoke about it. A mistress does not say "no" to her man, no matter how demeaning the command, no matter how disgusting the act.

Lieza Patrona had tolerated everything that was asked of her. She knew, or at least she believed, that she had a hold on Ari, a hold that no other woman or man possessed. Besides the sexual arrangement, her lover demanded more of her. She had become a member of his inner circle. She was asked to be his ears and his eyes, his confidant, his counsel, and his analyst. She learned all of the family secrets: where the bodies were buried; which politicians, aldermen, and police commanders were on the take; who murdered whom, how it was paid for, and who doled out the cash. Most of all she learned where the money came from.

As she had witnessed the demise of other trusted cohorts, she had realized that at some time in the future, her life, too, would be in jeopardy. And recently, she'd reason to believe that her time was approaching. Ari had been treating her differently. He no longer confided in her. Conversations ceased when she walked into a room. The late-night visits to her bedroom had become less frequent. Lieza knew something was amiss and decided to rely on her instincts; they had always performed well for her.

Her fate had been sealed when a special investigation team of the office of the Cook County State's Attorney and the Illinois Bureau of Investigation had deployed a detail to watch three key people in the crime family of Aroldis Gonzales Garcia: his mistress, Lieza Patrona; his bookkeeper, Celia Jaynes; and the inner-city street enforcer, Leon Du Perles. When presented with the preponderance of evidence, all three agreed to turn state's witness and testify against their former boss. Afterwards, there was the customary promise that once the case moved to the federal level, they each would enter the witness protection program.

Now two of the three were dead, and the sole survivor—the former mistress—would be on the move once again, unbeknownst to those searching for her.

Soon Lieza and her protector, Detective Theo Boycek, would leave their current spot. The next location was irrelevant to her as long as she stayed alive. Her past experiences had taught Lieza never to trust anyone, especially men, and now she had the worrisome task of placing her life in the hands of a stranger.

She feared that she was only an assignment to the detective, and if the situation became untenable, he would first choose his own well-being and toss her aside the way men had always done. But the situation forced her to trust the Polish cop, even though it was a feeling alien to her.

From the time she was a young girl, circumstances in her life had forced Lieza to become self-reliant. Her mother's dysfunctional relationship with her abusive stepfather had required Lieza to make her own decisions. She could not seek parental advice, nor would she heed the counsel of others.

And now, fighting against those very instincts that had served her well in the past, she had to rely on another: a man she'd met only days ago, a man whose reliability she was yet able to judge. She did not know where the next location would be, only that she would have to rely on a stranger to keep her from the army of assassins dispatched by her former lover, Aroldis Gonzales Garcia.

Chapter Ten

GENEVA, WISCONSIN

As I sipped my morning coffee the next day, I thought about the lack of productivity that had enveloped me. "Lack of productivity" was just my polite way of saying that I was being lazy. Yesterday, I'd wanted to patrol the area near the burgled homes, but I'd been interrupted by Bert's call asking me to immediately come to the French Country Inn. Patrolling was my bane. But sometimes I needed to stop driving, get out of the car and walk the crime scene. This morning I was determined to do so.

One of the burglarized lakefront homes belonged to a fellow named Teddy Scoville, Jr. Teddy's path and mine had first intersected when we were teenagers, while I was vacationing in the area during the summer. As adults, we would sometimes run into each other by accident and have a drink together, often at Kirsch's. Many of our conversations would revolve around his successes. I don't think he tries to brag or rub it in that he is richer than I am, I just think he prefers to talk about himself.

Teddy has been working in the family wholesale lumber business since the day after he graduated from college. He earned an above-average wage, drove a Cadillac, and saved his money to buy a lovely vacation home on nearby Lauderdale Lake. He was often overheard making the statement: "We don't want our lake to become another Lake Geneva." Many homeowners on the neighboring lakes in proximity to Geneva Lake make similar statements, as if to say,

"Geneva Lake is too big, too crowded, it has grown too quickly and attracted too much unwanted tourist attention and growth. We prefer our own quiet little wonderful Lauderdale, Delavan, or Como Lake."

Teddy's father, Theodore Scoville, Sr., had inherited the family business from his own father, Austin Scoville. During the building boom of the 1980s and '90s, Ted Sr. grew the lumber supply business into a Midwestern corporate powerhouse. Despite the company's growing wealth, and perhaps fearing that a high salary would corrupt his only son or give him too much of an independent streak as to make him uncontrollable, Theodore Sr. continued to pay his son only slightly more than a modest salary.

Unexpectedly, at the age of sixty-nine, the senior Scoville had died of a heart attack while vacationing in Hot Springs, Arkansas. Within months of his father's death, Teddy quadrupled his own yearly salary, divested himself of much of the inherited stock portfolio, sold his home on the quiet, wonderful Lauderdale Lake, and purchased a 7,000-square-foot home on Geneva Lake. Shortly after closing on the Big Bayview home, as it was aptly named, an extensive rehabilitation of the property began, and Teddy was never again heard speaking a derogatory word about Geneva Lake.

As I approached the house itself, my eyes were drawn to the large columns of the Greek-revival-style home. Unlike the lazy version of myself, who'd driven around the area the previous the day, this more robust and alert person walked around the neighborhood homes, side yards, and lake path searching for clues. I realized there most likely wouldn't be any clues lingering around the sites. I guess I was attempting to glean some idea of what had happened here last month on separate occasions. Someone, no doubt a professional, had gained entry to the homes and stolen some very special, very expensive articles.

While I was gawking at the magnificent structure, I heard Teddy Scoville ask, "Have you arrested the cat burglar yet?"

His voice sounded like the unfurling of $100 bills.

"You too, Teddy?"

"What do you mean by 'you too'?"

"There is no such thing as a cat burglary…unless you're stealing cats. It's a plain, old-fashioned burglary, the typical garden-variety type… well, perhaps it is a little more sophisticated."

"I beg to differ, Chief. What do you call a crime where the perpetrator gained access through a second-story entrance?"

"A burglary," I stated.

"What do you call breaking and entering using agility, deftness, and cleverness—when it is committed while the homeowners are sleeping in the house?" he asked, most likely expecting me to answer "a cat burglary."

I didn't oblige him. "A burglary." Then I added, "Neither your burglary, nor your neighbor's, happened while someone was at home. Nor did the perp gain entrance from the second floor. As much as everyone around here wants to add a little Hollywood intrigue to these crimes, they are just common, generic burglaries.

Teddy seemed perturbed by my response. It was apparent that he not only needed to be rich, he needed to be correct even when he wasn't.

"Well I certainly wouldn't describe the stolen articles as being common or of a generic type."

There was a tone of condescension and anger in his voice, so I thought it best to mollify his burgeoning emotions. "I didn't mean to imply that the items were common, only the crime."

I think Teddy needed to believe that it hadn't been some common thief who'd broken into his home and stolen his expensive articles. That would be too pedestrian for his liking. He'd probably created some scenario in his mind that the thief was another very rich guy, perhaps named Chip Harrington III or Paxton Quigley, Junior. Not only a very rich guy, but one who was jealous of Teddy's discriminating, high-end taste—someone who'd decided to steal the coveted items for use in his own estate.

It didn't typically work that way, though. Burglaries were usually committed by addicts looking for objects to sell or pawn in order to get money to feed their bad habits, or by some unemployed malcontent who supported his lazy lifestyle with stolen goods.

I kept thinking that these burglaries were the work of a professional because the culprit had not taken random objects that were smaller and easy to carry, store, and sell, but well-chosen items. Items that the burglar knew at first sight were valuable. Perhaps the perp had been in the house at one time and eyed the valuable trophies and then later returned for the theft.

I had Bert Burr and my new officer, Ral Donnert, going through the list of people who'd purchased tickets for the Horticultural Society's Annual House Walk, which had taken place last spring. Both Big Bayview and Norwood-Winston Home—the other burglarized residence, further down the lakefront—had been on the house tour. My theory was that the burglar had taken the tour, eyeballed or photographed the articles, perhaps with a cell phone, researched their values, and then returned to cherry pick the most valuable and transportable booty.

"Any leads, any prospects, any anything?" Teddy asked.

"Nothing at all, Teddy. I'm sorry to say that we are no closer to solving this case than we were three weeks ago when the items were first taken."

"I still say it was professionals, Chief. Someone who is capable of disconnecting my state-of-the-art security system screams out professional to me."

"Years ago I would have said that is true, but today all of these young people are tech savvy. It wouldn't surprise me if I discovered that some twelve-year-old kid short-circuited the system. Hell, you can learn how to build a dirty bomb on the internet, so I don't think it's out of the question to figure out how to disengage a security system." I added, "Even one as sophisticated as yours."

I was being a bit patronizing. Teddy's system, I had discovered, was not all that high end. It was a run-of-the-mill type that did not contain all the bells and whistles of the high-tech variety. Teddy should have spent less moolah on his collection of sauvignons and more on security.

It should have been more than adequate though, in spite of the fact that it had been circumvented. Teddy was a long-time second-home resident, and was well aware that burglaries were rare up here in Walworth County. Most of the break-ins were the result of mischievous teenagers who stole booze and partied in the homes, knowing that many of the lakefront properties were seldom occupied, especially during the off season. Maybe that was why he hadn't put out the big money for his system.

"We are checking the list of house walk visitors who toured your home last month and watching the national database for stolen and pawned properties. Officer Burr and my whole staff are also continuously checking eBay and the other internet auction sites to see if anything pops up."

I had already told these facts to Scoville, but I had nothing else to offer.

He promptly reminded me that I'd given him that same info a week ago, and he was hoping I had something new. Sadly, I didn't.

Once more, I went over the inventory of the burglarized items with Teddy. This time I asked him to elaborate, not simply on the value of the goods, but the subjective worth of each piece. Why, other than sheer dollar value, might someone want to own these pieces? Perhaps a collector needed an item to complete a set or someone desired a piece for sentimental reasons.

I was truly being a phony with this line of questioning and presenting myself as if I were sincere. I was substituting something for nothing. Down deep I knew most likely I would never solve this case nor find the stolen goods.

For one year, Dave Tedeski and I had worked together in the vehicle theft division on the Chicago police force. The only time we found a stolen vehicle was when it was abandoned on some side street—ninety-nine percent of stolen vehicles ended up in a chop shop disassembled for parts. The other one percent, well, who cares? Yet, ten times a day we would file a missing vehicle report and interview the owner of the car, telling him we would work to find his vehicle.

Shamefully, I felt the same way about Scoville's prized possessions. I believed he would never be reacquainted with them, and that I wouldn't locate or be able to arrest the thief who'd swiped them. Served him right for buying a $30,000 Max Ernst etching and a $1,100 silver flask that had been owned by Teddy Kennedy. I wanted to tell Scoville these facts of life, but instead I acted like some dumb high school sophomore sucking up to his algebra teacher by feigning interest in a boring, personal story.

It wasn't so much that I had a lack of concern about the crime. It was just the reality of the situation. I knew that if I verbalized my thoughts it might come across as if I were blaming the victim for being rich and acquiring expensive things. That was far from my intent. Accordingly, I thought it best to remain silent about the realities of the case.

After the perusal of the lakefront homes and my lackluster discussion with Teddy, I headed back to the station. I had no leads, no evidence, and worst of all, I had no interest in these two break-ins. The only thing I did have was a notion that perhaps Bert Burr was correct, that the burglaries and the theft of Navilio's newly acquired trophy car that had once belonged to Bugs Moran were somehow connected. Maybe the car, as I'd first believed, wasn't just borrowed. Maybe I should look for the stolen loot and the missing car in the same direction, and then I decided that direction should lead me to my favorite bartender, Scot Wild.

Chapter Eleven

CHICAGO, ILLINOIS

Awakened from her nap by Officer Boycek's recent cell phone discussion, Lieza Patrona entered the room dressed only in a cotton t-shirt that hung just below her thighs. She knew it was a provocative way for her to dress, but after living in close quarters for over two weeks with her bodyguard, she'd tossed away all decorum and the little sense of modesty she possessed.

Besides, the lovely thirty-year-old woman had made a habit of using her sexuality to attract and possess the men around her. Due to Theo Boycek's conservative demeanor, she particularly enjoyed teasing and leading him on. When she showered in the late morning, she always left the bathroom door widely ajar and the shower curtain partially open. She'd pranced and cavorted around the hotel suite in a short nightshirt sans panties, reaching for a tea cup from the top cabinet in the tiny efficiency kitchen, exposing her shapely, firm derrière.

Her caprices had been a constant source of consternation for Theo.

Under any other circumstances, Theo would have taken the bait and bedded the beautiful Latina vixen, but his professional discipline would not allow him to do so in this situation. Lieza realized this about him and from either pure boredom or wanton desire, she'd made every attempt to beguile the rigid officer into some type of sexual activity.

But Theo remained focused and never reacted to her overt flirtations.

He knew that more than their two lives were at stake. With the other witnesses now dead, it was only Lieza's testimony that could bring down Gonzales Garcia's organization, dismantle the drug-trafficking business, slave-trade prostitution houses, and the plethora of other major and minor criminal concerns. Only she could truncate his reach, but only if the veteran Chicago detective could keep her alive for several more days.

When Theo informed Lieza about the murders of the other two witnesses, she'd grown sullen and concerned. The one-sided, playful, sexual games she'd indulged in with her bodyguard were no longer foremost in her mind, nor the testimony that she had given to the prosecutors. All she could think of was whether or not she would live through the night.

"Do you think that they know where we are?" she asked.

"I don't think so, or they would already have paid us a visit. But that doesn't mean that they may not find out soon. There is a lot of corruption in the ranks of the police department, so I haven't told anyone where we are hiding. Not even my partner; he only has the untraceable telephone number and he calls me once a day to let me know what is going on with the case. He called me to inform me about the other two. I will tell another friend that I will be visiting him soon, but I trust him completely."

There was silence, and then Lieza said, "Poor Celia. I can't believe this is happening. I want to wake up from this bad dream. Please wake me up."

"It is not a dream, and there is no waking up. I have a plan, and we must leave here quickly."

Theo told Lieza to get dressed and gather up her belongings. He then walked to the closet and removed a large suitcase.

In the bedroom, Lieza dressed quickly. Flirtatious thoughts and playful games involving her bodyguard never entered her mind; she could only think about Celia Jaynes, Gonzales Garcia's personal bookkeeper, secretary, and confidante.

Although Lieza and Celia were not close friends, the two had been friendly with each other. They'd often shared inner thoughts and dreams over a cup of coffee or an early evening cocktail, but never discussed business. Secrecy was a code for all to honor.

What have I gotten myself into? she thought. For a moment she toyed with the idea of returning to her former lover, throwing herself upon his mercy, and returning to the life of richness and celebrity—but also one of debasement and self-loathing. Then she came to her senses. Ari didn't possess mercy. He would kill her outright, no doubt by his trademark throat cutting.

The reality of the situation caused her to break down and cry.

Theo heard her sobbing from the other room and joined her at the side of the bed, hugging her with his arm and shoulder.

"Look, kid, everything is going to be all right. I am going to take you somewhere no one would think to look, a place where we can't be found."

"You don't understand," she sobbed. "Ari has people everywhere. Santo Sotto, El Tercero, and his thugs will not stop until I am dead and cannot testify. The government attorneys told me I would be safe, that all of the witnesses would be safe, and now look what has happened. No place is safe."

Theo felt sorry for the Cuban woman, but he would not let his emotions stand in the way of his good judgment. "You need to be strong, Lieza. Now gather up only those items you truly need."

"Why did they not put me into one of those federal witness protection programs you always see in the movies?"

"This is not a federal case, Lieza. It is a state, county and city investigation. We asked for federal help from the FBI and the Attorney

General's Office, but they are too tied up with homeland security measures," Theo said. "They blew us off. Racketeering, murder, drugs are no longer a priority. They say they have their hands full looking for terrorists and preventing acts of terrorism. But once the indictments come down from the grand jury, we will seek their help again, but for now, it is the Chicago police force who will keep you alive."

Theo lied to the frightened woman. It was not the cops that would keep her safe. This job rested solely on his broad shoulders. His quick thinking, cynical nature, and street-wise abilities were a talent few of his contemporaries possessed. He also had one other gift that gave him an edge: Theo Boycek could play dirty. When the situation called for it, the Polish cop had no qualms about being as mean, nasty, or even as corrupt as anyone, perhaps even as dirty as Gonzales Garcia.

"Maybe we should call for some more police officers to help us," she said.

"I believe the fewer amount of people who know our whereabouts is the best situation. Someone is always bound to slip up, or brag to a friend or relative, and there are always bad cops who are on the take who will turn you over for the reward and to curry favor with El Hombre himself. Right now, I am the only one who knows where you are and where we are going. And I prefer it that way."

His words, although not very reassuring, made Lieza feel somewhat better, and she stopped crying. Her lithe, sinewy frame and unschooled manner belied her physical and mental toughness. A cruel word or an uncomfortable situation could send her into a state of self-doubt, but then moments later she could rise to the occasion and stand toe-to-toe with an adversary: unafraid, unabashed.

An abusive father might make someone quake in fear, but over time, this same cruelty can make a person stronger and instill a sense of self-determination in the victim. And Victor Torres, Lieza's stepfather, was as abusive as a character in a horror novel. When he wasn't verbally abusing her, he was physically and sexually abusing her. It was for the sake of her mother, also a victim of Torres's savagery, that Lieza had suffered in silence. The mental abuse left more scars on Lieza than the physical and sexual punishment. She had prayed to the Virgin Mother to send relief, but it never came, and then she promised herself she would kill him.

After her mother's death, she finally did.

As repulsive as they were, the stepfather's numerous visits to her bedroom had taught Lieza one very special thing: women have power over men through sex. They can obtain secrets, power, position, favor, fame, and fortune by using their sexuality in a manner that befits the situation. The more beautiful the woman, the more treasure she could obtain.

Lieza Torres, with her sexuality, learned to manipulate and control men the way a puppeteer manipulates its marionette. When she decided it was time for her stepfather to be dead, she executed a plan by using her sexuality to kill him.

She had sought out a notorious Latino gang member, and learned all about him: his temperament, his allegiances, his likes and dislikes. She had followed him and stalked him until, "inadvertently," they had met. To all involved, it had looked like a chance encounter, but Lieza had planned and rehearsed the moves over and over in her mind, often when in bed while smothered by her besotted stepfather.

In a very short time, the beautiful young Latina had manipulated her gang-member lover, playing on his jealous and possessive behaviors, his moods and protectiveness.

One night, as he often did, Victor Torres came home drunk. Lieza decided that night was the night she would complete her plan. She wanted him dead, but she did not possess the courage to pull the trigger or plunge the knife deep into his body herself. Instead she paraded around the house in a short, sexy dress, her dark, long black hair tied back to accentuate her long neck and high cheekbones, the blazing red lipstick spread bold and precise on her full lips. She wore no bra or panties under the tight-fitting taffeta dress. She reached for a dish in the top cabinet and bent over to pick up a magazine, the same moves she'd used to no avail on Theo.

This night had been the first time she'd attempted such maneuvers; her movements were gawky and stilted but they had the effect she sought. Victor grabbed her by her hair and pulled her into the bedroom. He ripped the garment off of Lieza, exposing her naked and supple body, then he violently pushed her to the bed. Lieza obeyed. She did not fight back; she said nothing. He licked her soft skin, skin that was much fairer than most Latina women.

On her back, Lieza patiently waited until she was positive that Victor was aroused enough that nothing would stop him from consummating the act.

Then she screamed, "No! No! Stop it. You cannot do this."

Victor began to hit the naked woman squarely in the face. The more she screamed, the harder he hit her. When Lieza was sure there would be a sufficient amount of cuts and bruising to her face and body, she acquiesced and allowed her rapist to complete the act. Victor quickly fell into a deep sleep atop his stepdaughter.

After she extricated herself from underneath Victor's corpulent body, Lieza looked in the mirror at her swollen and bruised face and she smiled in joy. She was pleased; the bruises were already turning black and blue, her lip and mouth were bloodied, but she had lost no teeth. She messed up her hair even more than it already was, then took Victor's car keys and wallet and slowly drove to her boyfriend Raul's home. She hoped the bruises would continue to darken and her face would swell even more during the slow ride.

She entered the living room of Raul's home as an ingénue might burst upon the stage of a Broadway playhouse for her first appearance in front of an expectant crowd, ready to recite the words written by the playwright. Only Lieza's words came from her own imagination, although they too had been rehearsed many times. They were a simple proclamation.

"He raped me," she cried. "He raped me, Raul."

Raul and a friend had been sitting on the couch watching a baseball game, drinking shots of Patron tequila and bottles of Modelo beer. They were stunned silent by Lieza's entrance and appearance. Lieza was pleased that Raul was drinking tequila; alcohol always made Raul angry and truculent. He would be easy to manipulate in this condition.

"He beat me and raped me, over and over, again and again. He would not stop. I begged him but he would not stop." She cried and wailed as Raul examined her battle wounds and attempted to comfort her.

"Who did this to you, mi amor? Answer me, who did this to you?"

Softly Lieza spoke, "Victor raped me. My own father raped and beat me."

Within hours, Victor Torres had been shot dead while he slept in the bed where he had often raped his stepdaughter, and Lieza had boarded a Greyhound bus bound for the city of Chicago. She had $275 in her purse, $950 in her bra, and a new name.

She'd decided her surname would now be Patrona, a tribute to the Patron Tequila that had helped fuel the temper of her boyfriend Raul. She would never return to Miami, although when she'd finally arrived in the City of Big Shoulders, she couldn't have anticipated where she'd end up—on the run from a man impossibly more powerful and intimidating than her stepfather had ever been.

Preparing for their next move, Theo Boycek opened the oversized suitcase on to the floor and asked Lieza to squeeze her five-foot, five-inch frame into it. She readily climbed inside with room to boot. He placed several items of clothing and her toiletries in the side pocket, then zipped up the bag, leaving it partially open to allow his human cargo to breathe. His own items and necessities he threw into a nylon duffle bag that now hung over his shoulder. He wheeled the large piece of baggage to the elevator, stopping only to dispose of two plastic bags that were filled with the clothes, sundries, and trash that he did not want to take with him to the next location. He wanted to travel light. His next destination would be only a short walk from the Algonquin, and the two would remain there for less than twenty-four hours.

Rush hour was over, and the crowds had left the downtown nearly empty. As Theo pulled the suitcase across the bridge that spanned the Chicago River, he prayed that neither the wheels nor the handle would break. He wondered what Lieza might be thinking of the click-ity-clack sound made by the metal casters as he pulled the bag over the bridge's steel-grate walkway. He could hear the Lake Street "L" train a block and a half away, making a similar harmonious clacking noise. The two together sounded like a street symphony played by handmade instruments.

The three-block journey from the Algonquin to the Renaissance Hotel went quickly and without incident. He registered at the new hotel under an alias, and paid in cash. Once in the room, Lieza exited the suitcase and immediately fell into a series of yoga poses to relieve her cramped legs and neck.

"What do we do now?" she asked. "Transfer me in the trunk of a car?"

"Not quite. Tomorrow I need to run some quick errands, and then we will be on the move again. Hopefully, it will be for the last time until your appearance at the grand jury. For now, you need to get some sleep."

Lieza looked around the small room and stared at the queen-sized bed.

"Where will you sleep?" she asked.

"In the chair with my gun beside me. If I get real tired, I will lay next to you for a nap."

She nodded her head in agreement, but said nothing.

When Lieza awakened the next morning, it appeared that Theo had already shaved and showered, but he wore the same clothes from the day before. His black hair with just a touch of gray was still wet and slicked back over his head with no part in it. He drank a cup of coffee from the pot he had brewed earlier. The hotel room door was double locked, and a chair was shoved under the handle for further security.

"We have no time to dawdle," he said. "Go take a shower. When you are finished, I will run an errand and then we will go."

"You're going to leave me alone?" she asked, surprised.

"I will be gone less than an hour, and I will leave you a gun. Do you know how to use one?"

"Remarkably well," she answered.

"Good."

Lieza came out of the bathroom with an oversized terrycloth towel wrapped around her body and another one around her wet hair. Immediately, Theo motioned her over to him and started to recite a series of instructions.

He showed her how to wedge the chair under the handle after he left. Told her not to answer either the phone or the door. He left her a number to call if he did not return within an hour and a half. The number belonged to his partner, who knew the situation and most of all could be trusted. He placed a Beretta handgun on the table and told her to be careful not to shoot him when he returned.

"When I do return," he said, "I will knock three times and then say, 'Open up, honey, I forgot my key.'"

Once out of the hotel, Theo moved quickly. From an outdoor parking garage, he called his next-door neighbor, Todd Dressel.

"Todd, I need a favor right now. Please don't ask any questions, and just follow my instructions."

"Sure, buddy, name it."

"You still have a spare key to my house?"

"Yeah."

"Good. I need you to go over to my place and get the Explorer. Then drive it to the Dunkin' Donuts on Harlem Avenue, just across the street from the Lake Street 'L' stop. Make sure you're not tailed. Drive around a bit, go through some red lights or something, but don't be followed."

"What's this all about, Theo? Are you in trouble?

"Don't worry, Todd. I'm always in trouble. Make sure the car is there by noon. Also, go inside and give the owner—his name is Orman—a twenty-dollar bill. If a car sits there for more than two minutes the son-of-a-bitch will have it towed. Let him know it will be there only till the afternoon. You got all that?"

"Yeah, sure. I'll do it right now. No questions asked."

"Thanks, buddy. I'll pay you back the twenty when I see you again."

Theo made consecutive stops at a CVS Pharmacy and then an Old Navy. Next, he picked up two disposable cell phones with prepaid minutes. Within the hour, he was back in the hotel.

Theo knocked three times and said, "Let me in, honey, I forgot my key."

Chapter Twelve

GENEVA, WISCONSIN

Harpoon Willie's is a neat little tavern that serves thick cheese-burgers and ice-cold beer. No saloon keeper ever went out of business serving that combination. In Wisconsin, it is a requirement, especially when you add a bratwurst to the menu. Harpoon's, and its larger sister restaurant, the attached Italian Café, Calamari, is located on the premier corner of Williams Bay, the quiet little burg that was next door to my own quiet little burg. Chances are, Scot Wild would be at Harpoon's this afternoon. Even if he wasn't working, he'd likely be hanging around.

In the Harpoon's parking lot, there were four pickup trucks nestled among a half-dozen cars. The trucks were all different ages, makes, and colors, but they had one thing in common: each had a dog inside of the cab. In the grey pickup, Dave Whiting's truck, there was a black lab; in Ray Kriete's black Silverado was his black lab, Butterball. I was at a loss to remember who owned the beat-up yellow vehicle of indistinguishable variety, the one parked in the handicap spot despite having no handicap sticker or plates. Inside was—what else—another black lab; perhaps the dog was the one who was disabled.

The fourth vehicle, Scot Wild's red Toyota Tacoma, stuck out like a Chicago Bears fan at Curly Lambeau Field, but not because the foreign make of the vehicle. The glaring difference was this: inside there was no Labrador retriever. Scottie's best friend was Killian, a Golden Retriever.

In the tall office buildings and wide shopping malls in major cities and states, one day a year was dedicated to "Take Your Child to Work Day." The rural Wisconsin counterpart to that event was "Take Your Dog to Work—Every Day."

The eccentric Wisconsinites took their dogs to work, not just one day a year, but, weather permitting, every day. These men's best friends sat patiently in the pickup trucks, waiting for their owners to let them out for their relief time during their fifteen-minute morning coffee breaks, and then was back in the cab 'till lunchtime. Another break between three and three-fifteen, and then after work it was "go to your favorite bar" time until dinnertime came around. It sure beat being cramped up for hours in a small cage in a studio apartment in downtown Milwaukee or Chicago. As a politician might say, "These people cling to their dogs more than they love their guns and wives."

My eyes were drawn to Ryan Starker, who was holding court with a couple of the local beauties. The yellow pickup in the handicap spot, I now remembered, belonged to him.

"Starker, get your truck out of the handicap space right now, or I'll drag you in for aggravated stupidity."

"Sure, Chief, I'll do it now."

I had come to Harpoon Willie's to visit with Scot. As the most popular barkeep in the county, he heard more rumors, scuttlebutt, and tidbits of information than a Hollywood gossip columnist. Most of the chatter he got, passed around from person to person and bar to bar, was…well quite honestly, it was just that, plain old-fashioned gossip. Occasionally however, there was a nugget of truth mixed in with the tram load of raw bull.

I walked up to the bar and caught Scot's attention.

"I'll have a Pink Lady."

"Are you the proud saleslady of the year for Mary Kay Cosmetics?" he asked.

Scot and I—as I do with most bartenders—have this little game we play, where I ask for some type of frou-frou drink like a Brandy Alexander and he gives me my usual. With a gesture I waved him off when he reached into the beer cooler, so he poured me an ice-cold Sprecher's root beer from the tap. Technically I was not on duty, but I wasn't exactly in my civvies either, so I thought it best not to have a beer—or a Pink Lady.

"Hear anything of interest lately?" I inquired.

"Tom Dooley got hung from an old oak tree," he answered sarcastically, referring to The Kingston Trio song that was playing in the background.

"I'll write up a report."

"If you're talkin' 'bout the missing Bugs Moran vehicle or the rash of cat burglaries, I have nuthin."

"Okay, what's with everyone referring to these as 'cat burglaries'? Was there some sort of feline involved?" I asked, somewhat ticked. "They are burglaries. Just your simple, garden-variety break-ins, not cat burglaries, not dog burglaries, not skunk burglaries; they are just plain, old-fashioned burglaries."

I caught my breath and then added, "What is this cat burglary crap anyway? Is this a 1950s Cary Grant movie or something?"

"Don't get yourself all worked up, Chief. It's just a term. Anyway, if you ask me, I think they are related, the car theft and the ca—" He caught himself before he earned himself another rant. "The burglaries."

"Why so?"

"The items that were taken from the lake homes and Bugs' car are high-end. They can't be sold on the open market like a camera or a cell phone. These things were taken by a disinterested third party, for a specific client."

Scot poured himself a quarter of a glass of club soda and then continued: "Take the car, for instance. The owner will never be able to get plates or registration for it, nor drive it in public. It can only be for an aficionado who wants it for his private collection. Same is true with the artwork and antiques from the lake mansions. This guy's not going to put a signed painting on the internet that can easily get traced back to him. He'll get caught in record time."

He stared at me, perhaps waiting for a response, and then said, "I've got nuthin' else." He added, "Talk to Norman, he may have somthin'."

Almost by rote I answered, "I plan to."

Scot moved down the bar to tend to another patron, and my attention turned to Jay Thorton, who was sitting at the far end of the bar. I hadn't previously noticed him.

Thornton was a particularly disagreeable person. The type of a guy who you wouldn't be surprised to hear had slapped around a defenseless pimply-faced teen or cursed out a nun because she was driving too slowly. His boyhood nickname "Bully," which no one dared speak to his face as a youth, had stuck with him through adulthood, and now all openly referred to him by the moniker.

When he visited a bar, which was often, most tended to keep their distance from the grumbler, excepting the foolish and uninformed. Many a fight had been instigated by Thornton. Because of his age, which seemed to be mid-forties, he wasn't as tough as he used to be, but he sure was as mean as ever and he would say, if he saw fit, whatever to whomever.

Perhaps it was a bit of ill-fate or simply the way events seemed to transpire at Harpoon's, but on this calm autumn afternoon an equally disagreeable person decided to occupy the vacant barstool that was next to the one Bully Thortnon was sitting on. It was evident by the look on Bully face that he wanted the man to sit elsewhere. Before the other man's rear end had even settled into his seat, he had ordered a bottle of beer.

"When your beer comes, drink it elsewhere," Bully said.

"Sorry, is someone sitting here?" the man asked politely, but with a gruff voice.

"No," replied Bully.

"Expecting someone?"

"No."

"Then why should I move?" asked the stranger.

"I don't want you sitting next to me."

"Then go sit somewhere else."

"This is my spot, and I don't want anyone sitting next to me."

The stranger, not knowing Bully's reputation, nor intimidated by his size or confidence, looked Bully up and down, stared straight into his eyes, and said, "Go fuck yourself."

Both men leapt from their chairs and began to throw punches at each other as if they were mirror images. In the few seconds it took for me to navigate through the small crowd that had gathered to catch a glimpse of the donnybrook, damage had already been done. Not to the bar mind you, but to the two pugilists. Blood flowed from over Bully's left eye, and his cheek was already red from the punches thrown by his adversary.

The other man had a cut lip and bloody nose. He held a beer bottle by the neck and was ready to slam it across Bully's head when I dislodged it from his hand. I twisted the man around, using his own force against him. I was as careful as a hockey referee attempting to break up a fight between two players. I didn't want to catch an errant punch or purposeful beer bottle atop the head.

Bully immediately recognized me. Surely not wanting to spend time in the town jail, he backed up a step or two. The stranger was less eager to let the matter come to an end, but when I grabbed him by the throat and told him I was the police he became subdued on his own accord. Then the finger pointing began.

"I just came in for a couple a cold beers," said the stranger, "when this guy starts a fight."

I regarded the man. He was 6'0" or 6'1", with white hair, a sinewy torso and muscular arms; he had more tattoos than an NBA player. Okay, maybe not that many, but if he had two or three more he could play for the Bucks.

"He invaded my space," Bully retorted.

"What are you, a couple of teenagers?" I asked rhetorically. At least I guessed it was rhetorical because no one answered.

"How many drinks did Bully have?" I asked the bartender.

"That was his second," the bartender said, nodding his head toward the half-full bottle still on the bar where Bully had been seated.

"Okay. Bully, you leave right now and don't come back or stop anywhere else. I'm going to drive past Foley's later, and if you are there, I'm taking you in and you'll spend the day with Bert Burr.

Bully didn't fear a night in jail, but listening to Bert's stories for hours could have a chilling effect on someone. It is a fate worse than going home to the wife or listening to an insurance salesman.

"You from around here?" I asked the stranger.

"No, just visiting."

"Where you stayin'?"

"Down the road a bit, at the French Inn."

"You mean the French Country Inn?"

"Yeah, that place. I just walked down to get some fresh air and a beer."

"C'mon, I'll drive you back there."

"I can walk, I'm all right."

"I know you are, but I just want to make sure you get back safely."

I could envision Bully Thornton lying in wait to start up the brouhaha all over again. On the ride back to the inn, I commented that the man knew how to handle himself in a fight. He didn't respond.

"What brings you up here?" I asked.

"Just wanted to get out of the city."

"Chicago?"

"Yeah."

"What do you do down there?"

"Independent consultant."

"What kind?"

"A number of different jobs."

During the five-minute ride to the French Country Inn, I grilled the stranger about his background and the reason for his visit to the area. There was no amount of pleasantry in his voice, no openness to his responses to my questions. I could see I would get no useful information from the guy, so I stopped trying except for one last question.

"What's your name?" I asked.

"Fred."

"Fred what?"

"Fred Smith."

Yeah right, Fred Smith, I said to myself.

I dropped Fred in front of the French Country Inn, circled around the property, and then parked my car in the east lot and entered through Kirsch's Restaurant. I poked my head in the bar and saw my good friend Fred already on a stool with a friendly bottle of beer before him. I went to the front lobby via the parlor. Debbie Vanderstappen was at the front desk.

"Afternoon, Debbie. How are you today?"

"Just fine," she answered. "And you, Chief?"

"I'm fine too. Do you have a Fred Smith staying with you?"

Debbie took hold of the computer mouse as if it were a delicate Faberge egg and manipulated it across the pad, then said, "Yes, we do."

I inserted myself behind the desk and asked belatedly, "May I?"

She did not reply, since I was already in position and reading the computer screen.

Fred Smith, 6363 North Milwaukee Avenue, Chicago, Illinois

Source of payment: Cash

"Okay, thanks, Debbie."

"Is there a problem, Chief?" she asked.

"No, just a little curious," I said. "He looked familiar, but his name didn't ring a bell."

Smith really didn't look familiar; I had only said that for Debbie's sake. The address, on the other hand, did, but I couldn't quite pinpoint it—I knew 6363 North Milwaukee Avenue was in a Polish neighborhood, lots of commercial buildings and six flats. I tried to figure out Mr. Smith's angle, but nothing came to me. Maybe he was meeting a woman and he didn't want to use a real name or address. Or maybe it was nothing devious at all, he simply wanted to come up to the lakes area for the same reason most others do at this time of the year: to get some R&R and to enjoy the changing colors of the foliage.

But then again, Mr. Fred Smith, despite the black rose tattooed on his forearm, didn't look like the botanical type to me. Nor did he look like a "consultant," unless he was consulting on how to cause trouble. His close-cropped white hair and long, gaunt, craggy face with a hundred or more deep wrinkles in it gave the appearance of trouble. His broad shoulders and thick arms told me he could dole it out as easily as absorbing it. It didn't surprise me that he had gotten the best of Bully Thorton.

I grabbed hold of the handle to the front door, and through the window I could see the innkeeper, Jocelyn, moving toward the lobby. I knew she would start jabbering about Navilio's missing vintage automobile so I backed away several steps. Through the door that leads from the lobby to the bar I could see Mr. Smith, beer in hand, leaving the bar and taking a seat on the lakeside terrace.

Perfect timing, I thought, as I was able to avoid both Jocelyn and Mr. Fred Smith while I snuck into Kirsch's. I took a seat at the bar. I tried to hide myself alongside a thirty-something couple; they were drinking a cosmopolitan and another drink that was most likely an appletini.

"Sometimes I hate this place," I thought to myself.

The man said, "Excuse me, were you speaking to us?"

"Did I say that out loud?

"Say what?" he asked.

"Never mind," I said and turned my head in the other direction.

I guess my timing wasn't as perfect as I'd thought because at the other end of the bar I could see a woman I had once dated entering the room. She'd always referred to me as an "old flame," which was definitely a misnomer. I wasn't exactly an old flame of hers—more like a burn victim. We only went out a few times, a mere diversion for me, but she acted as if we had been childhood sweethearts who'd been an item since junior high. When I stopped calling on her, she trash talked me to just about everyone in the township who would listen. And of course, in this small town, everyone wanted to hear whatever manure one could fabricate or exaggerate.

"Well, hello, Chief. How are you doing these days?"

"Hi Clare, nice to see you. It's been quite a while."

Clare gestured to the man next to her. "This is my fiancé, Alex. Alex, meet an old beau of mine. He is the chief of police here in Geneva. You can just call him Chief."

We shook hands and exchanged pleasantries. Then Clare spoke again.

"Now don't get jealous Alex, but Chief and I were pretty hot and heavy for a couple of months."

A couple of months? It seemed a lot longer than that to me. Geez, I hoped I didn't say that out loud too. I looked at Alex's face. I wondered if she'd trash talked me to him the way she did to everyone else she met. He seemed unconcerned.

"Alex is on the board of trade… in Chicago."

I was glad Clare added Chicago, so that I didn't get it mixed up with the other board of trade, the one in Williams Bay.

That was another thing I hated about Clare—there were so many—she always had to identify you with your achievement, occupation, or what you owned. With her it was never, "This is my friend Tom or cousin Bob." It was always, "This is my friend Tom. He has a home in South Beach," or "This is my cousin Bob. He owns a yacht at Belmont Harbor." Of course, with Clare, the home in South Beach could really mean the south shore of Lake Como, and the yacht could be a dinghy on Paddock Lake. That was why so many people referred to her behind her back as "Clare, Clare, wants to marry a millionaire."

I often wondered why I'd even dated her in the first place. Sometimes, I wondered if I was drawn to women who eventually and intentionally wanted to do me harm: The Femme Fatale Complex, I called it.

Long ago I was watching the Turner Classic Movie Channel, and the host and a guest were talking about the role of the "femme fatale" in the classic movie genre. They defined her as a woman who was always trying to do harm to her man. Though not usually a narcissist, I immediately began to think of the women in my life who wanted to do me harm, especially in my previous life back in Chicago.

Clare, of course, came to mind. I thought about the lies she had spewed about me. She described me as homicidal, suicidal, incidental—you know, in the size department—unintelligent, selfish, boorish, and worst of all Liberal in my political views. In southeast Wisconsin, calling someone a Liberal is as low as calling them a Chicago Bears fan.

My ex-wife Rita also fell into this category, as well as a few others I'd dated in Chicago. I surely hoped Annie did not.

Alex excused himself and headed toward the men's room. In his absence, Clare pulled herself closer to me and whispered, "Gimme a call sometime soon. Alex is only up here Thursday through Sundays and the nights get a little lonely."

"Can't do that, Clare. I'm usually busy Monday through Wednesday. But it's been wonderful seeing you again. Give my regards to your fiancé when he returns." I stressed the word "fiancé" to Clare, but I was sure the irony of my tone was lost on her.

In an attempt to distance myself from the irritating woman, I turned my back to her and grabbed my phone, pretending like I was checking my email messages. That would have been quite an accomplishment, since I was techno-Amish and didn't fully comprehend email, or texting for that matter.

I then moved to a chair that had a clear vision of Mr. Fred Smith, who was still seated on the deck, and yet was far from Clare. I played with my phone as if I were emailing, but I was really thinking about women.

I didn't even know why Clare had dated me in the first place. I certainly was not wealthy and probably never would be. If Clare truly wanted to marry a millionaire, she'd hooked up with the wrong guy. Not only did she try to do me harm after we broke up, but she did so even while we were dating. It appeared she wanted to see me debased in the eyes of those who surrounded me. She exaggerated my faults, bared my peccadilloes, berated my looks, and commented on my girth, which at the time was a little more robust than it is now. Of course, once we parted ways, her attempts to harm me grew exponentially with the length of my avoidance of her. Yet, with all of my shortcomings, I guess I was still good enough for her, at least for the three days a week when Fiancé Alex was away.

While considering the other women who had harmed me most prominently, my brief liaison with the murderess Greta Olsen came to mind. My tryst with her was most re-Greta-able, as I liked to say. That erudite bitch wanted to use me as her alibi in the only cold-blooded murder to take place in the township in the past quarter century. I was sure she'd stayed awake at night, plotting and scheming how she could manipulate this small-town yokel to her benefit.

"Say, I wonder how I can kill my best friend and then stay above the entire investigation by having beguiled the moron chief of police of the Town of Geneva? I know—I'll sleep with him, pretend I'm in love with him, and frame the unwitting chef at Kirsch's restaurant by planting seeds of false evidence in the mind of this dimwitted, love-struck gumshoe."

Oh, Greta Olsen, you certainly had all the makings of the patented "femme fatale." Robert Mitchum and Jane Greer would have been so proud of you.

Then, of course, there was Rita, my ex-wife. I knew I had to keep my thoughts about the harm she'd done to me for another session of daydreaming. My little mind could not handle any more self-abuse.

All the while, through my musing, I watched Fred Smith. There was something about him that aroused my curiosity. I decided I would place him in my unofficial book of suspects, even though I didn't know what I suspected him of doing.

He sat drinking his beers on the deck, quiet, unanimated. Then, suddenly, like a man who had remembered that he had something very important to do, he rose and left. He had a determined look of a person who had something important on his mind.

Chapter Thirteen

Geneva, Wisconsin

Fred Smith was angry with himself. When it came to his work, he believed he was the consummate professional. To minimize occupational risk, he planned every detail in advance, contemplated potential elements of surprise, and predetermined an exit strategy in case things went horribly wrong. While on his jobs, he preferred to remain generically plain: no ostentation, no boastfulness, a simple, quiet Mr. Peepers that no one would notice. And now, here in Jerkwater Town, USA, he'd allowed some two-bit bully to goad him into a disturbance that had brought him to the attention of a local authority.

In his room at the French Country Inn, Fred looked at himself in the mirror, rubbed his calloused hands across his face, and tried to calm himself down by taking a series of deep breaths.

"It's not that bad," he said.

That small-time cop doesn't possess the skills or mental capacity to even consider that I am more than a casual visitor, simply trying to get away from the worries and complexities of big city life. But then he started second guessing himself.

I shouldn't have used Fred Smith as an alias, he thought. By its own simplicity, it calls attention to itself. I should have used something more ethnic. He knew his somewhat swarthy appearance allowed the use of names of Polish, German, or Slavic origin.

Now he was angry for needlessly and uncharacteristically whipping himself into a near state of panic. He took several more deep breaths in order to calm down and logically plan his next move.

He had been told by his employer to bring the merchandise he had been hired to appropriate to Chicago, but Fred had refused. He wanted to get paid first. Even though he had carefully plotted his itinerary, there was great risk transporting stolen merchandise across state lines, and he wanted to get paid in full before undertaking such an operation. He had been told by his employer to remain patient, because there were more important things at hand. Apparently manpower could not be wasted by sending couriers to Wisconsin to deliver his $30,000 in cash. But now his impatience grew in concert with his degree of worry over coming to the attention of the chief of police of tiny Geneva Township.

He agonized about calling his contact, but even with considerable doubt still in his mind, he made the call.

"Amigo, it's me, Fred Smith."

"What is it you want, Mr. Smith?" the voice at the other end of the cell phone asked coldly.

"There has been a change of circumstance, and I cannot stay here any longer. I will need to get paid right away so that I can deliver the merchandise to you."

"Bring the merchandise to me here in Chicago, and I will have the money waiting for you when you arrive."

Smith considered the man's request, even though he knew it would be a tactical error. The risk in obtaining the item was not as great as the risk in transporting it across state lines—a federal crime. He determined he would be persistent in wanting to get paid before transport.

"No, amigo, I need to be paid first and then the delivery. Certainly you have many subordinates who are capable of such a minor deed."

The voice said, "We have more important things to do at this time. Great matters that I cannot share with you."

Smith determined that there was some hesitation on the speaker's part, so he said nothing in return.

Then the voice asked, "How far are you from Kenosha?"

"Around thirty miles."

"Some of my men will be in Kenosha soon. I will have someone call you at around 6:00 a.m. about your payment, perhaps tomorrow or the next day. They will call you at this number when they are ready to see you. But do not make the delivery until I give you the date."

"As I said, things have changed, and I may need to leave soon."

"Well, soon will have to mean a couple of more days. If you must, take the property to a new location until I call you for delivery."

Smith knew that the current location was secure and that changing his position prematurely was more dangerous than standing pat, but he chose not to bandy words with his employer and agreed to the request.

The voice said nothing more and simply hung up the phone without even saying "adios" as he often did.

The stolen merchandise was not the only reason Smith was in Wisconsin; it wasn't even the primary reason. He was also here, on orders from his partner in Chicago, to spy on the very same chief of police who had just driven him to his hotel.

Instead of remaining anonymous and operating in the shadows, he was now at the forefront of the mind of the man he had been sent to observe. Smith was fully aware that at some point in the near future he may have to confront Chief, but now because of this unwanted meeting, Smith considered abandoning his primary mission. Plus, he knew that coming to the attention of the local police would make it more difficult for him to successfully carry out his other mission.

Reluctantly Smith made a second telephone call, this one to his partner.

"It's me," he said. "Unfortunately, I may have to leave here soon."

"Why?" asked the voice on the other end of the line.

"As luck would have it, I have come to the attention of your friend, the Chief. I think it best that I come back, now."

"No, absolutely not," said the voice. "Things are coming to a head. I will soon know what I must do and then you will know what you must do or not do."

The two men usually were equal partners in their business, most often making decisions together, through consensus, but this situation was different. The stakes were higher, the plan had to be more exact. The consequence of failure would be more onerous.

The partner's steady, calm voice did not reveal that he was scared, nor that his life was in jeopardy on two different battlefronts. Smith decided to defer to his partner's age and experience.

Beside his deference to his experience, Smith was beholden to his partner. It was he who had taught Smith, mentored and molded him. Introduced him to his cronies, brought him into the circle of power, money, and corruption. When the time was right and the apprenticeship complete, it was he who had promoted Smith from junior partner to senior partner.

"Your friend, I think he is an idiot, even if you think he is smart, but he may figure things out for himself. Then what will we do?"

"If you think he is aware of the real reason you are in the area, then at some point you will have to eliminate him too."

Smith could not believe what he had just heard from his partner. "Kill a chief of police? That would be insane, even if it is the chief of a small town."

"Don't get soft on me, my friend. Remember if I go down, it is unavoidable; you will go down with me too. We kill who we must kill and keep alive who we must keep alive. Those are the facts of life."

Smith was soberly aware of that truth. His partner's potential order could mean he would need to quickly spring into action. To kill or not to kill, he thought to himself as if he were Hamlet contemplating Yorick's skull. But unlike the Danish Prince, he was not morally conflicted with death. He only pondered if it would be necessary to kill the chief or not.

Events that would occur ninety miles away in the next hours or the next days would determine the answer to that question.

Chapter Fourteen

GENEVA, WISCONSIN

I couldn't stop thinking about 6363 North Milwaukee Avenue. I just couldn't come to grips with the address Fred Smith used when he registered at the French Country Inn. It was like when the words of an old tune get stuck somewhere in the back of your brain and simply won't come to mind.

I was heading back to Harpoon Willie's in Williams Bay to finish the conversation with the bartender, Scot Wild, that had been all too brief. The ruckus between Bully and Mr. Smith had put an end to that possibility.

There was a small condo building nearby that was filled with a lot of Chicago greaseballs. I wanted to ask Scot if any of them had been in to Harpoon's recently. If not, I wanted to suggest that he start a conversation about the burglaries and the missing Bugs Moran car if they did show up.

Perhaps it wasn't politically correct, but the burglary, the name Navilio, and the missing mobster's car had "Italian" written all over it. I was beginning to sound like my friend Frank Murphy, raconteur and Kirsch gadfly, who blamed everything, including global warming, on the Italians. I was starting to be concerned that the "thought police" would smash my windshield.

I slowed as I approached Harpoon's. The place was brimming with activity, and I realized because of the crowd within I probably wouldn't have Scot's attention. I decided to move on as he had suggested and visit Norman instead.

A quarter mile up Geneva Street is the Bayside Motel, a.k.a. the Bates Motel. The proprietor at the time was Norman Bates. That wasn't his actual name. I hadn't used it in so long that it would take me some time to remember, but it didn't matter anyway, because everyone called him Norman. If you removed the Santa Claus beard from his round and corpulent face, he resembled the Cheers sitcom character, Norm Peterson, more than the Psycho character, Norman Bates.

Norman, as usual, must have seen me pull into the parking space in front of his residence, which was adjacent and connected to the motel office. Before I could knock, Norman opened the door widely and handed me a Smithwick's.

"Sorry, can't today, Norm, I'm on duty."

"Well, punch out for a while and enjoy life."

"Good idea," I said and took the bottle of ale from his still-outstretched hand.

"What's the rub?" he said.

"The rub?" I repeated. "I'm looking for info, and it's not from the 1980s. That was the year I last heard anyone ask, 'What's the rub?'"

"It's from Shakespeare," he said.

"Oh, didn't know that. Have you heard anything about the lakefront burglaries?" I asked.

"Nothing at all. I just assumed it was the usual teenage crap that's been going on up here for ages: kids looking for mayhem, and a place to drink beer and get laid. When you and I were teens, just like every other jacked up, hormonal idiot, we did the same."

He stared at me, waiting to agree with his description of teenage tomfoolery, but I didn't. In our younger days, Tedeski and I used to swim out to the large cabin cruisers moored offshore on buoys to drink and make out with our ladies.

"That was my initial thought too," I said. "But there are a couple of oddities. First it's still early autumn, and there were a lot of people around. The mischief break-ins usually take place later in the season, when there are fewer potential witnesses, but still before the cold winter days set in. Plus, there is just too much high-end stuff missing."

I took a couple of swigs from my ale and waited for Norm to say something in response. He didn't, so I continued.

"But the main thing is the burglaries and the property that was stolen. It appears the items may not have been taken at random. There may have been some order to the theft."

Again Norman looked at me as if he wanted me to continue uninterrupted.

"Then there are the burglar alarms. Each home had them, good ones, but not state of the art."

The alarm part got Norman's attention. "Shit," he said. "These kids today are so techno smart that a fifteen-year-old could disarm the Pentagon's security system in minutes while whackin' off to a Playboy centerfold with his left hand."

A gross exaggeration on Norman's part, not to mention the comment's crudeness, but it was certainly filled with some half-truths. I realized I wasn't going to get anything out of Norman today. He didn't know anything or didn't care to share any knowledge, if he had any. I decided to switch topics and ask about my new friend Mr. Fred Smith.

"Have you seen a guy up here in the last few days? Tall, thin, white and gray hair that's closely cropped? He has a floral tattoo on his left forearm."

"Sure have." Norman chugged down the last of his Smithwick's and moved to the refrigerator to get two more. He handed me another even though I wasn't finished with the first.

"Mr. Fred Smith. He's staying in room number eight on the corner. Actually, I shouldn't say he is staying in number eight, more like he's renting it. I haven't seen him since the day after he checked in. I don't believe he has slept here at all, but he paid in cash for the whole week."

"Can I see his check-in receipt?" I asked.

"Receipt? What part of paid in cash didn't you understand, Chief?"

I laughed. At times I loved Norman. "Do you remember what address he gave you?"

"Yeah, I jotted it down on a piece of scrap paper." He thumbed through a bunch of papers on the side table. It was a pile that looked destined for the trash can, or more appropriately, a paper shredder. "Here you go: 6363 North Milwaukee Ave, Chi-town."

"Do me a favor. Check that address on Google Maps for me."

Norman turned on his iPad and his stubby fingers deftly worked the keyboard.

"Internet is down," he said. "Sometimes bein' up here is like living in a third-world country."

Then it came to me as fast as Norman chugged down his second Smithwick's. He went to retrieve a third from the fridge, but saw that I was still backed up with my second, so he left me alone.

Milwaukee Avenue was an old-line Polish area. Smith looked like he could be a Pole; he had that swarthy look about him. Maybe he had one of those unpronounceable Polish names and had changed it to Smith.

"Do you recognize the address, Chief?"

"I sorta know the area. Polish area, but the block doesn't seem that familiar."

I quickly changed the subject. "What kinda car was Smith driving?" I asked.

"He wasn't. He has a truck. A twenty-five-footer. He asked if he could park it in the garage, but I told him it was full. Then he asked if he could leave it next to the garage. I told him there was more room in front, but he insisted on parking it next to the garage. I sort of got the impression he didn't want it seen from the street."

Each time Norman said garage, he pronounced it as "gay-raj," clearly enunciating each syllable. His accent became more pronounced with each subsequent bottle of Smithwick's.

"The next day, Smith asked if there was an indoor space where he could park the truck for several days. I told him about the storage units I manage for Brian Staunton off of Highway 50 near the Dairy Queen." Norman paused and stroked his beard as if he were trying to remember the facts more clearly. Or he could have been thinking about some detail he wanted to omit. Maybe the three quick beers had impaired his thought process, but that couldn't be it. I was sure Norman drank at least ten beers a day, seven days a week.

He continued, "Then as dusk approached, he asked if I would rent him a space and take him over to the storage facility. He asked me again if the space was big enough for his truck to fit in. He started to piss me off. I had already told him twice it would be snug but it would fit."

I loved getting info from this bearded, fat man. Not only did he always seem to know what was going on in the area, he related the stories in clear detail like a trained watchman.

"Once at the storage units, he backed the truck halfway into the space then went around the back. I couldn't see what he was doing, but I could hear him fussing in the rear and I think maybe lowering a ramp. He said he might be there for a while and that perhaps I should leave. I asked if he would need a ride back to the motel. But he said no.

"Then he stopped doing anything and just stood there thumbing his keys, waiting for me to leave. I told him again it was no problem for me to return to pick him up. He didn't answer this time.

"He seemed like he was being sort of secretive with his actions. So I decided later I would go back and snoop around to see why he was being so sly." Norman held up his near empty bottle as if he were going to make a toast. "Want 'nother?"

"No, thanks, I'm on duty," I said. He smirked in response. "Did you go back to the storage space to look around? What did you find?"

"Don't get ahead of yourself, Chief."

I backed off with the questions and listened as Norman spoke.

"Well, first of all, he shows up back here at the Bayside about an hour later. I didn't even hear him approach the place, even though I was sitting right here where I am now."

"How did he get back here, in the truck?" I asked.

Norman gave me the eye. "You're as impatient as a newborn looking for his mother's teat," he said.

"Sorry."

"Okay, where was I? Yeah, now I see him astride a 100cc Yamaha Mountain Bike, the top-of-the-line 200 series. I never seen him or heard him pull up 'til I see him right out here in front of my window. I went outside and he asks me how much I'm owed for the parking space.

"I told him seventy-five bucks for the week. Figuring he might complain, I'm ready to tell him we only rent by the month, but he whips out a hunnert and says thank you and keep the change. Funny thing about his bike."

Norman paused. I wanted to ask him what he meant, but I didn't want to get admonished again, so I waited and asked nothing.

I felt as though Norman wanted me to ask him what he meant by, "Funny thing about his bike," so that he could use one of his cute little folksy aphorisms to put me down. Nor did I ask if he gave Smith a receipt for the "hunnert" bucks. I knew the answer, and I didn't take the bait. He continued.

"That damn mountain bike was the quietest vehicle I had ever heard... or I should say, never heard. It had a purr like a fat cat after she'd rolled around in a field of catnip. You know, those bikes usually have the loudest engines you could imagine, but not this one. It was like a stealth machine, never even know'd it was running."

"Did you go back to the storage unit to check around?"

"Yep, I did; stopped on my way to the Farm and Fleet store to buy a sump pump, you know they are cheaper there than the big box stores. But there was nuthin'. The truck was backed into the stall all the way to the rear wall. No one, not even the skinniest little kid, could have climbed into the rear box. Of course the door was closed and locked with two of those kryptonite bicycle locks, one on each side."

"What about room #8? Will you show me it?"

"No need to, Chief. There's nothing in it; checked it this morning. Bed hasn't been slept in, towels not used, and no luggage inside. Very peculiar, but it's not the first time someone has paid for a room and didn't stay there."

"Why would someone do that?" I inquired.

"They check in, but then stay elsewhere, with a girlfriend, relative, or someplace else where they are perhaps meeting someone they don't want others to know about. Who really knows? It has happened before. But still it's peculiar."

"Very peculiar," I said.

Norman and I finished our beers and talked about the weather, the start of duck and deer hunting season, and Halloween, which was approaching. Then I left.

On my way back to the station, I pondered the many questions concerning Mr. Fred Smith that were bouncing around in my head. Most prominently, why had he rented a room at the Bayside Motel but decided to stay at the French Country Inn? Maybe he'd checked in to the Bayside, didn't like it, then saw the inn and decided to stay there instead. Not wanting to hurt Norman's feelings, and having already paid for the room, he decided to absorb the cost. But Mr. Fred Smith didn't seem like the type who cared about hurting someone's feelings.

And why would he rent a storage space and not leave the truck at the Bates Motel? And then finally there was the address. As I spoke with Norman about the address I realized I had known the area but not the exact location. Was there a reason he used that particular address, or was Mr. Smith playing games with both his name and his address? I hoped I would find the answers, but for now I decided I would pay a little more attention to Mr. Fred Smith of 6363 North Milwaukee Avenue.

Chapter Fifteen
Gevena, Wisconsin

Norman Bates: a man for all seasons. I wasn't referring to his intellect, but the amount of beer he drinks all year long. Yesterday's conversation with Norman had gotten my juices flowing about Fred Smith. My gut was correct; it was obvious Smith was not here to enjoy the change of season and the colors of the trees. There was purpose behind his visit.

During my drive to the opposite side of the lake, I was thinking of possibilities. Was he here to steal the Bugs Moran car, or was he the one who burgled the lakefront homes? Could he be responsible for both? Were they related, as Bert Burr believed?

I was so deep in thought that I hadn't really paid attention to where I was driving. I couldn't figure it out after a quick look around, so I pulled over and put the address of my destination into the GPS.

After having visited and lived in this area for close to thirty years, one would think that the town of Geneva would be as familiar to me as the words to the Miranda rights, and generally it was, but there was one exception: the Como Subdivision, on the north shore of Lake Como. It was as confusing as a teenager's logic. The streets were laid out in what was supposed to be a grid system, but the topography and natural boundaries made it incomprehensible. The Jeep given to me by the township was equipped with a GPS that I used only when I left the county or when I needed to find a home on the North Shore.

Right now, the north shore of Lake Como was where I happened to be, searching for 221 Alberta Street.

I was on my way to serve a restraining order to a young man, barring him from entering one of the local drinking establishments. I liked the lad, but his argumentative behavior and angry disposition had worn thin on Gus Baldwin, the tavern owner, who also had an argumentative and angry disposition. Henry Stimach had been thrown out of Muddy's Tavern more than once, and had been told never to return, but when he sobered up, he claimed he didn't remember that he'd been told never to return. Finally, Gus had had enough, and he sought relief from the court.

"If anyone is going to cause trouble in Muddy's or harass the clientele," Gus liked to say, "it's going to be me."

Sometimes I thought my main duty around here was serving restraining orders. I'd often said if it weren't for bar fights and restraining orders—or peace bonds, as they were often called—I could cut my force by half. Because of the often-explosive nature of a restraining order, I preferred to handle them myself. I tended to keep the situation from getting out of hand.

I had driven straight down to the lake off of Highway H and Whatley Road and was now traveling southwest, toward Lake Shore Drive, when my phone rang.

I was hesitant to answer the phone, but was glad I did when I heard the voice of Theo Boycek, a friend and fellow cop. Theo was one of several men who had been a mentor of mine in the old days at the Chicago Police Department. He was calling because he and a companion needed a place to stay. He would be arriving in a day or two, but was reluctant to give me an exact time. He asked that I keep the phone call and his request a secret; he stressed for me to tell no one of the call and his impending arrival. The conversation was brief and to the point. I was curious. Was his friend female? Were they being pursued by an angry husband, or perhaps a jealous boyfriend? My curiosity would have to wait until the pair arrived.

The reason I hesitated to answer the phone call in the first place was because the caller ID displayed "Unknown Caller." Usually when that happened, nothing good came out of the conversation; it was often either a salesman, a crank call, or someone looking for volunteers for a pointless cause. Instead of "unknown caller," it should read: "Don't take this call because it's going to irritate the crap out of you."

My initial thought when I saw "unknown caller" was that it was probably a lawyer, and most likely my ex-wife's lawyer, and that was never good.

It was fitting that I had assumed that the phone call might be connected to my ex, because at that exact time, the GPS instructed me to "turn left, turn left, now." The voice on the GPS sounded exactly like that of my ex-wife. The tone was imperious, the timbre strident, and it made the hair on the nape of my neck stick out like the quills on a porcupine.

The main problem was that if I had followed the voice's instructions, I would have driven directly into the lake. Last winter when I first activated the GPS, I had been at this very location traveling along the road on the north side of Lake Como. The voice had said to "turn left ahead at the next street." As I drove another several hundred yards the voice instructed me—it actually demanded—that I "turn left, turn left, now."

Had I turned as directed, I would have found myself upon the ice in a very treacherous area of the lake. Due to some natural flowing springs, the water off this shoreline never actually freezes thick or solid. If a snowmobiler or an errant cross-country skier goes in to the cold water of Lake Como, it generally happens at this bubbling springs area.

And now once again, months later, the sardonic voice ordered: "Turn left now."

"Is that you, Rita?" I asked the voice.

I felt foolish talking to a computer-generated voice, but I was sure it was Rita. Someway, somehow, my ex-wife had figured out a way to jerry-rig this system in order to do me harm. She wasn't satisfied humiliating me, taking our modest home, and confiscating our meager savings; she actually wanted to see me drowned in this picturesque lake I loved so much.

I was glad I wasn't driving in Chicago or Milwaukee. Rita's GPS voice of doom possibly would have instructed me to drive the wrong way down an expressway ramp. I could see the newspaper head-line: "Wisconsin Chief of Police Killed in Auto Accident."

The story would follow: Police car demolished in head on collision with tractor-trailer while traveling wrong direction down an expressway exit ramp. No alcohol or drugs were detected in his blood, but friends say in recent weeks, the Chief complained of hear-ing the voice of his ex-wife, Rita.

Despite the directions of the demonic GPS, I managed to stay out of harm's way, restraining myself from driving into the lake, or into a hundred-year-old oak tree. When I reached my destination at 221 Alberta Street, I switched off the automated system and hoped that I did not have to use it again for many months to come. Just a simple remembrance of times past with my ex was enough to cause me a week of anxiety; the sound of her voice, or a facsimile thereof, could drive me into a binge of despair and self-loathing, not to mention a bout with excessive drinking.

This whole malarkey about the restraining order and why Gus had petitioned Judge Goggin to issue one keeping Henry Stimach out of Muddy's and at least one hundred yards away from Gus himself did not sit well with me. Henry was an affable guy who had patronized Muddy's since he'd come of age; it was like a second home to him. He was a bit obnoxious and loud when he drank too much, but then, that described a lot of people around here, both male and female. I tried to talk to Gus about it, to no avail. Once he had made up his mind about something, it was like talking to a granite slab. You could never move it with mere words.

Henry looked like he had just awakened from an afternoon nap when I served him the order. We stood on his front porch as he listened to my words. I told him this was a serious matter, and that he should stay away from Muddy's and from Gus for the ninety days while the court order was valid.

His facial expression resembled that of a seven-year-old who had been barred from the boys-only treehouse.

"Chief, I don't understand this. I don't act up any more than any one of the other guys who hang out at Muddy's. It's almost as if Gus has it in for me, but I don't really interact with him that much other than orderin' my drinks and sayin' hello and goodbye."

"It's his bar, and he can ban whomever he chooses. Maybe he just doesn't like your looks."

"My looks. What's wrong with my looks that Gus doesn't like?"

"Nothing's wrong with your looks, Henry. I mean Gus can bar you for any simple reason that his crabby little mind dictates. It could be the way you part your hair or wear your pants. It's his option."

I prayed Henry wasn't going to ask what was wrong with his hair, and thankfully he didn't.

"Look, I'll talk to Gus in a couple of weeks and see if I can get him to change his mind, but I'm not promising anything. You understand?"

"Sure, Chief, thanks."

On my way out of the subdivision, I thought about activating the GPS to see if Rita would now instruct me to "turn right" and steer me directly into the lake one more time, but then I thought I shouldn't tempt fate. The voice on the GPS after all—like Rita—was a fickle woman.

Chapter Sixteen

Chicago, Illinois

"Are you okay?" Theo asked Lieza.

"Sure, couldn't be better," she answered. "I am a bit hungry, though."

"We will get something on our way."

"Our way where? Another hotel?"

"I'll let you know when we are on our way. We have some preparation to do, so come with me."

He led her to the bathroom, and asked the woman to sit on the side of the bathtub. He removed a pair of scissors from the CVS bag and began cutting Lieza's long hair. She did not protest or ask what he was doing; instinctively, she knew she was going to be disguised. Once the locks were shorn to a boyish length, Theo asked, "Blonde or redhead?"

"Blonde," she said. "They have more fun."

As clever as it was, neither of them laughed at her remark. Both were fully aware of the gravity of the situation. There was no levity in being chased and hounded, or being at the top of someone's kill list.

Theo performed his cosmetology duties as if he had once worked in a fashionable Gold Coast salon, which, of course, he hadn't. After Lieza blow-dried her hair, Theo admired his work of art, and was satisfied with the outcome. He then ordered her to remove her t-shirt.

"I have nothing on underneath," she said, with incredulity in her voice.

"Don't you think I noticed?"

"I can never tell what you are noticing or thinking," she said. "You are a mystery to me. Sometimes I think you are gay."

"Please," he said. "Just do it. We don't have time to banter."

Silently and without further protest, Lieza removed the shirt, and stood, topless, before her Polish protector. For the past several days, before she had learned of the other murders, Lieza would have been excited by standing naked in front of Theo. But there would be no titillation for either of them today. The situation was too dangerous for there to be any feeling other than dread.

Theo removed a long, wide Ace bandage from the bag of supplies he had purchased earlier and began to wrap Lieza's firm, supple body with the wide elastic. He wanted to hide her breasts under the wrapping.

"Is that too tight?" he asked.

"No, it's comfortable," she responded. "What else do you have in mind for me, a fake mustache?"

"No, nothing that dramatic," he answered.

Actually, Theo had first thought of making Lieza into a teenage boy, but he realized there was no way to hide her femininity. She was simply too beautiful, too curvy, and too refined in appearance. Trying to disguise her as a male would only draw attention to her by making her appear to be an effeminate male teen. Instead, he opted to attempt to make her look like a young female who, if she could manage to adapt certain mannerisms, possessed some tomboyish traits.

Finally, he dressed her in blue jeans, an Old Navy-brand navy blue sweatshirt and a blue baseball cap with the Nike insignia on the front. He stepped back from her to scrutinize his creation. "Good job," he said to himself. He was sure that anyone who saw the two together would think she was his daughter, much younger sister, or perhaps a niece. Her clothes were simple and non-assuming, the type that would not draw attention.

Theo then gathered up all of the items that he would dispose of in the trash, and cleaned up the room and bath; he packed Lieza's and his belongings in his nylon bag and asked her if she was ready.

"You're not putting me in that suitcase again, are you?"

"No, we'll leave it in a utility room. You are now free to move about Chicagoland with me as your pilot. Just don't be too feminine. Try and act like an unsophisticated dopey teenager, but don't be loud or do anything to draw attention to yourself. Understand?"

She nodded.

"Now, what shall we call you?"

"How about Maria?"

"Too ethnic."

"Yolanda?"

"Too black."

"Ingrid? I am a blonde?"

"Too Swedish; too sexy."

"Okay, then you pick one."

"How does Sophie sound?"

"Also ethnic, but I can live with it." Then she hesitated and sadly said, "But hopefully not die with it. Can we go now? I am nervous and hungry."

Side by side, the two walked to the elevated platform at State Street and Lake, and waited for the Green Line train to arrive. Although he felt secure they were not being watched or followed, Theo's eyes darted at the fellow commuters: several students, a tall black man wearing a Chicago Bulls sweatshirt, an elderly woman carrying a shopping bag from Macy's department store, and numerous others. He searched their faces for any change of expression which would alert Theo that someone had noticed something odd or familiar about the couple: he, strong jawed with tanned leathery skin, wearing a wrinkled sport coat and khaki pants; she, a blonde teen in jeans and a sweatshirt. The newness of her outfit was enough to make Lieza stand out in a crowd. Theo had now wished he had spent the extra money and purchased a pair of denims that had the washed out, faded look of his old Levi's—the ones that were so beaten and moth-eaten he never wore them anymore.

"I realize you are worn down and nervous," Theo whispered to Lieza, "but I need you to be alert. Pay attention to everything and everyone. If you see something out of the ordinary, or someone who looks familiar or is acting strange, let me know immediately."

She nodded that she understood.

The "L" train ride ended at Lake Street and Harlem in Forest Park. The two walked across the street to the Dunkin' Donuts where Theo ordered half a dozen donuts and two coffees. After having cohabitated with Lieza in the hotel suite for many days, he knew her peculiarities. Coffee with extra creams, low on sweets, high on carbs. He did not need to ask her preferences.

"Anyone looking for me, Orman?" Theo asked the donut vendor. "Did anyone ask about the car?"

"No, no one asked about you or the car, Theo. Some guy just dropped off the car and said you would pick it up later. Why do you ask?"

"It's not important, but if anyone asks if you have seen me, tell them no."

"Sure thing," Orman said as he handed the change and merchandise to Theo.

"Hey, the guy told me you would give a twenty when you picked the keys up."

"Nice try, Orman."

Then, with the two coffees and donut bag in hand, the two were out the door as fast as they had entered.

Once in Theo's car, Lieza chowed down on an old-fashioned unglazed donut as if it were the last indulgence she would have before facing a firing squad. The hot coffee burned her lip, and she let out a tiny meow, then asked Theo if they were now leaving for the final destination.

"Yeah, I have already made the arrangements. But we will be on the run for a couple of days first to make sure we are not followed. I'm sorry I lied to you. I feel safer this way."

Theo picked up one of the disposable cell phones with prepaid minutes and looked at it with jaundiced eyes. He thought about the call he'd made to his old friend and one-time partner who now lived in Geneva, Wisconsin. He worried he had made more than just a tactical error—that the conversation was a total blunder. He thought about the words he had spoken, and then beat himself up over each one: "Please tell no one of this call, Chief, or that you have even seen or heard from me for a long time. Understand—no one."

He only worried that his friend's talkative personality may cause a casual slip of the tongue, that he might unknowingly mention the conversation to a girlfriend or a fellow worker. He thought about changing his plans, but then decided that it would be good to have a friend's help during these last hours before he had to take Lieza back to Chicago for her final testimony before the grand jury. He would need someone to rely on in the interim, and Chief would be that person.

"What are you thinking about, Theo?" asked Lieza.

"Just making plans, and thinking about trust," he answered.

Theo had no basis to mistrust Chief. He knew torture itself couldn't pry a betrayal from his old friend.

Chapter Seventeen

GENEVA, WISCONSIN

I looked at my watch and knew I'd better hurry. I'd promised to meet Annie for a cocktail at Kirsch's. Or was it a Bloody Mary at Muddy's? Too early for Kirsch's; must be Muddy's.

Annie and I pulled up to Muddy's at the exact time. Not as eventful as having achieved simultaneous... well, never mind.

"Glad you're on time. I'm starving for a cheeseburger," she said.

"If I were late, you could have ordered without me. I wouldn't have minded."

"That's something you would do: order and then eat, instead of waiting for me. But that's not me."

"Hey, I grew up in a neighborhood with lots of Italians. When the internal lunch bell rings, it's time to eat. No delays, no excuses, no apologies."

I didn't like the way this conversation started, and worried it could deteriorate further.

"Everything okay with you, Annie?" I asked. "What's on your mind? Does it have to do with this new position you mentioned?"

"What does 'does' mean?" She looked confused.

"I just meant to say, 'does' the criticism of me possibly ordering and eating a fictitious meal before you arrived have anything to do with the new position that you had previously and briefly mentioned to me?"

I spoke slowly with the other half of my brain trying to figure out how I can wiggle my way out of this spider's web of words I was getting myself entangled in.

"You're being obtuse," she said. "I'm not criticizing you, merely stating that if we were meeting up to eat together, even simply catching a quick cheeseburger, I would wait for you to come before I ordered, whereas you would have no problem ordering and eating said cheeseburger before I even arrived. An observation, not a criticism."

It sure sounded like a criticism, and I wisely decided not to interject further.

"Did I tell you about my new regimen of reading books, increasing my vocabulary, and doing the Tribune's daily crossword puzzle?"

"No, you didn't," she said. "What has caused this new erudition?"

"Erudition? I'd better look that one up in case it is tomorrow's crossword clue. I was thinking about Chandra Harper—you know, the woman who was killed last winter at the Inn."

"No one around here is going to forget her anytime soon."

"Well, I kind of admired her. Not her personality, mind you, but her intellect. That side of her was rather fascinating. So I decided to emulate her by reading more and sort of working on my mind the way an athlete works on his body. Exercising the mind."

I half expected her to say something like: "In that area you are definitely a ninety-pound weakling," but she didn't. The conversation was becoming sort of clumsy so I dropped it post haste.

When I said Annie was a problem solver, I meant it. I was glad she asked to meet for lunch because I wanted to ask her opinion on a couple of items.

"So there is this Chicago guy, Fred Smith. Norman Bates told me he rented a room at the motel, but I know he is staying at the French Country Inn. Who does that? Rents two rooms?"

"It's suspicious, but maybe he's married and meeting another woman, and he wants to keep it a secret."

"Norman said something like that too. Then the guy has a truck that he puts over in Staunton's Storage. Backed up nice and tight so no one can get into the back. I'm thinking it's the loot from the lakefront burglaries."

"Suspicious," she said. "Why not get a search warrant?" Then she answered her own question, imitating the crusty Judge Goggin: "Evidence my boy, you need evidence first."

"Then there is this situation where a beaver creates a dam that forms a pond that cuts Jonah Martel off from a cabin on his own property."

I abruptly stopped talking; I'm sure I was sounding like a rambling idiot. I reoriented myself and told her the whole story and asked if she had any thoughts on how to handle the beaver dispute between Jonah Martel and resource director Harland Bevis. Short of trapping the beaver and moving it elsewhere, I was stumped.

Annie seemed disinterested, but said she would think about both situations. Jonah had told me he and Jeri were heading to North Dakota to visit family and go grouse hunting, so I still had plenty of time to find a solution in the interim.

"So tell me about this new position," I said, realizing that, as usual, I was monopolizing the conversation and talking about myself.

Excitedly, Annie started: "I heard from an old high school friend of mine who moved to Lacrosse that there may be an opening for the position of chief of police in Pelham. It's a town just east of there. I mean, just east of Lacrosse."

"Annie, that's wonderful, it really is, but I'm happy right here in Geneva. It's the right size for me, the right fit and the right location. I have no desire to go elsewhere and start all over."

She threw an icy, mean glance at me, and I didn't like the look of it.

Coldly, she said, "I wasn't talking for you. I was talking about it for me. An opportunity for me to advance."

I got a lump in my throat.

"Annie, I am so sorry. I'm so self-centered I thought you were saying it was a good fit for me, but you were saying it was a good position for you. Of course. You would make an excellent chief. Better than I am, of course. You are more organized, more articulate, better at solving problems, a multi-tasker, skilled in police work and investigation…"

I realized I was going on too strongly and laying it on as thick as a cement worker pouring a slab of concrete. I decided to quickly stop talking.

There was a lull in the conversation. Annie's face was expressionless. Then she spoke. The excitement that was previously in her whole body and expressed in her voice was completely gone.

"Pelham is looking for a new chief of police, and they are giving special consideration to female applicants."

"You see," I interjected. "That rules me out right from the get go. I'll never have a chance at getting that job now."

I denoted a sense of laughter or at least a smirk wanting to come out of her, but she resisted. My sense of humor had defused another potentially bad situation just in the nick of time.

She said, "My friend Audra is good friends with a town board trustee who is on the search committee, and she has already discussed my credentials with him. He was very impressed."

"That is absolutely wonderful. What an opportunity." I was at a loss for words. "Did we order yet? Gus, can we get a menu here?"

"Menu? What the heck?" Gus looked astonished. "Don't you have it memorized by now? The specials are on the blackboard."

I looked up at the blackboard. Nothing was written on it.

I was hoping to buy a little time in order to collect my thoughts. I'd seen many situations like this on TV. The plot goes like this: Boy meets girl. Girl threatens to move away for a new opportunity. Boy must decide to make a commitment so girl will not move away. Chief changes channel so he does not have to deal with an uncomfortable situation.

"What are you thinking about?" Annie asked. "You look like you are a thousand miles away."

"An old TV show I just remembered, and I'm trying to decide what I want to eat. Not sure how hungry I am."

"You are always hungry. What are you thinking about?"

I think she knew, but I felt we had to talk about it even if it made me uncomfortable.

"Let's order," I said.

We both had cheeseburgers and ginger ales, no Bloody Marys as previously planned; we wolfed them down as if we were late for a concert, with neither of us speaking. I threw $20 on the bar and said, "Let's take a ride."

I drove the Jeep up Schroeder's Road, across Highway 50, and past Wood School to the aptly named winding drive called Snake Road. The autumn foliage formed a multi-colored dome over our heads. I wished the Jeep had a sun roof.

"Are you thinking about interviewing for the Pelham position?" I asked. Before she could answer I added, "Are you going to leave me, Annie?"

Isn't it the woman who usually asks a question like that? I thought to myself. I was uncomfortable talking about it. I wanted to change the channel, or at least push the mute button.

"Would you care if I left?" she asked.

"Of course I would. I love our relationship. You mean so much to me, and I couldn't picture my life here in Geneva with you living in Lacrosse. Isn't that at least three or four hours away?"

"It is a long drive, and I don't think we are the type to have a long-distance relationship. Plus I think it would be me driving back here a lot more than you driving out there."

I couldn't dispute that, but I always say that I hold up my end of the relationship, even though it is a lie.

I moved up here to southern Wisconsin in order to get a little sliver of peace back into my life. I thought I had found it in my relationship with Annie, and then this cropped up. We were going to have to make a decision in our relationship, and, quite honestly, I was pleased when Annie asked to be dropped off back at Muddy's.

She said, "I have some errands to run."

I think she meant she had some decisions to make.

Chapter Eighteen

GENEVA, WISCONSIN

Yesterday's conversation with Annie had been uncomfortable to say the least. We'd had a brief, uncomfortable lunch, followed by an even briefer uncomfortable scenic ride, before we split up and went our separate ways—she to run "errands," and me to pout alone. And now, another day had flashed by without any meaningful police work to show for it.

Never got around to asking Annie about Navilio's missing Bugs Moran car and whether she thought it was related to the lakefront burglaries, as did Bert Burr and a couple of other officers. She would have no proof about the cases, of course. I simply wanted to get her gut feeling about a possible relationship between the two.

Burlington, where she works, is a big town with a large police force. I wanted to ask her what her fellow officers were saying about our little crime wave here in the Township.

At least I got to tell her about the new regimen I'd started. The one centered on Chandra Harper's intellectual pursuit.

It wasn't for the reason one would expect, but the murder of Chandra Harper last winter at the French Country Inn had been a watershed moment in my adult life—not to mention a pretty big event for Chandra herself. I'd come to admire the woman's love of literature and her passion for detail, names, and vocabulary. Even though I found the little minx offensive and self-centered, when it came to intellectual pursuit, she'd been truly inspiring.

The woman had total recall of dates, places, character's names, and literary minutiae. From the many books she had devoured, she could repeat details that would put a Jeopardy champion to shame. Chandra could match little-known authors with their obscure characters, and she could give an oral dissertation about their secondary works. Maybe I was so impressed by her because I was only an average student throughout my entire schooling, doing only the bare minimum to get by with my schoolwork. On some level, Chandra's abilities appealed to me.

After wrapping up her murder case, a la Chandra Harper, I decided to improve my intellect and immerse myself in literature. Perhaps immerse is too strong of a word, more like dipping my toe, maybe up to my ankle, into the intellectual waters of literature. The Catholic priests at my high school always stressed the importance of reading. It was the source of a growing intellect, they would often say: reading improves and stimulates one's mind, heightens one's ability to reason, expands one's knowledge, and elevates one's analytical thinking skills. Or something to that effect.

Since then I have read at least one book per week, well maybe every two weeks. To supplement the broadening of my knowledge, each day I've worked the Chicago Tribune crossword puzzle, compiling a list of unfamiliar words that I then look up afterwards. I call it my Pursuit of Intellectualism, inspired by the late Chandra Harper, the only person, I am sad to say, who was murdered while on my watch as Chief of Police.

I am especially proud that, during the past few months, I'd managed to keep it all to myself, but not so much out of a sense of humility.

The fact is, I know myself. Years ago when I quit smoking, I went around bragging and boasting about having the unflinching discipline of a Tibetan monk in my ability to quit. When I inevitably did fall from the Himalayan opinion perch that I had placed myself upon, the fall was higher and more humiliating because of my boasting and superior attitude. The same was true each time I proclaimed I was dieting, on the wagon, or starting a great workout regimen. I decided that with this new endeavor I would simply better myself and my atrophic brain in strict privacy.

Except I would tell Annie, of course.

All of the questions I wanted to ask Annie would have to wait until our next time together. I decided I would make plans to take her to dinner at Kirsch's at the French Country Inn. She loved the place, and was always in a great mood when we had dinner there.

Chapter Nineteen

Geneva, Wisconsin

I had been reading Raymond Chandler's *The Big Sleep* when The Big Nap occurred. The phone ringing woke me; it was Dorothy at the station.

"Chief, it's me Dorothy."

"Yes, I know. What's up?"

"I'm supposed to remind you that you wanted to personally deliver Cheryl Kintrick to the Chicago authorities."

"Thanks, Dorothy. I'll be in soon to pick up the lovely lady."

I yawned and stretched my arms out wide. I'd had a great nap and felt refreshed and eager to be on my way. I needed the nap, because I'd barely slept last night. The recent conversations with Annie weighed heavily on my mind. I would fall asleep, wake up, turn the TV on, fall back asleep, wake right back up, and the cycle would start all over again. Between sleep and TV, I thought about Annie. Was she using the possible position in Pelham to force me to make a commitment? Generally, she was not the type of woman to play games with our relationship.

I decided to put all thoughts of her out of my mind and focus on the job at hand.

Briefly I thought about Theo's impending arrival. I wasn't exactly sure which day he was going to arrive, but I figured I could always shoot back up here if he showed up when I was in Chicago.

I was not excited to go to Chicago; the city no longer had the allure it once did. However, I was excited by what I was planning to do once I dropped off Ms. Kintrick at the Chicago Police Department.

Cheryl Kintrick was a scofflaw who'd fled Chicago to avoid nearly six thousand dollars in unpaid parking tickets. I love these Chicagoans. They think by moving up here across the state line they have foiled the "down under" Illinois authorities. They believe it's like running off to Thailand, that Wisconsin is so remote they can avoid their past. The same is true for the locals up here. They run into trouble and flee down to the south side of Chicago to live with their auntie and believe they will be safe for the rest of their lives.

Those greedy, thieving Cook County politicians might not pursue you for a Class-X felony or even a murder rap, but by God, six thousand dollars in unpaid parking tickets? They will go to the ends of the earth to collect that money.

It was nothing personal with Ms. Kintrick; I wanted to deliver her to downtown Chicago because I had some personal business to attend to in the City of Big Shoulders and corrupt politicians.

After I delivered Ms. Scofflaw to her destination, I planned to head over to view one of my favorite classic movies, *The Maltese Falcon*, which was going to be playing at a small North Side theatre. A copy of the book by Dashiell Hammett was sitting on my desk; it was the next book I was planning to read in my classic detective series.

In between the delivery and the movie, I would pay a visit to an old friend of mine named Mike "Night Train" Layne. His drinking establishment was only a few blocks from the theatre. Mike's place, a hangout for Chicago cops, was a repository of information—but not always good information. Rumors, conspiracy theories, who killed whom, and who's sleeping with someone: it all ends up there.

I wanted to talk to Night Train to see if he knew anything about the likes of Fred Smith, the burglaries, or the missing Bugs Moran car. I knew the latter two were a stretch, but I thought Smith might have crossed paths with someone at his place, especially if he hung out around the 6300 block of Milwaukee Ave.

When I decided to begin my literary journey, I promised myself I would not simplify my intellectual pursuit by relying on shortcuts such as Cliff Notes—not that there would be one for the Falcon anyway. I wanted to make sure I not only read each and every word, but that I would ponder the substance of the work itself. But never once did I vow that I wouldn't see the movie prior to reading the book.

I arrived at the station, picked up my charge, and then headed south. The trip down south to Chicagoland itself was most annoying.

Miss Kintrick jabbered on nonstop. She blamed all of her parking ticket woes on her ex-boyfriend and then the Chicago cops, who had it in for her. Finally, she concocted a conspiracy theory involving the local alderman, who supposedly had a thing for her.

She tried to get me to let her go, first by appealing to my sense of fair play, then by cajoling me with flattery about my good looks and animal magnetism. Finally her pleas turned to outright bribery with sexual favors as payment. She was very persuasive in her description of the favors she would perform if I agreed to let her go.

That was the only time the trip went quickly, and I was surely glad the little slut was in the back seat with her hands shackled in the mandatory handcuffs.

Chapter Twenty

Chicago, Illinois

The sound of El Tercero's heels hammering on the oak floor as he paced back and forth finally got on Aroldis Gonzales Garcia's nerves. Saying he sounded like a Flamenco dancer, Gonzales Garcia ordered Santo Sotto to sit down.

"They will be here any minute. Perhaps traffic is heavy this morning," El Tercero said.

Just as Gonzales Garcia was to give his second-in-command a dressing-down, there was a rap on the door, and two men were escorted into the study by one of Gonzales Garcia's armed guards. The first man was simply another one of the crime lord's trusted soldiers; it was the second man who was the one of great importance. His name was Jacob Tandy, and he was a twenty-five-year veteran detective of the Chicago Police Department. In his hand was an 11-by-14-inch manila envelope containing photographs and typewritten information that was of concern to the two men who sat facing the officer.

"What do you have for us, my friend?" asked Gonzales Garcia.

Tandy pulled two 8½-by-11-inch glossy photographs from the envelope, and handed one to each man.

"This is the man we believe is holding Lieza. He is a Chicago police detective named Theo Boycek. No one has seen him for almost two weeks, but he is not on any assignment that appears in the police log. Officially, he is still on duty, and collecting a paycheck; I personally verified that fact with the payroll office. He has not taken a leave, nor is he on vacation. Yet he has disappeared. Even the four cops who were hiding out with the fake Lieza at the Palmer House do not know if he is with the real Lieza or whether or not he is on the case at all."

The cop spoke confidently, but wished he had more information to present to the two crime bosses. The reputation Tandy had among his peers was that of a conniver, someone who was seeking the upper hand by always looking for an angle. In his "me-first" world, Tandy walked a fine line between not-so-good cop and very-bad cop. The 51-year-old, balding, grey-haired, veteran cop kept himself in peak physical shape. His only physical impairment was that he was as bow-legged as a rodeo clown. Silently, he stood in front of Gonzales Garcia, waiting for the boss's response to his short presentation.

"Is that all, that is all you have for me? And what makes you think that he is the one who is guarding the woman?" asked Gonzales Garcia, who was loath to mention his former lover by name. "And please don't tell me you have a hunch. Hunches are for betting on horses, not betting on lives."

"First of all, Señor, he is nowhere to be found. I have accounted for all of the veteran officers who would be the likeliest to receive such an assignment. He has not been to his house in at least two weeks. His mail is piled up on the floor, newspaper delivery stopped. Even his partner, who is also his best friend, doesn't know where he is, or at least he isn't saying."

"Wife?"

"Not married."

"Girlfriend?"

"None. He's a loner," answered Tandy. "To me, it makes perfect sense. If I were in Lieza's shoes, Theo Boycek is the man I would want to guard my life, plain and simple."

"If you do not find the bitch soon, then perhaps you had better get this Boycek to guard you."

Gonzales Garcia's words were a not-too-subtle hint to the detective, and to El Tercero, too. Find the girl, or else they would be in the unenviable position of facing the wrath of their superior. The detective was not usually intimidated by anyone, but that was not the case with the Chicago crime boss who was currently threatening him. It was not so much the words and questions that came from the man, it was the cold, glassy stare in his eyes that upset the detective.

"Look, Señor. I am not a miracle worker. I don't have the where-withal to perform any task you command. I am only a detective, and I don't have the clout to be in on the decisions of the inner circle; they may not even know where Lieza and Boycek are located. Theo could be acting in a lone wolf capacity, could have ripped up the script and be off on his own. If so, he won't return until the grand jury convenes."

Sotto jumped up from his seat and got in the detective's face.

"We cannot wait until then. We have to find her now. Right now!"

Tandy was unmoved by Sotto's outburst. He was more scared by the big boss's stare, which continued to be fixated on him. He had been on Gonzales Garcia's payroll for years, but with few exceptions had worked with Sotto or one of his underlings. The gravity of an audience with the man himself was not lost on him. The loss of the bimonthly cash stipend he received from the organization was the least of his worries.

"I am working on this day and night, and so are all of my people. We will find him. I spread the money El Tercero gave me all over the city and suburbs with photographs of the two. Someone will give us a lead, and we will find them, and then she will be history."

"Have you checked the lakefront?"

"Yes. I have a crew on a boat in the water as we speak. I have sent men to Milwaukee and to the Indiana and Michigan shores. I have men watching his house, his partner."

"You have put all of your efforts into finding this one detective, believing that he is the guarding the woman. And yet you don't even know if he has the bitch."

Gonzales Garcia rose from his seat, and stopped within inches of Tandy. Their faces were so close that the detective could smell the harsh aroma of cigar on his breath.

"If this Boycek has no girlfriend or no wife, then I suggest you find his old partner or his friends and squeeze them for information," Gonzales Garcia said.

Tandy rebutted, "He only has one friend and one partner. We are watching both of them. And you don't know these guys, Señor; they are not the type of person who can be intimidated... even if they did know where Boycek was."

"Then pick them both up and make them talk. Everyone has a tipping point. Find this Boycek's partner, and his friend, and make him tell you where he is, or where he thinks he might have taken the girl. If you do not have the cojones to do it, I have someone who does."

Gonzales Garcia looked at El Tercero. "Set him up with Goshi Chao. Given time, Chao can break any man."

"His old partner and his friend are not just any men. They are hard men."

The words came out of his mouth with a tone that the detective immediately regretted. He searched Gonzales Garcia's face to see if he had gotten an unwanted reaction.

"Tell me, Mr. Tandy, do you have a tipping point? Do you know what will happen to you if you have miscalculated about the woman being with Boycek?"

"Yes, Señor," Tandy answered. "I will be very wrong...and I will be very dead."

Chapter Twenty-One

Chicago, Illinois

The Southport Irish Tap was a shot 'n' beer joint tucked amid the rehabbed greystones, chic taverns, and expensive cafés on Chicago's Near North Side. Despite the influx of yuppies into the neighborhood, the Tap managed to retain its character. It was a Chicago version of Muddy's on the lake, except the Tap's barkeep was not nearly as harsh as Muddy's proprietor, Gus Baldwin.

Its owner, Mike "Night Train" Layne, was a gnarly retired Chicago cop who served cold beer and burnt hamburgers to the local patrons. It was the unofficial hangout of city workers, blue-collar Joes, and police officers from the 19th and 20th district who didn't feel at home in the other nearby establishments.

I wanted to surprise Night Train, so I didn't call in advance to warn him I would be stopping in for a visit. I knew he would be there because, well, he is always there. The Tap was his home, literally and figuratively; he lived in a small, but efficient apartment, upstairs from his small, but efficient tavern downstairs.

Besides, I wasn't sure how long the transfer process of Miss Cheryl "I Will Screw Your Brains Out For Life If You Let Me Go" Kintrick would take. I was willing to cut short or completely eliminate a visit with Mike Layne, even though it was the more important of the two reasons I came to Chicago, but under no circumstances did I want to miss a widescreen viewing of *The Maltese Falcon*.

As it turned out, I had time to spare for a visit with my old friend. Night Train Layne, as I expected, was behind the bar when I entered. His chubby face lit up when he saw mine, and we started to reminisce about the days we worked together. We talked for an hour about the old gang, especially Dave "The Duke" Tedeski. The Duke had been Night Train's favorite; Tedeski was everyone's favorite, and not just after he had died. Everyone spoke kindly of a person after death, but Tedeski was a rare individual: he was everyone's favorite even while alive. People liked to be with him, to be part of his inner circle. In the wee hours of the night of his wake, many had gathered afterwards right here at the Irish Tap. I had confided that Dave was the only person in my entire life who I wanted to be like. At least half a dozen friends and coworkers admitted unabashedly that they too wanted to be like Dave Tedeski.

The more beers Night Train and I had, the more maudlin we became about death, the old days, and growing older, so I changed subjects and asked about my two cases from up north. I knew it was a stretch, but I tossed them out there anyway.

"You hear of anyone trying to peddle a vintage auto that once belonged to Bugs Moran?"

"That's out of my league, Chief, but I can ask around."

"Do that, Night Train." Then I described some of the stolen goods and asked if he'd heard anything about them.

Nothin', Chief, sorry. But talk to Paddy Downs."

"The cop in Deering?"

"No, the fence on Roosevelt Road. I'll give you his number."

Before he scribbled it down, I described Fred Smith to him, adding the little I knew about the mystery man.

"I tink I've seen the guy, at least someone who fits that description," Night Train said. "Comes in here once in a while, has a couple of beers. Most of the time I've seen him talking with one of the dicks, but I can't tink of who it is."

"Which detective? Was it Theo?"

"No not Theo, I'll tink of it, and when I tink of it I'll call you."

It was only when I was about to leave that Night Train told me about a couple of strangers who had stopped in a few days earlier, asking a lot of questions about me and a couple of other officers, past and present. He apologized and said he had almost completely forgotten about it.

"Sorry, Chief. It completely skipped my mind. I was so happy to see you, I didn't even tink about it 'til just now when we was speakin' 'bout that Smith guy. Only then did it jog my memory."

"Who are they?" I asked.

"They looked like a couple of thugs—Latino types, probably Mexicans or Central Americans. They were not the usual variety, you know, the sloppy tattooed ones. These guys were dressed in suits, definitely carrying," he said, referring to being armed.

"They were suspicious acting, so I told them nothin'. One of them had a picher and asked me if I knew any of you guys. Of course I told them no."

"What do you mean a picher? A picture?"

"Yeah, that's what I said; they had a picher of you."

"They had a picture of me? How odd is that?"

"It was that picher of you, the Duke, and Theo. You know the one when you guys were fishing up in Wisconsin, way before you moved back up there?"

"What else did they say?"

"They said they heard this was a hangout for cops, and the guys in the picher were cops, and it was very important that they got to see Theo Boycek. They pulled out a wad of hundred-dollar bills, and offered me some for info. But I told them nothin', absolutely nothin'."

"Did you see them again?" I asked.

"Are you kiddin' me? I threw them out because they was botherin' everyone, showin' that picher around, askin' all kind of questions.

After that, they was hangin' around the area, watchin' the joint from the outside for a couple of days, and then I stopped seein' them after that and completely forgot about 'em til we was talk'n' bout Dave and me seein' you."

"Did you tell Theo about them?"

"No, I told Rory to tell him, but he said no one has seen Theo for weeks. They think he's on vacation, or somethin'."

"Theo on vacation? That will be the day." I said, half-laughing. "Theo Boycek has no life outside of work. Why would they want to know about me? This is strange, real strange."

Night Train said, "I think they wanted to find Theo. I got the feeling they was askin' bout you just because you were in the picher. They thought you might lead them to him or something. They don't look like nice guys, Chief. I suggest you stay clear if you do run into them."

I purposely did not tell Night Train about the recent phone call I'd received from Theo. Boycek had asked that I tell no one, and I would hold true to his directive.

I gave my old friend my card and asked him to call me if he saw them again, or if he heard from Theo.

Night Train then gave me a sketchy description of the two Latinos, and I told him I had to leave. I had others to meet. It was true. I was off to the Music Box Theatre to see Mr. Humphrey Bogart and Miss Mary Astor. I had a date with *The Maltese Falcon.*

Chapter Twenty-Two

CHICAGO, ILLINOIS

The Music Box is a vintage movie theatre in the same trendy neighborhood, not far from The Irish Tap. It showed cinematic gems from a bygone era that usually appeared only on television. But for those who wanted to view the classics in a widescreen format, The Music Box is the place to go.

It was 10:15 p.m., and the evening showing of *The Maltese Falcon* had just ended. This 1941 black-and-white classic—a story of murder and intrigue—was the consummate "whodunit." Set in San Francisco, it involved a cast of colorful and devious characters who were seeking the mysterious, priceless, and ever-elusive Maltese Falcon.

I loved the movie and had seen it many times, but not because it was based on crime writer Dashiell Hammett's long-popular novel, nor for the crisp dialogue of screenwriter John Huston, who'd also directed the film. I liked the movie because I had this silly seam of vanity that liked to think I was comparable to the main character in the film, a gumshoe named Sam Spade, played by the great Humphrey Bogart.

Just like Spade, I am fearless, aggressive, and possess a vein of cynicism that could only be created by a pulp fiction wordsmith. However, I am more edgy than Spade, possessed more of the devil-may-care attitude, and, although strong and wiry, do not physically resemble Bogart. I often vainly said to myself, "So this is how others see me; how interesting."

It was a silly notion, because I knew I was really not like Bogey or Sam Spade. I was cynical all right; I possessed a lot of the edgy qualities of the protagonist, but down deep I didn't have the discipline to be that kind of individual. Maybe I did when I first became a cop, and perhaps, if I had remained in Chicago, I may have evolved into someone like the Spade character. The Chicago Police Department had a way of hardening an individual. It corrupted you, put a lot of hard calluses in your mind and over your body. Once I left Chicago for the suburbs, and then made my move to Geneva, I became softer and leaner in my thinking and my demeanor.

As I walked down Southport Avenue, my thoughts were engrossed in the film I had just seen. I did not notice until it was too late that the two men who had walked past me had quickly turned 180 degrees and were now only steps behind me, nor did I hear the screech of a van as it stopped abruptly. In a stupor, I was suddenly inside the van, trying not to pass out from the blow that had been delivered to my head.

When I awoke some time later, I was in a dimly-lit warehouse, duct taped to a chair.

I forced myself to become lucid enough to immediately appraise the situation. Damn duct tape, I thought. I'd like to kill the guy who invented it. It's so much easier to free yourself when tied with rope. This wasn't the first time I'd been bound with duct tape, so I knew it would be futile to try to struggle free.

I looked around the room; it was bare like it hadn't been occupied for quite some time. I didn't really care where I was, why I was here, or even who had brought me to the place. My only thought was how I might extricate myself from the shackles of the thick gray tape. The chair I sat in did not appear to be overly sturdy, and each of my legs was duct taped separately to the chair's legs. This was good. If I could crush the chair by rocking myself against the wall or on to the floor it might easily break. Each leg could then be free for me to run and kick while I fled. In the distance, I thought I heard Spanish being spoken.

This was not about a missing car or a couple of burglaries. This had to do, I was sure, with Theo—his phone call, and his impending visit to Geneva. Did I step into something bad, real bad? The Latino guys Night Train had told me about must have been watching his place, lurking about, and waiting to see if Theo would show up there. I'm sure he must have been their intended target. I'd simply had the bad luck of appearing in a photograph these goons had picked up somewhere.

As more bad luck would have it, they spotted me instead, ambling around like a naïve tourist taking in a late show. The Music Box Theatre was right near The Tap; they must have followed me there, then, while I was inside, they'd put together a plan, worked out all the mechanics, and snatched me right off the street when I came out of the theatre.

Were they that good or was I simply that bad? Why had I not been more vigilant? Night Train had warned me about these guys hanging around the neighborhood. If my hand weren't duct taped to the arms of the chair, I would have given myself a good pimp-slap to the face.

My thoughts now shifted from how I'd gotten here to how I was going to get out of here, but nothing came to me. With these guys, I had the feeling my powers of persuasion would do me no good.

The murmuring of Spanish I'd heard from before came from a trio who now stood in the shadows next to a wide column.

A short, sinewy figure and a wide-bodied one approached. The wide-bodied man stopped and stood still while the shorter of the two came closer to me. It was an Asian woman dressed in a black t-shirt and white karate-style pants. Expressionless, she stared at me. She made no attempt to hide or disguise her face. That was always a bad sign.

"Ni hao ma?" I said to her.

With quickness, she drove the heel of her foot squarely into my face. I and the chair, as if it were an appendage to my body, fell backwards to the floor.

This chair may be a bit stronger than I thought, I said to myself.

The wide-bodied man remained in the shadows, not bothering at this time to insert himself into the situation. He watched unemotionally as the woman struggled to raise me and the chair to their upright position. She looked at me squarely in the eye.

Unafraid, I asked, "Konnichiwa?"

With a one-two punch that would be the envy of a speedy, bantam-weight prizefighter, the woman landed two blows to my head, one to each temple. She was quick, and her punches stung, but not the same as if they had been delivered by a man.

My first two questions to the woman had exhausted my Far Eastern language skills, and I was glad I didn't know any other Asian greetings that might elicit more punishment. But the little Asian needed no excuses, and immediately went into a tirade of kicks and punches and body blows. She worked nonstop for what seemed to be a couple minutes or more. I tried to cry out for her to stop, just so I could ask what they were doing and what they wanted, but the blows to my mouth prevented the words from coming out. Sweating profusely and breathing hard, the woman finally stopped of her own volition.

The wide-bodied man stepped nearer to me, but his face remained in the shadows. He fit the description that Night Train Layne had given me of one the men who'd showed the picture in his bar. I wish I had taken the opportunity to stay away from these guys as Night Train had warned.

"Where is Theo Boycek?" he asked.

I spit a hocker of saliva and blood on the floor and asked, "Is this what this is all about? How in the hell would I know where he is? I am not his keeper."

A hard, open-hand chop landed on the side of my neck, and more blood and spit ran down my chin and landed on my shirt. The blow hurt me more than the others, but I was still glad it had been thrown by a woman rather than by a muscular male, such as my inquisitor. The man raised his hand to the Asian before she could cock her fist for another blow to my head.

"What is your name?" he asked.

I told him my name then added: "I'm Chief. Everyone knows me as Chief."

The man did not react to the indirect answer to his question. With the wave of his hand he held off the little Asian woman who was not amused by me; she appeared eager to beset me with more fury.

"I want you to tell me where Theo Boycek is, and who is with him. If you do that, we can all go home. If you do not, these unpleasantries will only continue. My little friend here is a professional. She will beat you to pieces and then take away your manhood."

I didn't like his description of what would take place, and I started to panic.

I lied. "Look, I haven't seen or heard from Boycek for months. He's a loner, a mystery man, always disappearing for long stretches, or doing something odd. I have no idea where he might be, or who might be with him."

"Where would Boycek go if he didn't want to be found?" asked the man. "Somewhere he could hide out for a couple of weeks."

"Wait a sec, let me clear my head for a minute."

I was trying to buy some time so I could figure out my next move. I wiggled my body in the chair. The duct tape had stretched a bit, but not nearly enough for me to free my extremities. I sensed that the integrity of the chair could be failing. Perhaps if I fell to the floor enough times, it might break to pieces. I thought about picking up a splintered chair leg and driving into my female tormentor the way a Romanian peasant drives a stake into the heart of a vampire.

In the distance I noticed a third figure, no doubt a man: his legs were crossed as he leaned effortlessly against the cement column. Just what I need, another person I have to elude if I can free myself.

Then I spoke out, in an eureka-type moment, as if I had just realized where my old partner might be: "Boycek likes to go to the gambling boats. He prefers the one in Michigan City, Indiana. Sometimes he stays at a cheap motel nearby."

Boycek didn't gamble, and I never remembered him ever going to Michigan. When he did leave the city, he usually went up north, to the west side of Lake Michigan, often stopping for a night in my little Wisconsin berg.

"I could take you there. I would recognize the place if I saw it."

As I was pleading my case, my eyes were drawn to the leaning figure in the distance. The man had changed position now, and stood facing me. Immediately, there was something familiar about the silhouette of the man: he was bow-legged. The only person I knew who was so bow-legged you could toss a Frisbee through the gap between his knees and not worry about touching anything was Jacob Tandy, another one of my former partners at the CPD.

That son of a bitch was just standing there, watching me get shit kicked. If I got out of this predicament, I swore I would show that bastard Tandy first-hand what it meant to get the shit kicked out of you.

That crooked cop bastard.

Then, my thoughts were interrupted by the big man, who said, "Unfortunately for you, detective, I don't believe you. Your story is quite lame. I hear Boycek is a straight-arrow man—doesn't smoke or gamble, barely drinks or cusses."

Now I was almost sure the man was one of the guys who had the picture that Night Train told me they were flashing in his bar. He had to know I was a friend of Theo's.

"Look, whoever you are, I am no longer a detective, or even a Chicago cop anymore. I quit years ago. I rarely see my old fellow cops or friends. I live out of state, I'm—"

The man stared at the Asian woman, and she moved toward me. I thought I noticed a slight smile of delight on her face. She really was enjoying this.

I saw a callous look in her eyes, and a feeling of dread came over me. Before I could begin to gather my thoughts, it all started again. Fists and feet, kicks and punches hit me all over my battered body. Then it stopped, as quickly as it had started. It was as if the Asian was attempting to get her adrenaline pumping.

A long, tapered object was placed in front of my face, and I recognized it as a chopstick. I feared that act two was about to begin. The woman placed the seven-inch-long object into my left ear, but not far enough in to cause any discomfort. Then, with the grace of a dancer, she moved herself around and stood in front of me, lifting her right leg upward so that her kneecap was touching her lips. She held the pose, presumably for my benefit, for a long time.

As beaten and battered as I was, I considered saying something like: "I would love to get you into my futon," but my boldness was fleeting. I turned my head and started to talk to the man who had retreated back into the shadows. I tried to shake the chopstick from my ear and wiggle to throw myself to the floor.

Before I could make any preemptive adjustment, she spun herself around like a ballerina and brought her right foot high into the air and hit the chopstick, driving it deep into my ear. I cried out in pain as the chair and I fell to the floor. I swore at the woman, calling her every foul name in my extensive four-letter-word vocabulary. Warm liquid began to build in my ear.

From my horizontal position on the floor, I could see a pair of bowed legs moving in my direction. I looked further up the figure, glancing at its face. It was indeed Detective Jacob Tandy, arm outstretched, gun in hand. He fired two bullets, instantly killing the wide-bodied man. His automatic was now pointed at the Asian, who moved to avoid his shot—but she, the one who had pranced so gracefully while pummeling me, was now almost flat-footed, as if she were moving in slow motion.

A single shot hit her in the forehead.

Tandy took a handkerchief from his pocket and placed it over my ear; I let out a murmur. He asked: "Are you all right?"

"You son-of-a-bitch, bow-legged bastard, what in the hell were you going to do? Wait for them to kill me?"

"I thought they were just going to give you a once over—you know, a good beating. When she kicked that chopstick into you, I knew I had to do something. C'mon, I'll get you to a doctor to look in that ear."

"What are you going to do about this?" I asked, referring to the two dead bodies. "We need to call the precinct station for backup."

Tandy thought about the situation while he cut the tape from me.

"If we do that, Theo will certainly die. Do you hear me, Chief? Theo will be a dead man. You can't go by the book on this, or Theo will be dead."

"Okay, okay, I get it. What will we do now?" I wasn't about to tell the bastard that I had received a call from Theo, and that he would soon be coming up to Geneva.

"I can't let the crime lab boys in here. I'll get someone to clean up the mess and dump the bodies elsewhere. This gun is untraceable. I've kept it for a situation just like this."

"What do ya mean by 'a situation like this,' you fuck? When someone is getting a chopstick stuck in their ear?"

"Shuddup and let's get outta here," said Tandy. "I've got to figure out what our next move should be."

While on the way to the medical clinic, Tandy told me the story of the Asian woman, Goshi Chao. Even though she had never laid eyes on me before, he said, she hated me. She hated me not because I was a cop, or because of my nationality: she hated me because I was a man. She despised all men. Being held captive and repeatedly gang raped by a band of thieves in her native China had had a lasting effect on her. She liked to endure pain, and even more so she liked to administer pain to others, preferably to the male of the species. If any of her rapists had survived the retribution she had meted out to them, they would have given testimony to the harsh punishment she was able to endure and inflict.

For a brief time, I had been in the unenviable position of being the embodiment of each and every rapist who had tortured and abused Chao for days on end in a rural province in China, until she was able to free herself, and become a tormentor and executioner herself. If it had not been for his intervention, Tandy added, given the opportunity by the man in charge, Chao would have tortured me until I was no further use to my captors, then she would have carved me up into unrecognizable pieces as she'd done to her rapists, many years before.

That bastard related the story as if he were some kind of hero for helping me out. I almost expected him to suggest that I owed him a dinner over the whole thing. He probably would want to go to Chinatown for a meal of dim sum and fried rice. What a great guy.

Chapter Twenty-Three

CHICAGO, ILLINOIS

I wished I had a Popsicle so I could stick it in my ear. My left ear canal throbbed and played an unrecognizable tune that sounded something like a medley on a Jamaican steel drum. Tandy gave me the six tablets of Advil that he kept in his pocket, in preparation for the many times he'd suffered from a bad hangover.

"I'm working undercover on this case," Tandy said. "I can't tell you anything about it, but Theo's in big trouble, and I'm the only one who can help him. You're gonna have to trust me on this one."

"Oh yeah, undercover. I figured that out already," I responded sarcastically.

"Undercover" was Tandy's way of saying he was on the take, and now he needed to eliminate the bad guys, and then figure out a way to place the blame on someone else. I worried I might be that fall guy. I was thinking I might end up like Miles Archer, Sam Spade's ill-fated partner in *The Maltese Falcon*. The Music Box seemed like weeks ago instead of only hours.

For now, I would let Tandy string me along—at least until I knew the truth. If Theo Boycek was in danger, I would not want to jeopardize his life, but once I knew he was safe, that would be a different matter. At that time, I would come down on that son-of-a-bitch Tandy's bow-legged ass.

"I'm lookin' for Theo. I think he has info that I need. Finding him will lead to wrapping up a lot of loose ends on my case, Chief. Take me to him or get me in touch with him. It's really important."

"What makes you think I know where he is? If I did, I would have told that ape back at the warehouse." If I didn't say anything about the phone call back in the warehouse while I was being beaten and tortured, I certainly wasn't going to be swayed by words spoken by Tandy.

"C'mon, Chief. You gotta have some idea where to find him. I'm in a big jam, and I gotta talk to him. It's important. It's a matter of life and death. Have you heard from him? He's hiding out, do you think he will come up to Wisconsin to your town?"

"How in the hell should I know? Look, I can't think with my ear like this. The damn things ringing like a church bell on a Sunday morning. Get me to that clinic on Roosevelt Road."

I had known Tandy long enough to never believe a word that came out of his mouth. If he told me it was noon, I would check my watch for the correct hour. While in the Mother Cabrini Medical Clinic, I tried to piece the parts of this puzzle together, but I couldn't concentrate. I only knew not to believe anything that Tandy said. I would have to be as cynical and skeptical as Bogart's Sam Spade.

For a brief time, almost twenty years ago, Tandy and I had been partners on vice in the 19th District. Putting two cops like us together—men with serious flaws in their character—on the vice squad was like giving the keys to the liquor cabinet to the alcoholic brother-in-law for safe keeping. Both of us shook down the local pimps and whores and the establishments where they operated. Tandy stole enough money to buy himself a little property on Bengston Lake, in Berrien County, Michigan, and had enough left over to drape both his wife and his girlfriend in furs and jewelry. I had squandered my graft on trying to keep an unfaithful wife happy. I also had a couple of other bad habits: gambling and booze.

But, unlike Tandy, after a year, I had transferred out of vice, and not because of a guilty conscience; at that time, I had none. My reason was that I'd developed a fear of getting caught. I also developed a sense of ethics. I call it my adult conscience, because I had none as a teen or a young man. Besides, I did not want to lose the only job I knew how to do, and I loved my work. I enjoyed the respect it garnered from some, and the fear it inspired in others. I had the curious streak of a nosy cat, and loved to pursue the bad guy; right now, I was curious about what was going on in the corrupt little mind of Jacob Tandy.

The nurse walked into the room, interrupting my thoughts. "The doctor says you're lucky. The object did not go that deep inside of your ear. You have a broken eardrum, and most of your hearing should come back."

"Funny, I'm not feeling lucky at all."

She ignored my comment. "Now don't be tempted to put a Q-Tip in your ear," said the nurse, who handed me the bottle of antibiotic ear drops and another with pain killers.

"Whadda think I'm a farkin' idiot?" I screamed at the woman as I left the tiny room.

I vaguely registered that I had been extremely rude to the caring nurse who'd attended to my damaged inner ear and bruised face.

Dismissing that realization, I returned to my thoughts. So Tandy wants me to trust him on this one? How absurd. The guy put me in a position where I got pummeled by a female Jackie Chan, had a chopstick burst my eardrum, witnessed two murders and a cover up and then he says, "Trust me on this."

I tended to mistrust everyone, except perhaps my dearly departed mother, a few friends, and of course my dog, even though I knew he could be bought off with a couple of strips of bacon. But there was more. Just like most of the cops who'd worked with Tandy, I knew he was corrupt and dirty, and would sell the last vestiges of his integrity to anyone who offered him a few shekels and a cheap shot of bourbon.

But this was big. Murder and kidnapping—these were capital crimes. As much as I knew about Tandy being dirty, I never would have figured him to get embroiled in something as dirty as murder.

Curiosity and concern for Theo got the best of me. If this corrupt bastard was looking for Theo, then he might indeed be in big trouble. I decided to play the part of a pawn in my ex-partner's game of chess to see where it took me.

Chapter Twenty-Four

CHICAGO, ILLINOIS

When I awoke the next morning, I felt like I had gotten hit by a bus and then been dragged underneath it for a block or two before a commuting blacksmith happened to drop an anvil on my face. I was barely recognizable to myself. I had slept with a bag of ice cubes on my face, switching it back and forth from my jaw to my cheek, the left side to the right. It was so cold in the bed I was sure I would wake up next to my ex-wife Rita.

The big question: How was I going to explain this new look? Cosmetic surgery was out of the question. I decided to choose one of three: a car accident, a mugging, or a jealous husband. I couldn't really tell the truth that a paid female assassin had beat me up and stuck a chopstick in my ear; two people had been shot dead before my very eyes, and now I was complicit in a crooked cop's cover-up of the whole matter. I decided the best story was the simplest: a jealous husband ran over me with a bus while I was getting mugged. The jealous husband was the same guy who'd dropped the anvil on my face.

After calling the station house to inform Dorothy that I had been detained in Chicago for a day or two, I raided the amenity refrigerator in my hotel room. I was pretty much out of it last night, but I did remember Tandy checking me into a hotel and using his credit card as payment. He was such a swell guy, always doing the right thing.

I took a bag of salted peanuts from the fridge along with three miniature bottles of vodka. I looked for some teeny-weeny blue cheese stuffed olives to no avail. I swigged the contents down with one gulp. I looked at the price list. The tiny vodkas were $925 each and the peanuts $645. I guess there wasn't much of a bumper peanut crop in Georgia this year.

They weren't really that high priced, but I wouldn't have cared anyway. I felt Tandy owed me for the severe beating I took, not to mention the probable partial loss of hearing.

My phone rang. It was Tandy.

"How are you feeling this morning, pardner?" he asked.

"Do you really care?" I said. "You had better tell me what's going on here, Jake. That was some serious crap that went down last night. You had better come clean. Who is your precinct captain these days?"

"Forget him. There are some serious guys looking for Theo. You need to tell me where he is. I ain't kiddin' you, Chief. Someone's going to get killed unless I find Theo, and I don't want that someone to be me or him. And now even you are in danger."

"Thanks for including me in your activities, ass wipe. I haven't seen or heard from you in years, and now I'm part of your little game here? I'm heading back to Wisconsin as soon as my face gets a little back to normal, and I don't want to see you or those bowed legs of yours for another couple of years." I was acting unconcerned, but was hoping to get some useful info from him.

"No need to get personal. I'm trying to save someone's life here. Have you any idea where Theo might be?"

I lied again: "No, but Night Train told me a couple of Hispanic types were looking for him and me. They had a picture they were showing around. Askin' lots of questions."

"That's what I'm talking about. These guys are part of the Cuban cartel. They're nasty. If I didn't save you last night, you'd be dead, chopped up in little pieces, and dumped in the incinerator at 103rd and Doty Street. Theo will be next unless I get to him first."

"You're quite the hero. Look stunod, I've been out of the loop for years. I get an occasional phone call, or hear a little scuttlebutt from someone passing through Geneva. But, if I see or hear from Theo, I'll tell him to get in touch with you. Okay? End of story."

"By not helping you're putting me in danger too, Chief. I don't want to have to... never mind."

"Never mind, what?" I asked the dejected Tandy.

There was silence. I almost thought he had hung up the phone.

"Jake, you still there?" I asked.

"Never mind; I have some work to do. I have some wrongs to right, sins to confess, and some atonement to honor. I need to... make a decision. It's Yom Kippur soon. I need to atone for my sins. Take care, Chief."

"Jake. Wait."

He didn't wait. I never got to ask him what he was talking about.

Now I almost felt sorry for the louse, because I knew he was into something way over his head and was desperate. No telling what a desperate man would do. But what I didn't know was this: Was Tandy working with the Cuban syndicate, or a lone wolf, simply trying to survive?

As much as I knew it was fruitless, I called Theo: first on his cell, and then at home. I didn't leave a message either time. I didn't want to leave any clues that could be traced back to me.

Later tonight, I was going to return to Lake Como, and I didn't want any Cubans coming after me or waiting for me. The Cubans were thorough, tossing a dragnet across Chicago, and maybe as wide as southern Wisconsin. If they followed me up to Geneva, at least I would be playing on my own turf with home-field advantage. I had a serious streak of self-preservation, and I didn't want to end up dead before my impending old age.

Chapter Twenty-Five

CHICAGO, ILLINOIS

Through his surrogate, El Tercero, Aroldis Gonzales Garcia sent a passel of his most competent underlings in teams of two north across the Illinois state line in search of his once-beloved Lieza Patrona. The men had been instructed to cut her throat from ear to ear.

What Gonzales Garcia did not know was that El Tercero had altered his boss's orders so that two of the men could run a special errand for the second-in-command. They were to deliver $30,000 cash to a Mr. Fred Smith at the Bayside Motel in Williams Bay, Wisconsin.

Based on a hunch and a photograph supplied to him by Jake Tandy, El Tercero dispatched his minions to search along the Lake Michigan shoreline. The photo was of three friends, beers in their outstretched hand, all smiling as if they did not have a care in the world. Sunshine, alcohol, a boat, and a body of water had that effect on most men.

These teams of underlings, armed with copies of the photograph, were searching lake towns along southern Wisconsin: Kenosha, Racine, the Milwaukee suburbs, and Milwaukee itself. The men would canvass the harbors, boat rental businesses, bars, and saloons, asking questions and showing the photographs of the three men.

At six o'clock in the morning, Cesar and Manuel were to drive westbound on Highway 50 from Kenosha to a point five miles west of the city of Lake Geneva, Wisconsin. They would call a telephone number, and arrange to deliver $30,000 to Mr. Fred Smith.

No receipt was necessary. The deliverers had no idea what was inside the black nylon bag, nor did they speculate between themselves the reason for the delivery. It was that type of thinking or questioning that caused one to fall into disfavor with their superiors.

As for Mr. Smith, he trusted that the amount would be accurate. He would follow through with the delivery of the merchandise.

Chapter Twenty-Six

GENEVA, WISCONSIN

I was back in God's country. After a day of rest in the North Side Chicago hotel, compliments of my dear friend Jake Tandy, I was trying to put the memory of a brutal beating and a burst eardrum behind me by admiring the multicolored leaves of a tall elm tree. Below the canopy of foliage stood three deer, foraging on the abundance of nutrients that lay on the ground. It was beyond my capacity for words to describe all of the tones and hues that were on display in the forest that late autumn morning.

My face, on the other hand, was almost as multicolored as the leaves, but instead of reds and yellows there were mostly blacks and blues and an occasional purple. I fought the urge to berate myself, and convinced myself not to reach under the seat to see if there was any vodka in my flask. I decided to remain upbeat and concentrate on the scenery.

A moment such as this, I concluded, was the true reason I'd moved from the urban sprawl known as the city of Chicago to rural Wisconsin. The simple pleasure of observing the flora and fauna in the countryside far outweighed the benefits a modern metropolis could ever produce.

I considered taking another day off to let my face mend. I didn't want to answer a lot of questions about the "accident" I'd had while in Chicago. Annie would surely ask about it, as would Dorothy. Bert, on the other hand, would simply ignore it, with the exception of a few snide comments. I decided the best story was that I had been involved in an auto accident while riding with a friend in his car. My air bag didn't deploy, and I hit the dashboard. "It's not as bad as it looks." I wouldn't mention the chopstick-in-the-ear episode at all.

Another reason to lay low was that I would bet dollars to donuts that Bert Burr and a few others would ask the old timeless and classic question: "Does your face hurt? It's killing me."

But luck wasn't with me this morning. The ring of my cell phone disrupted my ruminations. It was none other than Dorothy at headquarters, informing me of a disturbance at Muddy's; the call had come in to the stationhouse directly from Gus himself.

The disturbance at Muddy's didn't surprise me. Fights there were a fairly common event. I was surprised because it was early in the day, and that the call had been initiated by Gus himself. Bartenders, waitresses, or sometimes even a scared patron would place an SOS for assistance when there was some sort of a problem at the bar, but I couldn't ever remember Gus calling. The times he worked behind the bar, he generally handled problems all by himself, with the help of his friend Louisville Slugger.

Minutes later, when I arrived outside of Muddy's, I was witness to a donnybrook between Gus and Henry Stimach, the young lad I'd recently served a restraining order to, keeping him away from Muddy's. Actually, it was more of a yelling and shoving match than a full-fledged fight.

Sometimes, I thought that if everyone drove the speed limit and every bar in the township hired a competent bouncer to break up fights, my entire police department could be eliminated. Just two days ago I'd broken up a bar fight at Harpoon's between Bully Thornton and Mr. Fred Smith, and now here's Gus and Henry Stimach going at it.

I had hardly left my vehicle before Gus ordered me to arrest Henry for breaking the court order to stay away from Gus and his establishment. It was quite a sight to see the middle-aged Gus and the young Stimach pushing and shoving each other, both holding up their cocked fists, threatening to punch each other out. Just like most barroom hostilities between men who know each other, there was a lot of yelling, but no punches had been thrown. When I approached, both men stopped their activities and looked in awe at my face. Immediately they started their tirade all over again.

"What the hell is going on with you two?" I said, as I pushed them apart, careful not to catch an errant punch in my face. I just couldn't handle that in my current condition. I would have shot one, if not both of them dead.

"You guys are acting like a couple of teenagers," I added.

"I have a restraining order out on this guy, Chief. I demand you arrest him right now for violating it." The burly Gus screamed the words at me, his mouth contorted in anger.

"Just hold on here, Gus. Back off Stimach," I ordered, "or I'll kick your ass right here and now. Hear me?"

Gus paced back and forth like an angry street fighter waiting for the next round to start. Stimach, now docile, sat on a wooden bench, his saddened face pressed between his long fingers.

"Someone want to tell me what's going on here?" I asked.

Stimach jumped to his feet and started to say something about his mother, but before he could form a coherent sentence, Gus intervened and yelled to me again that it didn't matter, because a peace bond had been broken and an arrest had to be made. He ordered me to do so or else he would call in the county sheriff to do my job.

Gus's comments usually rolled off my back, but his orders and threats at this time did cause my temper to flare.

"Go inside, Gus, or I'll haul your ass down to the station."

He must have seen the anger in my eyes and heard passion in my words because he immediately turned and went into the bar.

"What are you doin' here, Henry?" I asked Stimach, who had returned to the bench. His face was long with gloom. "Well?"

He said, "I was talkin' to my mom."

Then he paused and was silent.

"About?"

"About havin' to stay away from Muddy's and all that. I said I seen other guys actin' up a lot worse and causin' a lot more trouble than I ever did, and Gus never threw them out for good like he did with me."

"Yeah, so what? It's his place, he can do whatever he wants."

"Well, Mom said it wasn't because of me. She said it was because of her. I asked her what she meant by that, but she wouldn't tell me. I kept harpin' on her about it, but she wouldn't answer me. All she would say was, 'You had better talk to Gus about it.'

"Each time I asked, she said, 'It'd be best if you talked to Gus about it.' So I came over here and asked Gus why. Why won't he let me back in to Muddy's? I told him what my mom said, and he got angry.

"Now, Chief I've seen Gus get angry, but I ain't never seen him get this angry b'fore. I figure there must've been something between Gus and my mother some time ago, and I wanted to know about it. Maybe it has something to do with my father leavin' my mother. You know, something like that. Did you know my father, Chief? Was he and Gus friends or maybe… enemies?"

"My roots with the locals don't go back very far, Henry. You remember, I am originally a flatlander."

Many Walworth County locals lovingly call the visitors from the big city to the south of us "Flatlanders." These Flatlanders, whose tourist dollars are the bread, butter, and gravy of the Geneva Lakes community, often become a local version of the Ugly American. When this Ugly Chicagoan rears its condescending and derisive head—to the dismay of harassed waitresses, insulted bartenders, and demeaned local authorities—there was not much love and admiration in the locals' hearts.

I asked Henry in a nice way to go home. I could see that he was troubled by what had occurred. I told him I would drop in on him after I talked to Gus.

Henry left peaceably and I entered Muddy's. Gus sat on a stool in front of the bar. He looked strange on that side of the bar, and I don't think I had ever seen him there before. If he wasn't behind the bar, he usually sat at a table in the corner. I also don't think I had seen him looking so sullen, and downright sad.

"What the hell happened to your face?" he asked.

"Forget about me. You want to tell me what's going on here, Gus?"

"Look. The kid was told—no, ordered—to stay away from here, and he came back and broke the court order. Now you goin' to arrest him or not?"

I looked Gus directly into his eyes and shook my head at him. "C'mon Gus, what's going on here between you and Stimach?"

Gus looked in my eyes, and he could tell that I had figured out what was going on between him and Henry. He put his head down and started to explain the situation to me. He rolled his head and gestured with his hands but said nothing.

Then he spoke quietly. "He's my boy, but he don't know it. No one does."

There was silence. Gus fidgeted with his hands and rubbed his fingers along the top of the bar then he started up again.

"He's my boy. I used to see Darla—you know, his mom. It was years ago. It wasn't love, or nothing like that; we never talked about being together. It was just a matter of convenience—for both of us, mind you. Just not convenient for me only, it was convenient for her too."

Gus spoke about his "convenience" like it was a TV dinner he'd popped in a microwave, rather than a relationship between two people. I wanted to slap him across the face.

"We talked about an abortion, but she wouldn't have anything to do with it. She's Catlick. When it comes to abortion you know those Catlicks don't want nothing to do with it. They look at it like it's murder.

"She told me to give her the money that I would have spent on the abortion, and that was all she wanted from me, nothing more. She said she would make up a story about the pregnancy, and that would be the end of it. But that wasn't the end of it, it never is." Then Gus stopped.

We sat in silence for a while. I thought he would continue with the story, but he didn't, so finally I asked him what he meant by "that wasn't the end of that."

"Several months after the baby's birth, she started blackmailing me."

"What are you saying, Gus?"

"I'm saying, after Henry was born, Darla said she needed money. She said she needed five hundred dollars a month and no one would have to know about me bein' involved. Then later on, after a few years she said five hundred wasn't enough, that she needed seven-fifty a month. And I have been paying the hush money for all these years. Finally it stopped when Henry was eighteen, when he got out of school and got himself a job."

I now realized that a pimp-slap was too good for Gus, only a hard punch in face would suffice. He needed a real good haymaker, one that would sting him badly and hurt for a couple of weeks. It would be a punch that was given not so much as punishment, but inflicted as a wakeup call. I was sure glad I didn't have a packet of chopsticks with me or I would have driven one deep into his ear.

"You dumb son of a bitch, Gus. Blackmail? What you're calling 'blackmail,' I think most people would call child support."

"Child support?" He was truly dumbfounded. He repeated the words then he went silent again. It had never occurred to the sorry bastard that he was reluctantly paying child support. He had never been asked to change a diaper or give a bottle to the baby; he had only been asked to contribute to the purchase of basic needs. Gus thought he was paying hush money so that he could keep his name from being attached to the birth of one Henry James Stimach.

What fools men could be at times. Once again, we sat in silence. This time for a long period. Then I spoke.

"Okay, Gus. Please tell me you realize that you need to tell Henry the truth about you being his father."

There was a puzzled look on my old friend's face and then he stated that he would talk to Henry.

"And let me give you some advice. Don't be your usual crabby self, Gus. Take the kid to dinner, to a nice place like Café Calamari, and tell him the truth. I'm not saying you need to act like a father and make him part of your life, although that wouldn't be so bad. Just stop acting like Henry is some type of leper that you need to avoid. Do you understand?"

The broken man nodded his head in agreement, and I sensed for the first time that my words had meant something to him.

On the drive over to the Stimach house, I reflected on fatherhood and wondered if I could ever be one myself. I didn't mean biologically; I was referring to being a proper father, doing the right thing, having a genuine relationship with a daughter or a son.

When I was a Chicago cop, I saw more than my share of young men whose lives could have been turned around by the presence of a father, real or simply a figurehead. It was a common occurrence when filling out a police report to write "unknown" in the slot allocated for father. There always seemed to be a mother or grandmother, but fathers were frequently an unknown commodity.

I wondered what impact a kind word or a father's attendance at a grade-school basketball game might have had on a young boy. What was the value of a parent's interest in a child's life, or boosting some-one's self-esteem through a kind word or welcome gesture?

Henry Stimach was a polite, hardworking young man. Darla Stimach did a fine job raising him on her own, but I wondered how much better of a person he could have been if Gus had offered him some encouragement.

In the process, Gus himself may have turned out to be a better person.

Now, it was too late to find out.

Chapter Twenty-Seven

Geneva, Wisconsin

This morning's interaction between Gus and Henry Stimach had been a scene right out of Mayberry RFD: two belligerent participants on the brink of fisticuffs, and me, swooping in like Sheriff Andy Taylor and settling the matter through calm reasonability. For obvious reasons, I disliked using references to Mayberry, Andy, and of course Barney Fife. I liked to think we were a little more professional, polished, and sophisticated—and a lot less bumbling.

Yet, there was Officer Bert Burr and his own brand of peculiarity. With his strange way of looking at things, Bert Burr reminded me of the goofy cousin who always got you into trouble with the words: "C'mon, I know what I'm talking about. You should listen to me. I've seen this type of thing before. Trust me."

When Bert started to speak, all I could see and hear was my cousin Louie, who, when we were kids, always got me in a predicament that I wished I wasn't involved in. Unlike Cousin Louie, whose kind of trouble was physical in nature, Bert put me in predicaments that were mental in nature. After we finished our little conversations, I spent entirely too much brain power thinking about situations and possibilities that I shouldn't really have to think about.

It was sort of like those TV shows about ancient aliens. Everyone knew that the Egyptian culture was not influenced by aliens, and the pyramids weren't built by extraterrestrials, but those damn documentary-style shows were so convincing—and, after all, they had credence because they were on the History Channel. Bert's theories hung on those same strands of possibility that lingered in your brain the way tabasco drops lingered on your tongue after you'd peppered your burrito with it.

When I came into the office this morning, after speaking with Gus, Dorothy reminded me that Officer Burr wanted to meet with me this afternoon. Before Bert arrived, I jotted down a note to myself, simply writing the initials T.B. for Theo Boycek, then added "Call Henry Stimach." I wanted to let him know that Gus would be calling him for a "get together" in order to put an end to the ongoing feud. I would say nothing about the history between Gus and Henry's mother Darla. That would have to be left up to Gus' dubious communication skills: "Hey, Henry. Years ago I was banging your mom, then you was born."

On second thought, maybe I should be there to act as referee.

I quickly put the consideration out of my mind as Bert Burr entered my office. By his serious manner I knew he had something unusual on his mind. To my amazement, he asked nothing about my face. I wondered if there were stories already circulating around the township that I would have to deal with in the days to come. Instead, he started off with a question.

"Chief, how well do you know Officer Donnert?" Bert was referring to our new officer Ralph "Ral" Donnert. Ral had been with the department for six months or so.

"Personally, not well at all. As you know, he has only been here for a short time. I know he hails from a small town outside of Baton Rouge. What's this all about, Bert? I checked him—" I stopped mid-sentence, then asked Bert: "What's on your mind, what's this all about?"

"There are some funny things going on here, boss. Strange events, inconsistencies, coincidences—and you know I don't believe in coincidences, Chief. I never have, never will."

"Continue." I really didn't want him to do so, but the time to close the door to this conversation had passed.

"First of all, he's dumb or is else playing dumb. Who writes himself a...?" Then Bert stopped himself. "And secondly."

"Secondly?" I asked. "What about first? What were you going to say?"

"It's not important for now. Second, he doesn't even know the difference between a burglary and a robbery. C'mon Chief, that's law enforcement 101. I had to remind him several times that a robbery is when you take things off of a person, and a burglary is when you take things off of a property."

Bert barely stopped to take a breath and continued: "He's so dumb about law enforcement and rules, but then he knows all about those antiques that were taken. There is something peculiar, Chief, something very peculiar."

Bert looked at me as if I were going to respond, but I didn't.

"Now about these cat burglaries..."

"Bert!" I yelled.

"Sorry, Chief, these burglaries. I've looked at them through all angles, and there is only one common thread that I could find. Do you remember the charity house walk in June that the Scovilles had for the Conservancy? And then in July, the widow Mrs. Helen Norwood-Winston had another for the Water Safety Patrol Fundraiser?"

"Yeah."

"Well I cross checked the guest lists—all of the tickets that were presold, they had names and addresses on them. It was easy to rule out the guests as possible suspects. I then figured if it wasn't any guest at the two fundraising events, how about the caterers or volunteers— you know, extraneous personnel, but even they didn't match up. I was about to go to a different angle—you know, back to the teenage thing, which I think we all ruled out.

"Then it hit me. What about security? Was there anyone hired for security purposes other than the volunteers? And there it was, voila. Officer Ralph Donnert worked both events."

Bert was rambling, but I resisted the temptation to interrupt and allowed him to continue unabated.

"While working security, Ral could've cased the place out, learned about the security systems, even determined which items were best to steal. Maybe going as far as taking pictures of items with his cell phone camera, and then checking out their value on the internet. How else could you explain someone stealing a Stanford White picture frame? Who would ever think a frame would be more valuable than the artwork?"

Even though he was sounding a bit like my goofy cousin Louie, his words were striking a chord with me. Crooked cop, inside job, great cover. It all seemed plausible.

"That's a powerful case, Bert," I lied, "but strictly it's circumstantial and coincidental."

"Chief, I already told you, I don't believe in coincidences."

"But they do happen, Bert, in spite of your beliefs. Do you think we could get Judge Goggin to give us a search warrant for Ral's camera phone, computer, or his home, based on your conjecture?" I answered my own question: "Probably not."

"I agree, but you can allow me to check the history on his office computer to see if he has been surfing websites or anything incriminating. Just give me the security code, or else you log in and let me check it out. It's a longshot that he would use an office computer to carry out his dirty work, but there may be a sliver of evidence there that we can build on."

Bert was too eager to act on his suspicions. If I allowed him to search Donnert's computer in his current state of mind, who knows what he might find. He probably would have learned that Officer Donnert was responsible for the Jimmy Hoffa and Judge Crater abductions—even though he was yet to be born. Besides, it wouldn't be proper for me to let Bert do it, so instead I told him I would it.

"When, Chief?"

"I'll do it right now."

"But Chief, Donnert will be here any minute, for his shift."

"Don't worry, I don't have to be at his computer. I can check up on it right here at my own computer. Which reminds me, Officer Burr. You are spending entirely too much time on the research of various crime theories. Give it a rest, at least here at the stationhouse."

I could tell Bert was embarrassed by my accusation of his wasting time, but he said nothing.

Out from my desk I pulled a little cheat sheet Dorothy had prepared for me. Now I was embarrassed for having to read instructions on how to use the computer.

"Stand watch, Bert. Let me know if Ral comes in. I'm not sure if anyone can tell if someone, through remote access, is checking up on someone else's computer."

I thought to myself, I should ask Nathan, my teenage neighbor whiz kid, if that is possible or not. It was Nathan who'd taught me everything I knew about technology, and that wasn't much, but I was learning something new every day. I made a mental note to ask the boy wonder if there was any way that Ral Donnert might discover that I had checked up on him through his computer. I realized that, as movie mogul Jack Warner might have said, "Mental notes—they are not worth the paper they are written on."

I swiveled my computer around, then unlocked my top drawer to get my steno pad, the one I kept with the various passwords that I used. Scanning down the list, I found it: PCW1234. That was the password I used most commonly—very challenging.

At the very moment I was to enter the security code I was interrupted by an almost-hysterical Dorothy. A matter of greater importance had arisen. Bert Burr's theory and our spying on Ral would have to wait.

Chapter Twenty-Eight
GENEVA, WISCONSIN

A call had just come in to the stationhouse informing us that a group of squatters at a remote farmhouse on the north end of the township was running a meth lab. The caller, Dorothy described, was a man whose speech was hysterical and almost incoherent. He babbled on about not getting his supply, how he wouldn't be taken advantage of, and that he was calling to get even with the lousy phonies who'd cheated him out of his money, so now he was ratting out those phony bastards. Every other word out of his mouth was the "phony" word, according to Dorothy.

Dorothy abhorred the F-word and avoided using it at all times, with the sole exception being her official work capacity, and then she only used it when quoting a third party. On those occasions she substituted the word "phony" for the all-purpose, four-letter verb, adjective, adverb.

The not-so-offensive "Flatlander" was then cast aside for the more harsh "FIB." Dorothy didn't like that name either. So, the few times she found it necessary to repeat anything derogatory about the tourist clientele, she'd often call them "PIBs" or "phony Illinois bastards," in lieu of the baser FIBs.

The lovable Dorothy had emphasized the "phony" word so many times that we were fully aware that the situation at hand was potentially explosive. As quick as a passel of teenagers bolting out of a classroom at the sound of the school bell, Geary and I—along with

Bert Burr, who was about to leave his shift, and Donnert, who had just come on duty—donned our Kevlar vests and grabbed shotguns from the rifle rack. Sirens blaring, we were on the road toward the location given by the mumbling caller. We dimmed our lights and turned off our sirens when we neared our destination.

The farmhouse was dilapidated, and appeared to be held together by old paint and rotted clapboards. Bert and I approached the front entrance, and with a wave of a pointed finger; I signed for Geary and Donnert to go to the rear of the house. Geary was a veteran, but I worried Donnert might have misinterpreted my signal as a gesture to bring me a Venti latte from the local Starbucks.

The front door was unlocked, and it squeaked when I pushed it open. Bert followed me up the three steps that led from the foyer to the small front room. From the outside, the lack of a vehicle gave the appearance that no one was at home, but the house had the definite feeling of occupancy. The living room was quiet but warm, a sign that the home was heated. When I stealthily moved several steps into the room, a smell overtook me. The fear of the situation at hand had allowed me to focus on the potential danger in spite of the aroma of a freshly prepared dinner that had now overwhelmed my senses.

"Police," I yelled out loud in my best baritone voice. I repeated "police" for all to hear. I immediately heard Geary's voice repeat "police" and then "clear" to let Bert and me know their location, and that, so far, the rooms were vacant. The process, room by room, was repeated until we were sure the first floor of the house was vacant.

While Geary and Donnert went to the basement, I checked the upstairs rooms. When I was assured the home was unoccupied and back on the first floor, I began my search for the other officers, especially Donnert, who was the novice of the trio. I called out his name and became concerned when I received no answer. From the rear of the house came an unsettling noise. In response I again drew my weapon from its holster and inched closer to what I believed to be the kitchen.

The nearer I came to the kitchen, the more my senses intensified. An aroma like the heat from a blast furnace slapped me in the face, breaking my concentration. With outstretched arm, hand, and gun, I spun around the door jamb and entered the kitchen. I was almost now almost paralyzed by the aroma that permeated the room. Once in the kitchen, I noticed Donnert standing in front of the stove. With a flick of his wrist, he wiped a slice of Italian bread around the inside of a pot of simmering marinara sauce. A casual observer might have thought he was attending a summer get-together instead of a raid on a possible meth lab. From either the intense garlic aroma or the savory taste of the sopped bread, his eyes glazed over and were filled with delight. In clockwise motion Donnert pressed and twisted his thumb and forefinger against his cheek giving the universal Italian sign of approval.

"Chief, you have to try this spaghetti sauce," he said. "It's unbelievable; I mean, it's really unbelievable."

I asked, sarcastically of course, "All clear, Officer?"

"Yeah, sure, Chief. All's clear… but really you have to try this spaghetti sauce."

As for me, rule number one was: Never eat the marinara sauce you find on the stove in a meth lab. My sarcasm had been lost on Donnert. I half expected him to start speaking in Italian while using wild hand gestures. Nor could I rule out the possibility he may break out in song, singing the Neapolitan favorite, "Funiculì, Funiculà." Bert Burr's description of Donnert as dumb, or playing dumb, came to mind, but I swept all thoughts aside.

Geary cried out, "Chief, take a look at this."

I entered a room on the first floor. Geary and Burr were peering into a corner closet.

"Look what we have here," Geary said smugly.

Inside the closet were items that appeared to be some that had been taken in the lakefront burglaries. Not a big stash—there were only a few items—but Burr recognized them, and started describing each item and which house it had been taken from. Burr always did his homework, and had immediately recognized the goods as the stolen property from the mansions on Geneva Lake.

"All of it is loot taken from the homes by the cat burglar," he said. "It's just a small portion of the total goods, mind you, but I am sure it's stuff that was taken from the Scoville house and the Norwood-Winston mansion."

I didn't know what to think of this situation. We came looking for a meth lab and found pot of marinara sauce and a few of the missing items taken in the lakefront burglaries.

Judging from the lay of the house—with lights burning, and food simmering on the stove—we must have just missed the occupants by minutes. Perhaps the same blusterer who had tipped us off about the meth lab had pangs of regret and warned his partners in crime about a possible raid. The place had the look of people fleeing in a hurry. The meth lab was a tiny operation, probably used to make a private stash for the distiller and a few of his buddies. Drug paraphernalia aside, I was sure the forensic team would find nothing for us; the landlord would have no useful info—he probably had received his rent payment in cash in advance. The DA surely would tell us not to move forward, because we didn't catch anyone red-handed and didn't have a search warrant allowing us to enter the premises, and there was no sense wasting everyone's time.

But at the very least we'd recovered some of the stolen goods, which was pure luck... or was it?

Tough luck for us all, or as Dorothy might have said, "It was bad phony luck that we just missed those phony bastards."

Chapter Twenty-Nine

Geneva, Wisconsin

L ater that evening, I reflected on my day. I didn't know what direction to go or what direction to think about the disparate events that had transpired. Action-wise, today had me in a dither.

First I had to listen to Bert's theories, conspiracies and what I'd figured at the time was plain nonsense. But now I wasn't so sure. I was wondering if all of the events—burglaries, the stolen vintage automobile, the arrival of the bi-located Fred Smith, Theo's mysterious, impending visit with a mysterious travel companion—were all related, or just coincidences? Bert's mantra: "You know I don't believe in coincidences, Chief," came to mind.

Then, by mere minutes, we'd missed making a drug bust and perhaps finding the burglar, or burglars, we'd been searching for over the last couple of weeks. The big accomplishment had been the discovery of some of the stolen loot and getting the meth lab supplies that had been left in the home. Possibly there might be some fingerprints that would give us a suspect or two or whose profile we could place in our database.

And, finally, where in the hell was Theo? If he'd had a change in plans, I thought he would have called me. Or was he in so much danger that me and my time and expectations were irrelevant?

In spite of the half-dozen cups of coffee I'd already downed, I was starting to doze off while sitting at my desk. I closed my office door, put out a "do not disturb" sign that I had pilfered from a knob at the French Country Inn, and told Dorothy to hold all calls and visitors, because I was going to do some heavy paperwork—my code word for heavy napping.

No sooner had I closed my eyes when my office phone rang; it was Dorothy.

"Chief, I know you told me not to disturb you, but there is a man out here at my desk who is from the Illinois Bureau of Investigation. I figured you would want to see him."

"Okay, I'll be right out." I stretched my arms, cracked my neck, and then unlocked my door and greeted the tall, angular man who was standing in the outer office. He greeted me by my full name, flashed his credentials, and introduced himself as Agent Ron Hurlbut of the IBI. We shook hands.

I asked what I could do for him. He called me by name and title, so I asked that he drop the formalities and simply refer to me as Chief, like most do.

"Tough day at the office?" he asked.

"Uh?"

"Your face, does it hurt?"

"Yeah, I know, it's killing you." My tone changed. "What do you want?"

"Chief, the bureau has been looking for a number of men who are paid enforcers of the Chicago crime boss Aroldis Gonzales Garcia. Have you heard of him?"

"Heard of him, yes, but we aren't drinking buddies."

He smirked.

"We believe that several may be up here in southern Wisconsin. IBI agents have been looking in Racine, Kenosha, Rock and Walworth Counties and a few of the border counties in Illinois as well. I have visited a number of departments, looking for information, and seeking—as we are with you—total cooperation." Hurlbut was professional and almost military in his speech and manner.

I regarded the man, and then stated, "My men and I will do our best in any way we can, Agent Hurlbut, but we don't get too much action from the Chicago crime syndicate up here, although some have been known to own vacation homes in the area. Mine is a simple, rural department, covering a tiny sliver of the county. Wouldn't it be wise for you to cover the larger towns and cities?"

"Normally, that would be good advice, but we believe the men we are looking for are trying to find a particular person who may be hiding in a rural area, such as your town of Geneva. Although we are canvassing the larger cities and towns, we are focusing our investigation and seeking help from the more remote departments, such as yours."

Hurlbut pulled a number of 8-by-10 inch glossy photographs from a file folder with a flap sealed by a small Velcro strip.

"These are the men we are looking for, Chief. Each is practically interchangeable in their appearance: All Hispanic. Some speak English well, whereas others speak with barely a trace of an accent. Around six feet tall, stocky muscular builds, almost always dressed in suits. They are well-armed and extremely dangerous. If you or your men see any of them, it would be very wise not to try and apprehend them alone. Contact us for additional help."

From the look on Hurlbut's face, I think he realized that he had just insulted me and my officers.

Considering I just got the crap kicked out of me a couple of days ago in Chicago, and therefore it might be a little hypocritical to think otherwise, I didn't like what he inferred. Here was another out-of-towner telling us cheeseheads—in my case a transplanted cheesehead—that we weren't smart enough or experienced enough to handle a situation on our own. The people from Illinois, especially Chicagoans, knew best. Their streak of superiority ran the gamut from business to politics to restaurants to law enforcement, as if to say: "You Wisconsin hicks are just too dumb and unsophisticated; we Illinoisans will show you the correct and most efficient way to do things."

Hurlbut began to apologize, but I interrupted him and told him my department would appreciate all the help we could get if we did encounter any of the men in the photographs. I had a very tough time speaking my words without showing signs of sarcasm in my voice.

I looked over the glossies. "Can't say I recognize any of them. Can I make copies? I'll post them on the board."

"You can have these," Hurlbut said.

He gave me the photos but kept the neat little Velcro-clasped folder, which I had been coveting since I had first seen it.

"Please don't post the pics in the open. This is a very sensitive case, and it would be better if perhaps you show them to your men individually and privately."

"I will do that, no problem," I said. "Can you tell me what this is all about, or is that too sensitive also? Who is this 'particular person' they are looking for, and why are they looking for him?"

Again I spoke without the slightest bit of strain in my voice.

"It's a person who can help us in our investigation of Aroldis Gonzales Garcia and his crime family. That is all I can say right now. This is the way the top brass at the IBI want us to handle things. Sorry, Chief."

He handed me the photographs.

Hurlbut and I shook hands. I looked him in the eye and said, "If I see any of these men or hear of anything suspicious I will call straightaway."

Hurlbut walked toward the door then turned and asked; "I don't mean to pry, but what did happen to your face?"

"I fell off of my bicycle."

"Yeah, right."

Then I asked if I could see his credentials once again. He handed me his picture ID and I noted his agency number in my head. I jotted it down before the door was closed behind him.

From the moment Hurlbut first entered my office and told me the reason for his visit, I knew I would not tell him anything about Theo's phone call and imminent arrival here in Geneva.

I also decided I would share with Theo only tidbits and pieces of the agent's visit, and perhaps withhold some details. I would feed him info on a need-to-know basis. Although I had always trusted Theo, even with my life, doubts had now arisen. Doubts, not by any of Theo's actions or words, but rather the theories and conjecture of Bert Burr had elevated my own sense of caution. I was suspicious by nature and cynical by design.

My motto: Trust everyone, but always cut the cards.

Chapter Thirty

Halloween was upon us, and the local stores were filled with arrays of costumes. I resisted the urge to buy a mask to hide my bruised and battered face from my girlfriend, Annie. The choices were plentiful, but I always preferred the ghoulish ones. I considered telling her that this was all make-up, that I hadn't realized that I had used indelible materials, and that now I was stuck with it.

When I was a kid growing up in Chicago, every year, my brother and I went trick-or-treating dressed as hobos. We would char the end of a cork over the stove burner, and then rub the soot on our faces. We'd put on old, ill-fitting clothes and a beat-up hat, and we were ready for a night of sugar-induced mayhem.

A few days ago, a Chinese karate artist had painted my face a multitude of colors using her feet as a paintbrush. Even after days of ice packs, the color of my face looked much the same as it had on Halloween night, many years ago, after I had rubbed the sooty cork on it. The swelling had improved a bit, but the discoloration was still quite ugly.

Annie would be concerned, and also ask lots of questions. I didn't want to lie to her, or tell her the truth and have to explain all the details. The only way to go was to stick with the story about getting in a car accident. Later, if I felt compelled to do so, I could tell her the truth.

Only hours after Agent Ron Hurlbut left my office, Theo Boycek and his mysterious friend arrived safely in town. Bert Burr didn't believe in coincidences, and I thought about taking up that same belief. What were the odds that I would receive a visit from an IBI agent asking a lot of questions and flashing around photos, inquiring about Latinos who may or may not be in the area? Then within minutes—without notice—I got the awaited call from Theo, saying he had arrived and was ready to check into the hideaway hotel I had chosen for him. Under cover of darkness, I moved the couple into the first-floor unit known as the Petite Auberge at the French Country Inn. The upstairs unit was vacant, and the building, also called the cottage, was on the quiet far west side of the property away from the main lobby and restaurant activity.

During the 1930s, the French Country Inn was the favorite hideaway of Baby Face Nelson, who used it in similar fashion as Theo was now: a place he could hole up while on the lam. The murderess, Greta Olsen, once told me a story about the hoodlum and bank robber Baby Face Nelson. Baby Face—particularly in 1934—was a frequent visitor to the French Country Inn, then known as the Lake Como Hotel. Nelson travelled with his wife, Helen Gillis, and he would often tell the guests of the hotel that they were on their honeymoon. In November 1934, only hours after leaving the inn, Nelson was shot seventeen times in an epic gun battle in Barrington, Illinois, while on his way back to Chicago. He died the next day.

I worried Theo and his guest might suffer a similar fate after leaving the French Country Inn.

Few words were spoken until we were safely inside the guest room. Earlier in the day, using a fake name for Theo, I'd reserved a room at the French Country Inn. I told the front desk that the couple was on their honeymoon, and did not want to be disturbed.

"Welcome, my friend," I gave him a half-embrace which he half-resisted. I looked at the pretty Latina who accompanied him and nodded politely.

"Nice face, compadre. Angry husband?" Theo said.

"I'll let you know later. Are you free to tell me what this is all about? Or if you prefer to keep me in the dark, that is fine too."

"Now that you are part of this, I think I owe you an explanation. For the past three days, since the time we left Chicago, we have driven a roundabout route throughout southern Wisconsin, moving from flea bag motel to flea bag motel. This is my lovely companion, Sophie."

I threw a glance in her direction and nodded a second time, ready to introduce myself, when Theo began anew.

"Sophie's real name is Lieza. We changed it along with the color and length of her hair. She is exhausted and a nervous wreck. I feared she might crack emotionally, so I decided it was best to stay in one location until she could give her testimony before a grand jury."

Theo talked as if Sophie was not present in the room, with little regard for her feelings.

"Testimony?" I asked.

"Sophie is the star witness against Aroldis Gonzales Garcia, the leader of Chicago's crime syndicate. You've heard of him, right?"

"I'm only nintey miles from Chicago, Theo. Not on the island of Malta," I said, to the delight of my friend.

"She is my responsibility now, but once she testifies against Gonzales Garcia, she will be under the fed's protection and all that they afford. I need to keep her safe for three more days."

By safe I knew he meant "alive," but I said nothing.

"This is a good place to hide out, Theo. You'll be okay here."

"Yes, great job, Chief. When I asked you to find a nice place that was not only secluded, but upscale and comfortable too, I had no idea you would pick a spot like this."

He looked in Sophie's direction. "I felt my companion here deserved a little luxury after having spent the last three nights in mom-and-pop motels in second-rate towns. And the day before that, in a suitcase."

Sophie smiled in response, but the gesture didn't reach her eyes. She did look pretty worn out.

Good thing I didn't suggest the Bates Motel, I thought to myself. When he said secluded yet nice, I'd immediately thought of the French Country Inn.

"So why are you on the run? Wouldn't you be better off in Chicago, in a safe house with some trusted allies?"

"Trust is the key word here, Chief."

Theo lowered his voice—this time, unlike before, in deference to Sophie's feelings.

"I'm sure Gonzales Garcia has some guys on the inside—dirty cops, real dirty. The other two witness were holed up in their own homes with multiple details guarding them day and night. Neither fared well. Armand Depke was almost killed in one of the attacks."

Theo glanced in Sophie's direction to capture her expression, but she was now curled up on the bed, her face on a pillow.

"You should be safe here."

"It's not that simple. There are some very bad characters combing the tri-state area, looking for the two of us with the sole intent to— well, you know. As I said, I need to keep Sophie alive until she testifies before the grand jury. After the state of Illinois completes its justice, the Federal Government will step in, and Sophie will become a ward of the feds and have the full force of the FBI to protect her."

"This is clearly a fed case. Why haven't they stepped in from the start?"

"National security, Chief. Homeland security now trumps all domestic crime, big and small. Had it not been for the feds' hyper-priority on homeland terror," Theo said, "the city of Chicago would not have been involved in this matter at all. Gonzales Garcia's organization would have been taken down by the feds using racketeering statutes. The Chicago Police Department would only have been used in a peripheral manner. In the meantime, I don't know who to trust; no one is who they appear to be. Everyone—stranger, co-worker, and acquaintance, except for you, of course—is a potential assassin."

Even though he pronounced me as a trusted one, he looked as if he was unsure of his statement.

Hurlbut's visit, followed so closely by Theo's arrival, aroused my suspicions, but I couldn't pinpoint what it meant. Keeping in mind my new-found respect for "there are no such things as coincidences," I'd originally planned to hold back some of the info about the visit from Agent Hurlbut, but Theo was completely open and honest with me, which was unusual to say the least. I was very surprised by his talkativeness and sharing of the details. I think he'd held so much of it inside, he wanted to get it out of his mind.

Theo usually didn't say much. To describe him as the strong, silent type would be a gross understatement. At times, he preferred to make his point with the nod of his head or the look on his face. Words, to Theo Boycek, were like bits of food on a deserted island: They were to be used sparingly. But this time, he'd told me what appeared to be the whole story because he needed my help, and I guess he figured, if I were to be his ally, I was entitled to know the circumstances.

When it came to my turn, I did share most everything with Theo: Hurlbut's meeting, the pictures of the Latinos, and everything else to boot. The conversations with Night Train Layne, the kidnapping off the streets of Chicago, and the beating in the warehouse with Jake Tandy coming to the rescue. But I withheld the details about Tandy's murders. Theo's high ethical standards would have demanded a report to his superiors and internal affairs.

"I think Tandy may be that dirty cop you think is on the inside of Gonzales Garcia's underworld," I said.

"That SOB. It doesn't surprise me one bit, except murder, Chief. That's unconscionable. I'm sorry you had to take that beating on my behalf. You're one brave compatriot."

"Not really. I would have told them everything I knew if they had given me a chance. Oh, did I not tell you about the chopstick in the ear?"

"Ouch, damn. Those guys are brutal."

I didn't tell him about the gender, or the diminutive size of the wannabe executioner.

"Tandy saved my ass only, I'm sure, after he put me in the awful position in the first place."

"He'll get his. Guys like him always do."

"One other thing, Theo. There is this guy I had a little scrape with. Goes by the name Fred Smith." I described Smith to Theo. "Night Train says he thinks he saw him hanging around having a couple of beers at the Tap. But that's all."

"Doesn't sound familiar. Next time I talk to Rory, I'll ask him.

Rory was Theo's one-time partner and longtime friend.

I told Theo that I would do as he instructed, without any questions asked.

"Listen, Chief. Don't draw any attention to our stay at the French Country Inn. No extra patrolling of the property, and you keep away from here too, in case you're being followed."

"Sure thing. I'm meeting my girl anyway."

"I thought you swore off dames after your divorce?" He smirked.

"More like dames swore me off—or more properly swore at me."

"You're a funny one, Chief."

Once the pair was safely tucked in their room at the Inn, and I'd moved Theo's car to my garage, I was able to stop worrying about my old friend and the danger that followed him. On my way home, I ran a little side errand to the Bay, stopping at Café Calamari to pick up some carry-out. Tonight, after work, Annie was coming over for dinner and a movie.

Recently, there had been a lot of disagreement over which movie we'd watch together, so we devised a solution. First we each chose three movies. Then we could each eliminate two of the other's choice; a flip of a coin determined who got to choose between the remaining two.

Annie was such a good sport that when she won the coin toss, she often chose my movie rather than her own pick. I, on the other hand, was selfish and never did the same. Let's face it: It's a lot easier to watch *Die Hard* for the 11th time than to sleep through *Sleepless in Seattle* once.

When we were in complete disagreement with no compromise in sight, the times when even a coin flip wouldn't suffice, we had a default position: Anything directed by Alfred Hitchcock. Earlier, Annie had texted me her three choices, and I'd texted back three of my own, ones I knew she would reject summarily. I really didn't want to watch any of my three; I only chose them because I knew she hated them all. I loved reaching my goal through manipulation. It was often quite gratifying.

That night, over dinner, Annie and I were going to watch *The 39 Steps*. Afterward, if I was a good boy, well, who knew?

When Annie saw my face, her eyes filled with tears. It was a good thing she had not seen it yesterday, or she would have had a complete meltdown. I told her it wasn't as bad as it looked. I skirted through the story about the auto accident; I hated lying, and I always got the non-facts mixed up.

"You stopped at Café Calamari, I see."

"Yeah, I had a taste for pasta Bolognese."

"I was hoping you would get Chinese," she said.

The very mention of the word "Chinese" made my stomach curl and my face hurt all over again. I hesitated and then answered, "I didn't feel like it tonight."

"What do you mean? You always want Chinese."

"I've sort of lost my taste for it. Let's not order it for a while."

"Lost your taste for Chinese? Chinese food is your favorite— plus, you love going to Moy's to ogle over that little Chinese doll you find so attractive."

"Yeah, I don't think she's that cute anymore."

"Well I never thought I would see the day that you wouldn't want Chinese food. That's a shock. No Chinese."

It was as if she were screaming the word "Chinese" at the top of her lungs and deliberately using it over and over again just to annoy me. Right now, I'd rather eat hummus and raw vegetables than even think about anything Asian.

"Can't we just enjoy the pasta?" I said, perhaps too harshly, because now Annie turned quiet.

We were enjoying our food—at least I was, in the Annie-induced silence. I replayed the first ten minutes of the movie because neither one of us had been paying attention to it. What Annie was thinking about I wasn't sure, but my mind kept skipping back to my cases: the missing Moran car; the Geneva Lake home burglaries; the farmhouse meth lab, which also had some of the burgled loot. I still had no solution for the beaver at the Martel homestead, and now I had Theo and company to worry about. I had almost forgotten my suspicions of Fred Smith: Tourist or villain, traveler or rogue? Or was he a guy just up for the week trying to get laid?

With few comments between us, Annie and I became engrossed in the movie. *The 39 Steps* was a thriller about a wrongly-accused man who gets himself involved in espionage, murder, and kidnapping. On the run from the police, the main character travels to Scotland to find proof of his innocence. He meets a lovely woman, gets handcuffed to her, and together they try to free themselves and uncover an espionage gang.

About two-thirds of the way through the picture, my mind began to wander. There seemed to be some eerie similarities between the movie's plot and real life. Life imitates art, as they say, or vice versa. The plot itself didn't closely resemble the events that had transpired right here in Geneva. Perhaps it was simply my overactive imagination that was at work here, but the situations and characters on the screen were putting ideas in my mind, ideas that I could not disabuse.

The movie had a character named Mr. Memory, whose brain had the capacity to memorize facts and could recall them at will—similar, but greater than the skills of the late Chandra Harper, who I was attempting to emulate. There were policemen who were fakes and a professor who was a spy. The movie started with a woman pursued by assassins.

I started to worry that maybe I, too, had such characters in my own midst. From the moment I 'd first met Agent Ron Hurlbut, I was suspicious of the real reason he had paid me a visit. This morning, Bert Burr had placed doubts about the credibility and reliability of fellow officer Ral Donnert. The mysterious local visitor, Fred Smith, had a military demeanor about himself; the bartender at the Harpoon Willie's had noticed it too. Was he a simple tourist, or was he involved in military intelligence? Then there was Mr. Memory, with his knowledge of trivia and minutiae; was he not so unlike Bert Burr? And then the coincidence of a visit from Hurlbut just before Theo and Sophie had arrived.

My thoughts were now starting to run amok like an Oliver Stone movie with conspiracy theories galore. I thought about Alfred Hitchcock's creative device, the thing he called the MacGuffin.

A MacGuffin is an unimportant item, a prop only injected to keep the plot moving forward. In *The Maltese Falcon*, the movie I'd watched the other night—before I was kidnapped and beaten to a pulp—the MacGuffin had been the elusive Maltese bejeweled falcon head.

Someone once asked Hitchcock to define a MacGuffin. His answer: "The things that spies are after." Were the burglary loot and the Moran car MacGuffins? Theo's predicament was similar to the movie man's on-the-run scenario. Were Theo and Sophie characters in act two of a play directed by Jake Tandy? Was Fred Smith a leading man in the cast, or simply playing a minor role? What were all of the spies after?

Internally, with my overactive mind and a barrelful of doubts, I was driving myself crazy. I put my arm around Annie and drew her close to me.

"This is a marvelous movie," she said, "but not too realistic."

"I hope not," I replied.

Chapter Thirty-One

Geneva, Wisconsin

Social critic Alexander Woollcott once said: "A hick town is one where there is no place to go where you shouldn't go." The town of Geneva—by Woollcott's definition and standards—wasn't exactly a hick town, because there were plenty of places one shouldn't visit. We had our share of strip clubs, biker bars, and few other dubious establishments where patrons wouldn't want their mothers to see them coming or going.

Muddy's Tavern didn't really fall into the category of a place one shouldn't go, except maybe for me. It was a place where sometimes I shouldn't go. Besides Gus Baldwin's tendency to drive me crazy, on the weekends, the joint was just too crowded, too loud, and too obnoxious. Particularly bothersome was the legion of smokers who stood outside the front door, puffing away on their cigarettes and stogies. They created a poisonous cloud that made me feel like I was walking through a farm field while it was being crop dusted. I am an ex-cigarette smoker myself, and while I still enjoyed a fine cigar from time to time, I made sure there was no one around to be bothered by the noxious fumes. Except for my frustrated canine companion, Dawg, of course, but he never complained.

Even with all of its warts and pimples, I decided to pay Muddy's a visit to see if something was amiss in Baldwinville. Besides, Gus—like all good barkeeps—was a trove of information. Maybe I could learn something new about something old. Plus, I wanted to check in to see if Gus had managed to talk to Henry yet. That wasn't a situation I wanted to stew for very long.

Fortunately the place wasn't very busy; maybe it was too early in the evening for the locals to come out to play. I looked around the room. Standing at the juke box was a man who was much too young to have his pants worn as high as he did. If they were any higher, he would have had to speak through the zipper of his barn door. A pretty blonde was helping him make his music choices. At the opposite end of the bar, there were a half-dozen men all wearing Green Bay Packer garb or John Deere hats and sweatshirts.

Icily, Gus asked what I wanted. By his demeanor I could tell he was still a little upset, or maybe embarrassed by the dressing-down I'd given him over the Henry Stimach situation.

"Stella Artois on tap," I answered.

He reached into the cooler and handed me a bottle after snapping off the cap.

"You want a crystal goblet for that?" he snickered.

"No, but a clean pilsner glass will do nicely."

"I don't know why I even stock that French crap. You and those yuppie types are the only ones who drink it."

"It's from Belgium, not France, and it tastes good."

"So are snails in garlic butter, but I'm not serving them either. Say, I have a favor to ask."

I figured his anger with me must have subsided if he was asking a favor.

"You remember that book I gave you last Christmas, Rodney Dangerfield's Book of Jokes?"

"Yeah, you mean the one you re-gifted from Ron Frankel?"

"No, it's not from Ronnie. I bought that book for you myself. I was sure you would like it because you love all those old Borsch-Belt comedians. Honest." He held up his right hand as a gesture of his sincerity.

"I believe you, Gus, but next time it would be better to check the front of the book first. That way you could tear out the page that has a note on it that reads, 'To my good friend, Gus. Enjoy and laugh. Merry Christmas, Ronnie.'"

"I think you're confused. But can I have it back?"

"Sure, why?"

"I want to send it to this old-timer who was telling me how much he enjoyed those old comedians, especially Rodney Dangerfield."

"Okay, let me get this straight. You want me to return the gift you gave to me, one that you re-gifted from Ronnie, so that now you can give it to someone else?"

"Well, when you put it like that, it does sound a little snarky, but yeah, I want to give it to this guy who I think will really enjoy it."

It appeared his anger toward me was in fact softening a bit, but one could never really tell with Gus. He always seemed crabby, even when he was having fun.

"I'll bring it in next time," I said.

While Gus ran some glasses through the glass washer and tended to the other patrons, I sat in silence, pondering quiet life in a small town. I loved autumnal Wisconsin. Even though both my parents died in October, years apart, and my wife left me the same month, October remained my favorite month, and autumn, my favorite season.

"You seem a little extra quiet today, Chief. Cat burglar got your tongue?" the returning Gus asked with a smirk of delight on his face. "What brings you out tonight?"

I ignored his comment about the cat burglar, which gave him a reason to say it again.

"No, seriously, cat burglar got your tongue? I heard you were ready to make an arrest, and then something gave you paws. Get it?" He spelled out each word "Gave you p-a-w-s, not p-a-u-s-e."

He waited for me to laugh, but I gave pause myself and decided I wouldn't give the codger the satisfaction, even though I thought his comments were clever.

"Where did you get that line from, Rodney Dangerfield?" When Gus didn't respond, I continued, "Actually, the reason I stopped in, besides wanting to see how you and Henry are doing, was to see if you'd heard anything about the burglaries or anything else that's going on. What are the guys talking about as they sit around at your bar?"

"To tell you the truth, not much. I heard some guys talkin' bout a little meth lab out on the north patch of town, but they said it was a real small deal. Some guy was makin' it for himself and a couple of his friends. No big operation."

"You heard right. We just missed hitting them by a few minutes, but it was a small lab. What about the burglaries, anything?" I didn't mention the few items of stolen booty we'd found in the meth house. "Also I wanted to know if you've seen any Latinos, well-heeled guys in suits, asking lots of questions, mostly about me?"

"Plenty of Mexicans, but none wearin' suits, not even on Sunday, and no one askin' about you. What's this all about?"

"Nothing important."

Gus pulled another Stella from the beer cooler and said this one was on him. I guess my perception was correct, his anger had subsided. Buying someone a drink was Gus's way of saying, "I'm good with you." I was going to broach the subject of him and Henry again, but I decided it best not to do so. Then Gus surprised me.

"The kid's a good guy," he said. "Darla did a fine job raising him all alone. Thanks for making me see the light, Chief. I'm glad the kid is in my life. I'm happy to know him on a different level, and I'm proud he's my boy even though I had nothing to do with raising him."

For all the years I'd known him, I'd never heard Gus speak so honestly, directly from his heart. I was shocked by his earnestness, and happy I had butted into a situation that I really had no business being involved in.

"It's never too late, Gus. I am sure Henry, even at his age, is happy that he now has a father in his life. I bet Henry's proud of you too. I'll deny I ever said it, but I am damn proud of you, Gus, and damn proud to call you my friend."

I put my hand out for Gus to shake, but he didn't take it. All he said was, "Okay, don't get all sappy on me now." Then he reached into the beer cooler, got me another beer, and stuck it in my hand. "This one's on me too," he said.

Alone I drank a third beer. Gus never came back to talk, and I was glad he didn't; it gave me time to switch off all the problems at hand and reflect on life. Alcohol had that effect on me, made me mellow even in the toughest of times.

I enjoyed being the chief of police in this small town. I enjoyed the people I worked with, the friends and neighbors I had, many of whom I'd met years ago, when I was ten years old, when our family first came up to southern Wisconsin.

I recalled a long-ago summer, back when I was thirteen years old; it may have been eighth grade, the week after my graduation from grammar school. School that year had seemed particularly long, especially the month of May. It had dragged on in slow motion, as if all the clocks had stopped and the all the calendar pages had stuck together. June, I'd worried, would never arrive—but then it did, and the school year ended, and it was back up to Geneva Lake to our summer home.

On the night of the first day of our arrival, I remembered lying in the grass on our front lawn and looking up at the sky. The sky up here was different than the one in Chicago; you could actually see the stars and the crater shadows in the moon. It was on that night I promised myself that someday I would live up here all year long. I would no longer have to stay in the city with the smog and the noise and people moving back and forth through crowded streets all twenty-four hours of the day. It took me almost thirty years, but I kept that promise to myself.

Life is good, and in the autumn in Wisconsin, it is simply better.

Muddy's was getting crowded, so I decided it was time to move on. It may have been the beer, Gus's kind words, or the reflection on my youth that had made me feel melancholy. Whichever one it was, I didn't care. It was time to return home and let Dawg out. Maybe too I would lie down on the grass in the front yard and examine the stars and the moon in the night sky.

Chapter Thirty-Two

GENEVA, WISCONSIN

I woke up the next morning and flipped through a small book of quotes that I kept on my nightstand. This morning's quote of the day: "There is nothing either good or bad but thinking makes it so," was from William Shakespeare.

I thought about it for a moment and decided to amend the quote to: "There is nothing either good or bad but drinking makes it so."

Perry Como's voice seemed to grow louder. I wondered if my mother's old Victrola had a mind of its own and adjusted the volume on its own accord.

The crooner's soft voice was peculiarly loud this morning. So loud, in fact, I could barely hear myself drink. I looked over my notes. I was preparing for this morning's staff meeting with my officers by writing an agenda and having a nip. But I wasn't drinking, per se, just having a friendly Bloody Mary to help get me through the morning. I used to look forward to these meetings, back when Annie worked for the township. It allowed me to strut and act the Big McGaffer in front of her without seeming as if I were putting on airs. Since she moved out of my professional life in order to move into my personal life, the likes of Geary, Shea, Burr, and the two new guys on the team, Ral Donnert and Efren Ovalle, don't quite give me the same thrill.

I sipped my morning drink. It wasn't really a Bloody Mary; it lacked the proper ingredients, horseradish and Worcestershire sauce. It was simply tomato juice with a couple of drams of vodka. Staff meetings always made me a little nervous, so I needed the potion to calm my nerves, and also act as the hair of the dog to ease the slight discomfort I had after an evening of self-indulgence.

After I left Muddy's last night, I'd returned home and had indeed reclined in the grass to observe the heavens and the universe, at least the tiny speck of it I could see from my front yard. It was spectacular. The night sky had never seemed darker nor the stars brighter. Unfortunately, I'd felt I needed some company to share this perfect moment of reflection and tranquility with me, so I'd brought my friend Smirnoff outside to sit beside me. That relationship didn't end well.

I looked over my notes. Even though I'd written them myself, they appeared illegible and indecipherable. I'd read somewhere that the human brain was categorized similar to the old library card catalogs, those little boxes sorted according to the Dewey Decimal System. I thought my brain might be different than most—more as if those drawers had been pulled out too far from the cabinet, and the index cards had spilled, all mixed up on the floor.

I gathered myself and my notes together in time for the morning meeting and headed to my car. As I walked from my car to the stationhouse, I decided to let Burr run today's session, but then quickly changed my mind. I wanted the meeting to be brief, a word that wasn't in Bert Burr's vocabulary. Before getting to the crux of the meeting— the burglaries, the Moran car, the meth lab farmhouse with a closet full of burgled items, and my questions about Fred Smith—I decided first to address any other situations that might have occurred.

I perused the week's report and then said to Officer Geary, "Tell us about this call you received that took you out to Theatre Road on Sunday night."

I should have waited to discuss the matter with him one on one, but, foolishly, I broached the subject to all.

"Well, Chief," he began, "we received a call about, well, you know what. A sighting… on Theatre Road."

"A sighting?" I repeated. The room fell silent.

"Yes, Chief, another sighting of the Beast. This couple said they were taking their trash out and then their dog started barking and going nuts. And then they saw it. It stopped, turned, looked at them for a few seconds and then went out scampering in the woods. The husband called the station. I was patrolling nearby and went over to take a look and write up a report, but of course the Beast had left, and the couple said they'd thought about it, and fearing ridicule, didn't want to make a formal statement after all. They described it the same way everyone else does: wolf-like, hairy, tall, big white teeth, walked on two legs then ran away on all four like a bear. I drove around Theatre down to Talbot Road and back again. Of course, I saw nothing."

Geary looked embarrassed and gazed around the room. He said, "That's it. That's all there is."

I made the mistake of asking if anyone else had anything to add. The question opened up a door, and all of us present at the meeting entered into an episode of The Twilight Zone.

"Chief, my brother-in-law saw it once. He says it's real, you could ask him," Shea said.

"The only question I want to ask your brother-in-law is how many beers he'd had when he saw it," Geary added.

We were talking about the Beast of Bray Road, also known as The Dogman. Bray Road is in the neighboring town of Elkhorn, the County Seat of Walworth, Wisconsin. To date there have been over two hundred sightings of the Beast, many by credible and prominent witnesses. Stories about The Beast of Bray Road have appeared on the History Channel, the Discovery Channel, and A&E. All described the creature as furry, wolf-like, seven feet tall, 300 or 400 pounds in weight, bipedal, able to leap twelve or more feet in three steps.

Sunday's sighting had been the second this year on Theatre Road, which was so named because for decades, there was a drive-in movie theatre located there just off Highway 50. The drive-in theatre closed over twenty years ago. I was ready to put the kibosh on any further discussion about the Beast when Burr asked for the floor. Foolishly, I said yes.

"Some of you may scoff at the legend of the Beast," he began, "but gentlemen, I submit the following." Then, with a clumsy hand gesture he opened his leather-bound notebook. No good ever came out of Bert's leather-bound notebook.

"I have been doing a little independent research about the Beast, and I have arrived at the possibility that there may indeed be such a creature right here in Walworth County.

"Anyone here ever heard of St. Anthony's Fire?" Bert asked, positive that no one had.

"Is that similar to St. Elmo's Fire?" Shea inquired.

"No, Elmo's Fire is nautical. St. Anthony's is agricultural. It's also called Ergot disease. It is a sickness caused by the ergot fungi from the rye plant, and other cereal grains. This fungus is known to cause some people to exhibit strange behavior, including delusions of being a werewolf."

"C'mon, are you kidding me?" came the grumblings from Bert's fellow officers. The mood of the meeting abruptly changed from interest to skepticism. Bert continued.

"Do not scoff at my research. Ergotism is real. It is a pathology that can cause a person to turn into a werewolf—or at least cause an individual to act like and believe he is a wolf. Many researchers of this disease have considered it to be an explanation for bewitchment, including those accused of witchery who were later burned at the stake after the Salem Witch Trials."

There was now silence in the room. I half-expected Bert to announce that he had proof that the Dogman had jumped off the screen of the old drive-in movie theatre, escaping while a 1950s-era horror film played and was now hiding in the nearby woods.

It seemed the wolf-man psychosis Bert talked about had disappeared across the entire globe, except in the Transylvania region of Romania, and in Walworth County, Wisconsin.

"Good report, Bert," I lied. "Now let's move on to the next item on today's agenda."

I was afraid we would not be able to recover from Bert Burr's dissertation on werewolves, so I decided to cut the meeting short and only broach the topic of the burglaries.

"Anyone have anything new on the burglaries at the lakefront homes?" I asked. "Anyone hear of any rumors, gossip, anything at all?"

There were a few grumblings from the crowd. My eyes met those of Officer Ral Donnert. I decided to put him on the spot.

"What about you, Officer Donnert? You have any thoughts you would like to share with us? About the burglaries that is?" As an afterthought I added, "Or the Bugs Moran car."

"Nothing, Chief."

"C'mon, officer. At least tell me your opinion, tell me what you think about these two cases."

"Well, Chief, if I had to guess, and mind you this is just a guess, if we figure out who was running the meth lab, we will discover they are the burglars too. After all, we did recover some of the loot in the house. As far as the Moran car, whoever lifted it is keepin' it for his own use. The men and I discussed that it is too rare to be sold on the market. It's gotta be like this those art thieves who steal a Picasso or Monet. They can't sell 'em, they just keep 'em for their own pleasure."

I almost got lost in Donnert's Louisianan accent, which had just a tinge of Cajun in it. It was almost as if he could turn it on and off as he spoke.

"Good, that's good, Ral. Very intelligent," I said.

It wasn't; it was nothing more than the same old dribble everyone else around here was repeating. Perhaps Bert was correct, and Donnert was not a smart cop.

"Is there anything you want us to do about the meth lab, Chief?" Donnert asked.

"I'm sure those guys won't return, they can't be that dumb. It wouldn't hurt, though, for you to keep tabs on the place, but don't spend too much time on it."

"I agree with you. I don't like spending time on a wild goose chase," Donnert said.

After the conversation with Donnert, there was silence from all. I looked at Bert. If he made a move toward his leather notebook I was prepared to take him down with a stun gun.

I looked over the faces in the room. My gaze settled on another new guy, Officer Efren Ovalle, our sole Hispanic officer on the squad. I decided to ask the usually quiet Ovalle a question.

"Efren, do you have anything to add, any idea about the ladron?" To put the new guy at ease I figured I would toss in one of the few Spanish words I knew. He seemed pleased with my attempt.

"El ladron gato, señor? Nada," he answered, with a big grin on his face. I figured it was best to end the meeting now, and immediately dismissed the crew.

Before they could leave the room, as an afterthought I said, "I have one more question. Have any of you seen a guy who has been around here for the past several days? He goes by the name Fred Smith."

I added a detailed description of Smith, and told the officers the locations where I had observed him. Geary said he saw a guy fitting that description smoking a cigar outside of the French Country Inn, but that was all. Then Officer Ovalle sheepishly raised his hand. I was hoping he wasn't going to say something more about the "cat burglar."

"Yes, Efren."

"Chief, I saw this man. I think maybe it was this man. I was driving past the Bayside Motel early in the morning. It was Thursday, my day off. I saw him talking to two men, Hispanics. I noticed the two men because they were dressed in suits, business suits. I'd never seen these two men before, and, well, I usually don't see Latinos dressed in suits around here, except maybe at nighttime or on Sunday. But this was in the morning, maybe six or six-thirty."

Efren hesitated a moment and I jumped in with a question. "These Mexicans, what were they doing? Were they acting suspicious in any way?"

"No, not suspicious. I think they were looking at a photograph and papers they had taken out of a manila envelope. They gave the white-haired guy a small nylon bag, like a small overnight bag. There was a lot of talking going on—and, Chief, I said they were Hispanic, but they're not necessarily Mexican."

"What do you mean, Efren?"

His answer left me cold, as if the blood had been drained from my legs.

"They were Latinos all right, but not necessarily Mexican. They had that Caribbean look about them—you know, Puerto Rican, Dominican, or maybe even Cuban."

Chapter Thirty-Three

Geneva, Wisconsin

"When I was born, I was so ugly, the doctor slapped my mother."

That was my favorite one liner from the Rodney Dangerfield's Book of Jokes, the re-gifted present that Gus Baldwin had given me last Christmas. A gift he now wanted back so he could give it to someone else. This morning, on my way to the staff meeting, I'd tossed it in the Jeep so I wouldn't forget about it. It was now a few ticks before noon, and this morning's vodka and tomato juice had whet my appetite for something more substantial, so I headed over to Muddy's under the pretense of returning the book. But what I really wanted was a Bloody Mary, and Gus makes the finest in the county.

By the time I came through the door, Gus was already half-finished preparing the drink. He was adding the final touches: Worcestershire sauce, and a healthy dose of freshly-grated horseradish root.

"Here's your book, Gus."

"Here's your drink, Chief." After a moment, he said, "Funny you should stop in here this morning, Chief."

Gus kept his voice low, like he didn't want anyone else to hear what he was saying. There was only one other person in the bar; an old man who was sitting in the corner drinking from a bottle of beer. I couldn't see his face from where I sat, and hadn't noticed him when I entered.

"Why's that?" I asked.

"When you were here last night, you asked if I heard any chatter about the lakefront burglaries. At the time I hadn't. But just a little later, after you left, when the place got crowded, I heard two guys talkin'."

"What did they say?"

"They said the cat burglar has to be Carlo Rapini. 'Has to be,' they kept saying. 'It makes perfect sense. It's got to be Carlo Rapini.'"

Gus was almost whispering now. I asked him to speak up, but he said he didn't want him to hear me. He nodded in the direction of the man seated in the corner.

"Don't worry about him. I can't hear you and I'm right next to you."

"That's him. That's Carlo Rapini right there," Gus said, and nodded once more in the same direction.

I knew Carlo Rapini had served time for burglary. It was years ago, and, as far as I knew, he'd been clean ever since. His reputation far exceeded his skills, but he was a local legend, held in high esteem by those who idolize such people.

Gus continued, "It does make perfect sense, at least to me. He once served time for burglary. It was years ago, but a leopard never loses its spots."

"I thought he was dead. Hell, he must be seventy years old, or older. Could he still have it in him?"

I looked over my shoulder, but still couldn't see his face.

"Go talk to him. I'll bet you anything he's the cat burglar."

I finished my Bloody Mary and asked Gus to give me whatever Carlo was drinking. With a second Bloody Mary in one hand and a Miller in the other, I approached Carlo Rapini.

"Mind if I join you, Carlo?" I placed the bottle in front of him.

"Anytime someone buys me a drink, they are welcome to join me," he said.

"Carlo, you have been on my mind," I lied. "I've been wanting to talk to you."

"Is this about the burglaries?"

"Yes, but I want to start off by saying that in no way are you a suspect. But I just wanted to ask if you had any ideas about how the two burglaries might have been pulled off, or if you'd heard anything from anyone. Does the M.O. fit a particular perp, or type of person? You must have read about the crimes in the paper."

There was silence as Carlo pondered his words.

"Well, Chief, a few of my cohorts and me, we have a cat burglars' club. We meet every Thursday night at Foley's. I could ask around see if a few of the members have heard any scuttlebutt or if any of them had pulled off the jobs themselves."

If it were possible for someone to give a look of complete ridicule and derision, that would be the stare emanating from Carlo's face.

"Okay, Carlo. I guess I deserve that—"

He interrupted me to say, "It's been thirty years since I last pulled a job, and none were ever in the area where I lived. I never crapped where I ate."

"I just wanted to know if you had any thoughts," I said.

"My thoughts are that you should mind your own business and not pigeonhole people because of their past. I paid for my sins years ago, so leave me alone."

Just as I was about to apologize, Carlo's son, Dante, entered Muddy's. He walked to the table and asked his father if he was ready. Carlo said to his son, "The Chief here thinks I had something to do with those two lakeside burglaries. What do you make of that, Dante?"

Carlo threw a ten-dollar bill on the table and yelled to Gus, "This is for both of the beers, Gus. You should be careful who you let in here. Your place could get a bad reputation."

Dante calmly approached and stood directly in front of me. Our faces were only inches apart as he regarded me up and down with a gaze similar to his old man's. His eyes were like two deadly weapons ready to be thrust into me as if they were stilettos. Abruptly, he turned and the two left Muddy's.

"That didn't go well," Gus said.

I said nothing in return as I finished my drink. I felt bad for the way I'd approached Carlo. It was difficult to rid a false notion. Carlo was angry that, for many people in this town, including me, he was only known as the guy who'd served time for burglary, even though it was thirty years ago.

The statute of limitations might run out on a crime, but never on a reputation.

I tossed a ten spot on the bar, bid farewell to Gus, and walked to my Jeep, where both tires on the left side of the vehicle had been punctured.

Chapter Thirty-Four

Geneva, Wisconsin

The town road crew came right out, jacked up my Jeep, and took the two tires into the shop to get them repaired. I went back into Muddy's and ordered another Bloody Mary. Gus made some sort of snide comment about me not driving over broken glass. I was amused, and retorted that if he didn't watch his mouth, he would see some broken glass coming down on his head.

I picked up a copy of the Lake Geneva Regional News that was sitting on the bar. There was another story about the two lakefront burglaries. They repeatedly used phrases like: "burglaries remain unsolved," and, "according to the Town of Geneva authorities, there are no leads." Perhaps I was reading between the lines a little too much, but I got the feeling the writer of the article was actually insinuating that the burglar chose these particular Geneva lakefront homes because they were in my jurisdiction, and that I was so inept and lackadaisical about my job that there was zero chance the culprit would ever be caught.

I reread the article and determined the writer was insinuating no such thing. It must all be in my own mind, I thought to myself; I was simply questioning my own capabilities. There could be some truth to my self-doubt, because I had lamented the fact that the burgled homes weren't a little further down the shoreline under the purview of the City of Lake Geneva.

All of Lake Como, including its entire shoreline, was located within the confines of the town of Geneva. A mere half of a mile or so, as the crow flies to the south, lies the majestic 5,800-acre Geneva Lake: spring fed, deep, and as clear as a September morning. Its shoreline was expensive, manicured, and home to the wealthiest and most prominent people in the Midwest. It used to be: "Make a million dollars and buy a home on Geneva Lake." Now, it required multiple millions to own such a trophy property.

The road crew returned promptly, and put on my repaired tires. They said it looked like the puncture marks could have been made with a stiletto-type knife, or even an ice pick. I decided not to dwell on Rapini's handiwork and get back to work.

I wanted to take another look at the area near the burglarized homes on the Geneva lakefront, hoping some idea would enter my brain. Dave Tedeski used to say: "Just like putting your feet in someone else's shoes, sometimes it is wise to put your brain in someone else's head." I think he may have pilfered the line from Yogi Berra. Both burglarized homes were among the smaller ones on the lakefront. The homes along this stretch were not even close in size to the McMansion properties that were sprouting up elsewhere on the lake. All were more modest in their size and opulence. Well, at least as modest as a two- to three-million-dollar home could be.

Perhaps the perpetrator had singled out this location, not because it was located in my Geneva Township, but because of the size of the homes.

It would be a lot easier to go through a ten-room home than a twenty-room one. The perp wouldn't have to worry about stumbling across an estate manager or a state-of-the-art security system. My decision to return to the scene of the crime had been based on a desire to take another look at the entry points. This time, I wouldn't be lazy, and would walk instead of drive the surrounding area to see if there was anything thing I might have overlooked. The old gut feeling that we cops liked to talk about was active, and I wanted to see if there was something to my intuition.

But sadly, there was nothing. No new thoughts or suspicions crawling around in my head. Dejected, I headed back across the highway toward the station house.

While approaching the turn at the intersection of Highway 67 and Palmer Road, my eyes were drawn to a blue convertible travelling south on the highway. It was a sunny autumn afternoon, so the fact that the top was down was not particularly odd, but the movements of the driver certainly were. The car weaved back and forth while the driver whacked the back-seat passenger over the head, again and again, with what appeared to be a short two-by-four.

I sped up and pulled over the vehicle. I hadn't recognized the automobile from the road, but as soon as I exited my car and walked closer, I realized the woman behind the wheel was Mrs. Alice Donahue; her son Mike was in the front seat, and her other boy, Terry, was seated in the back. It was Terry who was the recipient of the beating with the presumptive two-by-four.

"Why did you stop me, Chief?" Alice bellowed, in her slight Irish brogue. "'Tweren't speeding, t'was I?"

"You were weaving back and forth, driving recklessly, and beating on your son with a two-by-four," I stated in a serious tone.

"Aren't no such thing," she said. "But I'm about ready to kill one of these boys. These impudent devils are goin' to be the death of me yet. Someday you're going to get a call that I did in one of my menacing boys. Me own flesh and blood they are, but they're going to drive me to an early grave. You can bet they are. An early grave I'm telling you. Especially this one, Terry here. His mouth is going to drive me to an early grave."

Alice rambled on like a person who was about to lose her mind. The poor woman had four teenage boys, and it appeared the troublesome youths were about to drive their mother over the cliff of insanity.

"Alice, please calm down. I'm worried you could get into an accident, and you can't go around beating Terry with a two-by-four."

"A what?" she asked.

"A two-by-four. You can't hit your son Terry with a two-by-four, especially while you are driving."

Alice reached into a bag of groceries, one of three in the front seat between the driver and her son Mike.

"I wish it were a heavy oak board," she said, "but this is what I was using."

In her outstretched hand was a long loaf of Gonnella Italian bread.

I felt a bit embarrassed that I had jumped to the conclusion that the woman was assaulting her son using a piece of lumber. I empathized with her. When I'd encountered impudent teenagers on my job, I'd wanted to use my billy club over the head of many a teenager in the same fashion that Alice Donahue had employed the loaf of bread, especially during the summer tourist season. Besides, I could actually see my own mother taking such "harsh" action against my brother and me when we were sassy teens.

No harm had been done to the Donahue family, and I certainly wasn't going to ask Terry if he wanted to press assault charges against his own mother, so I left well enough alone. I warned Alice to drive safely, admonished Terry for misbehaving, and asked Mike to make sure they all arrived home without further incident. I could tell Mike's thoughts were elsewhere and he was not listening to my instructions.

I asked, "Something on your mind, Mike?"

"Yeah, Chief." He paused as if he were having difficulty getting the words out. Then he asked, "I was wondering. Did you catch that cat burglar yet?"

I had to control myself. I resisted grabbing the loaf of Gonnella bread from the grocery bag to beat Michael Donahue about the head with it.

"There's no such thing as a cat burglar," I screamed, "unless it's a thief who steals a cat!"

The trio left, Alice talking to herself along the way, and the two boys embarrassed by their mother's actions. As for me, the cat burglar comment aside, I laughed it off as I usually do with such incidents, and then proceeded to my next destination.

As soon as I entered my office, Officer Burr approached me with his latest theory about the burglaries. Bert always had a theory.

"Chief, about the burglaries…"

I groaned but said nothing.

Bert continued as if I hadn't made a sound. "Well, I think we should look into the finances of the homeowners. Maybe they set this up in order to collect the insurance money. Well, what do you think?"

"As simplistic as your theory is, Bert, you have a point, but I've already received permission from both homeowners to check on their financial data and to talk with their insurance agents. They're both financially sound, and had no special coverage on the items taken."

Bert and I chatted for a few more minutes, and then, after telling him to keep up the good work, I dismissed him. I hoped his brain wasn't working overtime, trying to connect the dots around the idea that the burglaries could be an insurance scam by the homeowners. That scenario would certainly be on any A-list of possibilities, but not much brain power needed to be spent on it. One only needed to watch one of several dozen crime shows on the television and that plot was sure to arise.

In real life, the possibility of an insurance payoff was greater in a murder case than in a burglary situation. If someone knocked over a business partner or spouse, and then it was discovered that he or she was the beneficiary of a life insurance policy, that person immediately became the prime suspect. Yet there were plenty of foolish people who believed they were capable of committing the perfect murder and reaping the benefit of a hefty life insurance policy.

Insurance fraud by burglary was often more involved, and the odds of getting caught were greater. False evidence needed to be planted, and then the stolen goods needed to be disposed of—either destroyed, or sold to a third party. Tedeski believed a person who stole from himself was often reluctant to destroy a particular item they had once coveted. They preferred to keep the item in a safe, undetectable place, or sell it to a fence for pennies on the dollar. And, let's face it, no place is undetectable, and the more people involved—say the fence—the more probable it is that the perpetrator will get caught.

Bert was correct though. Insurance scam was always a probability.

Bert's father was an accountant and his mother a librarian. Certainly Bert had learned from them a particular way of thinking that was orderly and analytical. He didn't look at the big picture but observed, primarily, the tiny details in order to solve a problem. He was a proficient reader of crime novels, did the daily Sudoku. Minutiae, trivia and subtleties were his bailiwick. That was why I liked to have him with me at a crime scene. He could glean irregularities at a glance, ones that I would never detect. I'm not referring to forensic evidence, such as fingerprints or DNA, but an out-of-place bit of bric-a-brac, or an uncharacteristic word a suspect or witness might use.

Bert's peculiarities on crime theory sometime ran to the brink of outlandishness, however. I once interrupted him analyzing the records of female criminals. He was categorizing them based on the bushiness and thickness of their eyebrows. Bert had a theory that women with thick eyebrows were more prone to commit violent crimes. I told him, if his theory were true, the unibrowed Mexican artist Frida Kahlo would be the all-time serial murderess. At times, I even worried that Bert might implicate my lady, the voluptuous and eyebrow-enhanced Annie Madden, in a crime.

He called his thesis the "Fisher Theory," named after one Lavinia Fisher, born near Charleston, South Carolina, in 1793. Mrs. Fisher was considered America's first female serial killer. She murdered a number of guests at the hotel she operated, the Six Mile Wayfarer

House, aptly named due to its location six miles outside of Charleston. She was sentenced to death after her conviction for killing several male travelers. Evidence was found in the numerous underground passages below her hotel. Before the hangman could perform his duty, Lavinia jumped off the gallows' scaffold after screaming at the gathered crowd, "If you have a message you want to send to hell, give it to me—I'll carry it."

She was quite the innkeeper. I wonder what type of reviews she and her hotel might have received had Trip Advisor been available back then.

After reading the story of Lavinia Fisher, I found some eerie similarities between Fisher and the Wayfarer Inn and Greta Olsen and the French Country Inn. Although Greta was not the innkeeper, she did spend a lot of time at the French Country Inn; Greta had murdered a guest there, and she'd used the underground tunnels as a way to move about the property undetected. She'd only killed one guest, who also happened to be her best friend, but who knows? Given the right set of circumstances, perhaps Greta would have blossomed into the town of Geneva's own modern-day Lavinia Fisher. Oh yes, I almost forgot. Upon her arrest, and faced with the preponderance of evidence, Greta reacted like a deranged woman too.

She was still awaiting sentencing, and regrettably there was no longer a death sentence by hanging, but perhaps Greta, as did Lavinia, would make an equally stunning final comment. I'm thinking something like: "The devil and Chief made me do it! Vacation elsewhere!"

Chapter Thirty-Five

GENEVA, WISCONSIN

Another Saturday night, and Kirsch's Restaurant, as usual, was as busy as ever. I entered the bar using the door that took me through the hotel lobby entrance. The barroom was packed with an array of local patrons and hotel guests. The fall colors brought a host of out-of-towners to southern Wisconsin, tourists who delighted in the paucity of automobiles and lack of smog. Some believed it was the fresh country air that was the Dairy State's greatest attribute, going so far to suggest—facetiously of course—that the state motto be changed to: Visit Wisconsin and Smell our Dairy Air.

On this particular evening, Kirsch's was as busy as any bar one might visit in downtown Milwaukee or Chicago. There were women in short skirts and high-heeled shoes, and sport-jacketed men sipped their gin and tonics amid the fanfare of barroom chatter. It was a scene directly out of a 1940s movie, except it was in color instead of classic black and white, and there was no saxophone music. The jukebox tonight played songs from the 1950s.

I told Annie I would meet her at seven; it was now seven-fifteen. I checked my new cell phone for a possible text. Two days ago, I'd moved into the twenty-first century. After resisting for months, I'd accepted a new cell phone. It was the kind with all the functions that were necessary for me to run my office more efficiently, and stay connected with the office staff and officers at all times—twenty-four seven, as they say. At least that's what Officer Burr told me. I would now have unlimited access to the whole World Wide Web, which was simply mandatory in this day and age—those too were more of Bert's words.

I wasn't sure if that was a good thing. I believed the peaceful existence I had craved for so long had just gone out of my life for good. Now, I would instantly be connected to people I had gone to great lengths to avoid. What next is in store for me, a Facebook page? So I will instantly know when Bert buys a new sofa?

Surprisingly, I had already adapted well to this new, more complicated device, and I was pretty proud of myself. In the past two days, I'd only had to call the teenaged whiz kid, Nathan, six hundred times for help. I checked again to see if there was a text from Annie, but there was none.

I hated sitting alone in a crowded bar, always concerned someone would believe I wanted company—I did not—or someone would think I wanted to engage in conversation—I did not. I just wanted to enjoy my vodka rocks and wait for Annie. I furtively looked around at the faces of the patrons. I didn't recognize any, so at least I wouldn't be set upon by someone who wanted to curry favor with the police chief.

Not to be smug, but as chief of police of this little town, I drew a lot of attention. I'd been approached too many times by people who wanted to "friend" me, so that if I stopped them for a traffic violation or some other minor infraction, I would let them go with a verbal warning instead of a citation. I could usually spot that sort upon arrival.

I tried to do my job to the best of my ability, and I hired and trained my staff to operate with considerable restraint: Do your job properly, but don't act the tough guy with a sizeable chip on your shoulder. The guy going four miles an hour over the speed limit is not your enemy; there's no reason you have to give him a ticket.

Some of the police in the neighboring municipalities liked to go after the tourists, especially those from Illinois, but I never saw the logic in biting the tourist hand that fed Walworth County. I treated the tourists with the same respect that I treated a lifelong resident of the area.

I had my personal code of ethics, and it didn't always match the state law. If someone drove drunk, they went to jail. I'd forgive a snide remark or two, but if someone got in my face, they went to jail.

Public urination behind a tree, or on the side of a garage, got a pass. After all, when you had to go, you had to go. And I always tried to avoid the "gotcha" attitude, such as, "Aha! Did you know it is illegal to drive in Wisconsin with your bright lights on? It blinds the deer, and here is your seventy-five dollar ticket, you stupid sap."

Rick, the bartender, asked if I "wanted 'nother."

I nodded. "More olives," I added.

Ever since they started filling olives with blue cheese, it seemed the bartenders began rationing them as if there were a wartime shortage of Gorgonzola. "Stick a couple of extra olives in the damn drink." I said to myself. "What is this, communist Russia, for chrissake? The olives have to be cheaper than the vodka they displace."

I found myself getting aggravated, and it wasn't because of the dearth of olives. I checked my phone again for a text from Annie: still none.

Under the ridge of the bar top, I sent Annie a text message: "at Kirschs r u on ur way."

I was proud of the progress I had made, technology-wise. I rattled off the text under the bartop almost as well as a teenager could surreptitiously text a friend during a math class without even removing the cellphone from his pants pocket. Okay, perhaps I was not that fast or that accurate, but I had been getting better, tech-wise. Hell, I'd even mastered email, at least half of it. I was not yet proficient at sending, but I was able to receive them.

To add insult to injury, someone nuzzled up to me. I turned to view the culprit. It was Lambros Pierce, one of the local yokels, as I fondly called some of the not-too-swift year-round residents. I immediately wished I could leave, but I restrained myself and didn't. I was surprised to see Bros, as we called him, here at Kirsch's; Muddy's was more to his liking.

"How you doin', Chief?" he asked.

"I'm well, Lambros. How about yourself?"

"Good, real good," he nodded. His face looked as if he had nothing else to say, and I briefly thought I might be home free. He stood back-to-back with the seated gentleman in the bar to my right, attempting to squeeze into the tiny space between the two bar stools. Not wanting to encourage the pest, I did not lean to my right, but kept my body perpendicular to the bar.

"Alone tonight?"

"No, waiting for someone... Is there something you need, Bros?"

"No, just came over to say hi. But actually, now that you mention it, I have a question to ask you 'bout the seat belt law."

He stopped talking and just peered at me with a dumb look on his face. Why did I have to open up my big mouth and ask if he needed anything? An inordinate amount of time passed. I waited for him to continue, but he didn't.

Finally I asked, "Well, what is it?"

"You know that new policeman, Officer Donnert?"

I waited again for him to continue, but he didn't. I guess he wanted me to answer his question. I waited a sec and then when he didn't continue, I answered.

"Of course I know him, Bros. He works for me, I hired him. Get to the point." I was getting perturbed, but tried not to show it.

"Well last week, Tuesday—no wait, it was Wednesday, yeah, Wednesday—I got up early and decided to drive into town to get myself a McDonald's breakfast, an Egg McMuffin." He scratched his head. "You know, now that I think about it, it was Tuesday."

"Lambros, is there a point to this story?" I asked again.

"Well, it was early morning, I'd say about five o' clock-ish, and I'm driving to McDonald's, taking the back road, mind you. I wasn't even on the highway, but on the back road. Ya know."

I was worried he was going to wait for me to acknowledge his "ya know," but thankfully he didn't.

"This new guy pulls me over on McDonald Road."

He stopped and started to giggle.

"Hey, Chief, I didn't even realize that I got pulled over on McDonald Road while going to McDonald's. Ain't that something, a real coincidence."

"Like an episode of the Outer Limits," I said.

"Whadda mean?" He asked.

"Nothing."

He started up again. "Anyway, to make a long story short—"

I interrupted him. "That ship has already sailed," I said.

"Whadda mean?"

"Nothing, go on."

"Well this new guy, Donnert, gives me a ticket for not driving with my seatbelt on."

Lambros looked at me like he was a wrongly convicted felon.

"Did you have your seat belt on?" I asked.

"Yeah, but he said I was wearing it improperly because I had the belt under my arm at the armpit instead of over the shoulder. Can you imagine that, Chief? I was on the back road at 5:00 a.m., and this guy gives me a fifty-dollar ticket for this crap. Life's not fair. That just isn't fair."

I had to admit I was on Bros' side on this one. Although the officer was correct, at least a "by-the-book" correct, I sympathized with him.

"Technically he's right. I'll talk to the officer, Bros, but I won't promise you anything."

"Great, Chief, that's really great. Let me buy you a drink."

"No, no, absolutely not," I said. "Actually, we shouldn't even be seen together talking about this seat belt situation. It'd be better for you to go sit somewhere else. You get what I'm saying."

"Sure Chief, I get you. You want to make sure we're not doin' anything fishy."

Thankfully, Lambros left, and, to boot, he left without even knowing that I had basically insulted him for carrying on his pointless conversation. The only good thing that had come out of the conversation is that I learned that my new hire, Officer Donnert, had issued a ticket for improperly wearing a seat belt. Technically, looping your arm over the seat belt is a ticketable offense, but around here, we use it as a reason to stop a vehicle when you have some suspicion, some sort of gut feeling about the automobile or its operator, not as an offense in itself.

It had been Bert Burr who'd first questioned Donnert's professionalism, and now I was having the same thoughts. I worried that Ral, as Officer Donnert preferred to be called, might actually be as inept as Bert had thought. Once I was back in the office, I would review the most recent batch of tickets he'd issued.

Without trying to draw any attention to myself, I looked around Kirsch's, hoping I wouldn't recognize any more of the patrons, and trying not to make eye contact with anyone. I simply wanted to enjoy my vodka and not be bothered. I hated being bothered, and Bros' unwanted, impromptu visit was enough bothering for one night.

Not wanting to be bothered was the reason I attended the Spanish mass at Saint Andrew Parish in the neighboring town of Delavan when I went to church on Sunday. I didn't understand Spanish, and I barely knew anyone at Saint Andrew, and usually no one knew who I was either.

Father Sabatino was the parish priest at Saint Sabina's, which was located right here in the township. The English-speaking congregation was full of my neighbors, friends and acquaintances. Even though Father Bob was one of my favorite people, I didn't want to go to mass and feel obligated to shake hands, give hugs, and kiss fellow parishioners' cheeks, not even during the peace offering, when it was customary to do all three. It was the same uncomfortable feeling one might have when going to a doctor who was also a friend in order to have a prostate exam. Some things are better left administered by strangers.

At the Spanish mass at Saint Andrew, I was just another gringo face. If I didn't offer my hand during the peace offering, or after mass, or if I failed to smile and greet anyone with an hola or buenos dias, those in attendance would most likely assume I didn't like Mexicans or that I was simply a rude person. Which, of course, only the latter was true.

It was now seven thirty-five. Still no Annie, and I was getting worried. Actually, not so much worried as restless. If I were at Muddy's, I would be more relaxed, probably because I was in my own element at that crusty old bar.

Kirsch's was upscale and chic, and I always felt a little out of place, at least on a crowded Saturday evening. When Annie arrived I was sure I would be a bit more comfortable. I pulled out my phone and typed in: "r u ok waiting at Kirschs." I pushed "send" and felt smug at the way I'd mastered the whole text-maneuvering situation while barely looking down at my phone.

Minutes later, I checked the phone again, and there was a text. To my dismay, it was from Nathan, the teenager who lived next door to Dawg and me.

What the heck? Why is Nathan texting me on a Saturday night? I hope there was nothing wrong with the house or with Dawg. I read the text in the dim light.

"chief why do u keep texting me from Kirschs am i spose to meet u there or something."

I rechecked the phone. It appeared I had sent the two text messages meant for Annie to Nathan by mistake. I guess my proficiency was not as good as I'd thought.

My self-deprecation over my technological inabilities was short-lived as I glanced at the door and saw Annie enter the room. She kicked her lower leg out to the side, as if she were making some special dance move, and then proceeded in my direction. A thirty-something professional-type sporting a black sport jacket and slicked-back, jet-black hair with blonde highlights approached her and asked, "Can I buy you a cocktail, beautiful?" His nose was refined, and his face, sophisticated.

"Sure, as long as I don't have to drink it with you," she responded and then proceeded to the chair next to me that had just been vacated.

"I guess that was a bit rude of me," she said.

"Yeah," I said. "You could have left him with at least a modicum of dignity."

Annie motioned the bartender over and asked what the gentleman in the black jacket was drinking.

Rick answered, "Vodka-rail."

"Give him one on me, and tell him I am sorry for being so rude."

Annie knew it was always wise to ask the cocktail of choice before popping for a drink for somebody here. There were plenty of high rollers at Kirsch's, and she could get stuck with the tab for an eighteen dollar glass of a Gran Cuvée wine or a seventy-five dollar snifter of Louis XIII.

"Where have you been?" I asked Annie, perhaps a little too icily.

"Why the attitude? I'm only ten minutes late."

"No, it's already seven-forty."

"I know. We were supposed to meet at seven thirty. I'm ten minutes late, a woman's prerogative."

"Didn't you say seven?"

Annie took my phone and showed me the calendar screen.

"Here, look. I put it right here in your meeting calendar. She showed me the screen. It read: "Annie 7:30 Kirsch's." She gave me a big, fat "see."

"Besides, I was basically ready. Why didn't you text me that you were already at Kirsch's? I could have rushed and gotten here earlier."

"Never mind," I said.

"Who are you texting now?" Annie asked.

"Only Nathan. I forget to tell him something."

Chapter Thirty-Six

Geneva, Wisconsin

Without interruption from anyone save the wait staff, Annie and I enjoyed our meal together. She had a dinner salad adorned with goat cheese, roasted almonds, pomegranate seeds, and heirloom tomatoes, and drizzled with a truffle oil vinaigrette dressing.

I considered, for only half a second, the evening special of roast squab topped with a reduction of cabernet, but then went with the New York strip steak smothered in morel mushrooms and garlic mashed potatoes. I told the waitress to hold the side of baby carrots. "Best to let those little guys grow up a bit longer. At least let them become teenagers, so they can drive their carrot parents crazy," I said.

I didn't think the waitress, Tracy, understood what I was saying. She never really understood my sense of humor, but she nodded politely and smiled anyway. I ate the thick slab of meat and washed it down with three glasses of red wine from a bottle that Annie had picked out of the list of chef's recommendations. Chefs are always recommending what you should eat or drink. I think their recommendations are based solely on price and markup.

During dinner, we talked about each other's work. It was a topic we always said we were not going to talk about, but then we always did anyway.

"I think Burlington has been quieter than your little town, even though it has ten times the population. It has been quiet, except for a few small-time crimes. You know, Chief, I'm the assistant chief of police, but sometimes I feel more like a glorified administrative assistant. I get all of the crapola that the Burlington chief doesn't care to bother himself with." I knew that included a lot of the paperwork that every police officer detested.

"I know what you mean. Geneva can't handle the salary for a deputy chief, so I have to handle all of the minutiae and damned paperwork myself, although I can usually toss some of it in the direction of Dorothy or Bert Burr." Sometimes I called Bert my deputy chief, but he really didn't have an official title.

"Except for last winter's murder of Chandra Harper at the French Country Inn, and all of the peripheral crime that went along with it, things have been relatively quiet in my zone too. Notwithstanding a couple of lakefront burglaries and a missing vintage vehicle."

I said nothing about the current, troubling issues in Chicago that had drifted into Geneva with the arrival of Theo Boycek and company. I didn't want her to worry.

On the back, back burner was Jonah Martel's beaver-pond situation. I wanted to ask Annie if she had a solution to the problem. It was the type of thing that could easily be blown out of proportion if not handled properly, so I wanted to address it before the Martels returned home. I would ask Annie's opinion, but didn't want to at the moment.

"Anything turn up on the missing Bugs Moran car?" Annie asked.

"Not really," I replied. "On one hand, Bert has me convinced that it was stolen by the same person or gang that committed the lakefront burglaries. But on the other hand, I have a feeling it's not really stolen per se, but just missing. I think it will turn up sooner or later. I hope it's sooner, for the innkeeper's sake. I think she believes she is the one responsible for its disappearance."

"What's your definition of 'missing,' as opposed to stolen?"

"Maybe it's at the mechanics or a body shop, maybe a friend took it for a joy ride or as a prank?"

"I think it's stolen," she stated. "It's been several days, so if someone took it with the intention of returning it, they would have done so by now. Also just my gut, but I wouldn't rule out the possibility that it could be bundled with the lakefront burglaries. Fifty-fifty chance there, I would say."

"You're probably right. I think I'll put it down as a stolen vehicle with an asterisk next to it because it's historical. You sound like Bert. He's positive it's related to the burglaries too."

"He's a smart guy. You don't give him enough credit," she said, using a tone that was filled with a tinge of I-too-am-smarter-than-you. "Didn't the robberies take place months before the car went missing?"

"Five weeks," I answered.

"So the robbers committed their crime, and then came back five weeks later and took Navilio's car."

"Came back from where?"

"Illinois. Chicago. That's where I'd look," she said.

"You know, we have some of our own thieves and criminals up here, too."

"I guess that was a bit prejudiced."

I changed the subject and asked if the officers in Burlington would issue a ticket for improper seat belt use for looping the belt under the armpit than over the shoulder.

"Let's not talk shop tonight," she said.

After the meal, we returned to the bar for a nightcap. We both ordered sambuca and cappuccino. Annie ordered some sort of flourless chocolate tart. To me it tasted like a lump of chocolate spam, not that I had any idea what that would taste like.

At the far end of the bar, I saw my friend Mr. Fred Smith sitting alone. There was something about the guy I just couldn't put my finger on. I asked Annie if she had seen him before and she hadn't. I then asked her to give me a quick profile of the guy, based solely on his looks and his mannerisms. She sized him up for a couple of minutes then walked over to the juke box, which was closer to where he was sitting. Her eyes darted back and forth from the playlist to Mr. Smith. When she returned to the barstool, she began anew.

"He's single. No ring and no ring tan mark. Spends a lot of time outdoors, tan and weathered. Works out regularly, low fat to body ratio. Age, mid-forties, even though the lines in his face make him appear older. Piano finger hands, slight calluses tell me he works with his hands. Sits erect, shoes polished; creased pants could be ex-military. It appears as if he is well aware of his surroundings. He ordered another drink without speaking, but with simple eye contact and a hand gesture, which says he tries not to call attention to himself with his mannerisms. I'd say he is either an abbot on leave from the abbey or an insurance claim adjustor. Why do you ask?"

"You're funny. He couldn't be an abbot or a monk, though. He's drinking brandy," I said.

"It's Wisconsin; Everyone drinks brandy." Annie reminded me that Wisconsin has the highest rate of brandy consumption of all fifty states.

"There is something about him that's just not kosher, but I can't put my finger on it."

"Has he broken any laws?"

"No. Just a little skirmish at Harpoon's the other day. Nothing worth mentioning. But one odd thing. Norman over at the Bates Motel says he is renting a room there, and—"

She didn't let me finish. "Why is that odd?"

"Because he staying here at the inn. What do you think about that?"

"Yes, definitely odd. I'll have to think about that one."

Work talk aside, we were enjoying a wonderful evening. Soft music, warm lighting, no bothersome interlopers.

And then Annie turned the conversation to us. No good ever came out of the conversational trio of man, woman, and relationship.

"You seem a little distracted tonight. Anything on your mind, besides the work stuff?" she asked. When I didn't respond immediately, she continued. "Do you ever think of us as a couple? After all, we seem to be exclusive."

"Exclusive." Is someone filming an episode of Sex in the City in here? I wondered. I was at a loss for words. "Have you heard from your friend Audra about the chief of police job in Pelham?" I asked.

I didn't know if a possible change in jobs qualified us for a "relationship" discussion, per se, but I didn't know what else to say. I know she'd said she didn't want to talk shop, but I couldn't think of any other subject to broach, and the Pelham position was the elephant sitting on the adjoining barstool.

"Change the subject. That is so much like you. Nice, real nice. Now that you ask, at such an appropriate time, yes, I have put together a resume and filled out the job application Audra sent to me, but I haven't yet made up my mind whether to apply or not. I've been told I have time."

"I'm sure you will make the best decision," I said.

I didn't know if asking her to forego a promotion would be considered selfish on my part. I also didn't know if she would think I was making some sort of commitment to her if I asked her to stay. I was at a loss.

"Don't you think the assistant chief of police of Burlington, a city of over ten-thousand residents, is more prestigious than being the chief of police of the rural little hamlet of Pelham?"

I was hoping my voice didn't betray my true feeling: "Why would you even consider a move that isn't even a lateral one, but a backward slide?"

Annie started to speak, but I really wasn't paying close attention to her words. It dawned on me that there might be another reason underpinning this situation. My musings about her making a move that was not an advancement screamed "ulterior motive."

Could she really be pulling a stunt like this? I have never known her to be devious, except when questioning a perp. She was a master at using techniques in order to get a criminal to slip up on his story. But would she use this cleverness on me? Try and force me to make a commitment by threatening to move away?

She was still talking about the possible move to Pelham. I feigned interest by simply shaking my head in agreement. I hoped with my benign head gesture I hadn't just committed to moving in with her, or even worse, getting engaged.

Fortunately, our waitress Tracy came over and handed me my phone.

"Here Chief. You left this on the table." I'm sure I looked embarrassed and said thank you. I was pleased with the interruption. I didn't want to talk about Annie moving to Pelham anymore, and I wanted to stop having thoughts about duplicity from the woman who I was dating. I felt like I was in high school and some teenage girl was trying to manipulate me into taking her to the homecoming dance.

To please Annie, and perhaps ensure I would not be going home alone tonight, I decided to try to sound somewhat romantic, which of course I was not. All the romantic bones in my body were either broken or at least fractured. I could already tell Annie was getting a bit perturbed, because she was the one doing all the talking; her lips tightened when she was angry.

I hadn't really said anything controversial, but I thought it best to say something sweet. I decided perhaps it was time for me to use the "f-word" this evening.

I lifted my glass a couple of inches from the bar and sloshed the coffee beans in my Sambuca from side to side, and then in the most sensitive, sexiest voice I could muster, I said, "You know, Annie, I am really fond of you."

There was a long silence. I waited patiently for Annie to express how wonderful and sensitive a person I was, but still she said nothing.

The silence grew deafening. It blotted out the music and the chattering of the patrons. It overwhelmed the sound of clinking glasses and the moving of barstools.

And then she spoke. "You're fond of me. That's wonderful. You're fond of me. That is really precious. You are fond of me. Are you fond of Dawg too?" she asked. "I'll bet you are. I bet you are very fond of Dawg too."

I believed I could detect a bit of sarcasm in her voice.

"Yes, of course I'm fond of Dawg. Why such a silly question?"

Then she hastily rose from her chair and said she had to leave, something about a mound of paperwork. I pushed my stool away from the bar and turned to join her, but before I could move an inch she shoved her index finger in my direction. The look on her face told me not to follow her.

So I didn't.

Chapter Thirty-Seven

GENEVA, WISCONSIN

A lone at a bar. It was not the first time, and it certainly wouldn't be the last. I married Annie's leftover sambuca with my own and peered at the six coffee beans that were now in the glass. The supposed good luck of the beans was not working tonight. What's so bad about telling someone that you are fond of them? I asked myself. And why drag Dawg into the conversation? What did he ever do to deserve such a put-down?

I was being disingenuous. I knew that sometimes I was a fool. This would have been a good time for me to profess my love for Annie by saying those three simple words: "I love you." I knew that I had said it before, so why was it that tonight the words had stuck to the roof of my mouth like a steaming hot piece of mozzarella cheese from a slice of pizza?

Sometimes, I made the biggest fool of myself when I was trying to be cute and witty. Saying something humorous at a time that called for seriousness was a coping mechanism. I'd recognized this flaw in myself for a long time, but had yet to change my behavior.

Was that it? Or was I feeling trapped and manipulated by Annie's talk about moving to the grand metropolis of Pelham? Earlier, Annie had said I liked to change the subject, and that was exactly what I planned to do.

With her untimely departure, I decided to give my full attention to Mr. Smith. He was engaged in a conversation with a delicious-looking brunette. From the look on the woman's face, she was rather pleased with what he was whispering in her ear.

I asked Rick for a coffee to go. Sitting here watching Smith and company made me feel like a peeping Tom, so I decided to bring my peep show outdoors, where no one could see me. Across from the inn there was a vacant lot. It was high ground, where I could back up my car and watch unobserved the comings and goings of the entire inn, except for the east parking lot.

I lowered the windows and the balmy night air refreshed my demeanor, which had sunk quite low after Annie had walked out on me. Trying not to be overwhelmed by my own sarcasm, I thought, That is the last time I ever tell a woman my true inner feelings. I doubted I would even tell Dawg that I was fond of him, although he was a male and would understand lot more than Annie ever could.

With my apologies to T.S. Eliot, "In the room the women come and go / Talking of Michelangelo." The poet may have written those lines after watching similar theatre that was taking place this night at the French Country Inn.

A young couple rocked back and forth on a swing near the fountain on the west side of the lawn. People walked onto the pier, which jutted out a hundred feet from the shoreline of Lake Como. Cars entered and exited from the parking lot that was just a couple dozen yards or more from where I sat in the lot, across West End Road. If I were on duty, or had more energy, I might have stopped a few on suspicion of driving under the influence, but I would have had to give myself a sobriety test first.

Leaning against the pool fence was a gentleman who looked familiar. I believed it could be Ron Hurlbut, the IBI agent who had recently paid me an office visit, but from the distance, I wasn't quite sure if it was him or not. The man pulled a cigar out of his jacket just as Mr. Fred Smith and his brunette friend came out of Kirsch's and passed by. The man who might be Hurlbut asked Smith for a light, which he obliged. The two men stood together only briefly without much conversation.

Another coincidence, I thought. Or am I now entering Bert Burr territory where everything has a purpose and is explicably intertwined? I tried to keep my thoughts and suspicions from running wild. With a puff of the cigar smoke the man disappeared, and Smith and his female companion proceeded to the hotel. Ah, Fred was a high roller; he'd taken a room in the luxury building, the one they called L'Auberge, with rooms that had large fireplaces and two-person whirlpool tubs. So, tonight, Mr. Smith is going in for the kill. Figuratively, I meant, not literally. One murder a year on my beat was surely enough.

With Smith presumably tucked in bed for the night, I had no real reason to stay and watch the evening's goings-on at the inn, but I stayed anyways. I reached under my seat and pulled out a flask that had a smidgeon of brandy left in it. I poured the remnants into the coffee cup, and began to reminisce about the days when I lived in Chicago proper.

When we were in our early teens, my best friend Dave Tedeski and I would follow people. On many a Saturday we would take the Lake Street "L" downtown for a matinee movie. Afterwards we would randomly pick out an interesting-looking person or couple, and then follow them around, sometimes for hours on end.

We used to dream up fake facts about these people; we imagined they were spies or wanted criminals or simply nonsensical things. Dave and I were professionals when it came to nonsense. None were better. We would follow the people through the streets, sit on a bench and watch them eat at a street vendor, and follow them through the stores while they shopped. The large Loop department store, Marshall Field's, was our favorite venue for spying on our unsuspecting dupes. Sometimes we even followed them when they rode the bus.

The one thing Dave and I learned is that other peoples' lives are really just as boring and uneventful as our own. But it never stopped us from following and spying and hoping that something interesting would happen along the way.

My silly thoughts were interrupted when I noticed a figure sitting in the swing that had been vacated by the young couple. His continued hand-to-mouth motion indicated he was puffing on a cigar. I believed it to be a man, the same one who'd asked Smith for a light: IBI Agent Hurlbut. I decided to take a closer look.

I drove from my perch across from the inn and parked on the far side of the east parking lot. If it were indeed Hurlbut, I wanted him to think it was just a chance encounter. Besides, the short walk allowed me to gather my thoughts and choose the words I would speak.

Approaching the man, I stated: "I think he is tucked in for the night, but certainly not asleep."

"I beg your pardon?" he said.

It was Hurlbut. "I said, I think he is in for the night."

"Oh, it's you, Chief." He hesitated a second and then asked, "You aren't spying on me. Are you?"

"No, not at all. I just had dinner with my lady, but she got called away. She's a cop too."

"What did you mean by, 'He's in for the night'?"

"Smith, Fred Smith. The guy you're watching. Did you get a look at that brunette who left the bar with him? I don't think he will going anywhere tonight, except maybe halfway to heaven."

"What makes you think I know this Smith, and that I am watching him?"

"Just a hunch," I said. "There is something strange about him. He's raw, yet professional in manner. I figure maybe he's involved with those Latino guys you're looking for."

"Is that all you have for me, a hunch?"

"Let me see your credentials once again."

Hurlbut pulled out his badge and identification card from his sport coat. I struggled to examine the I.D., so the agent turned on the flashlight on his phone. Note to self: Learn how to turn on flashlight app on my new cell. I examined his credentials closely, and believed he was who he claimed to be: an agent for the Illinois Bureau of Investigation.

"You're a suspicious one," he said.

"Chicago does that you," I said, trying to use a harsh voice.

Wanting to put him on edge, I said: "Why would you ask a man you are tailing to light your cigar?"

"That was rather dumb," he stated, almost embarrassed. "I didn't realize it was Smith. I just thought it was a couple returning to their room. Smith had previously been alone, so when I saw this couple, I asked for a light. He showed no indication that he made me."

Satisfactory answer. Without hesitation I decided to share the little trinket of information Officer Ovalle had shared with me.

"One of my officers saw Smith a couple of days ago with two guys that fit the description you gave me: Hispanic, tough looking, suits. It was early morning, and he thought they may have passed a duffle bag to Smith. My officer said the guys looked more like they were from the islands, Puerto Rican or Dominican."

I didn't mention Cubans. I wanted to see if Hurlbut would share some info with me in return. "How would he know the difference?"

"He's Mexican himself."

"So diversity comes to small-town America. What next?"

"Yeah, I hear transgender bathrooms are arriving soon."

"They're Cubans. Part of Aroldis Gonzales Garcia's network. They're looking for a witness who is supposed to give testimony against him. She's the one and only witness against him. Alive, that is. The other two were killed last week."

Once again, he had an air of superiority in his tone. Sort of like he was saying: "I know stuff that you don't know."

I was sure Hurlbut was one of those guys who had to be the first one to telephone all of the relatives to share the sad news that Aunt

Maribel passed away. But he appeared to be talkative, so I didn't want to interrupt him. I nodded in agreement, much in the same manner I'd nodded earlier with Annie, except this time I was paying close attention.

"We believe she is being guarded and moved around from place to place by your ex-partner."

"Which one? If you include my ex-wife, I've had more exes than Hugh Hefner."

"Theo Boycek. Have you seen or heard from him recently?'

"If I were in danger, Boycek's the guy I would want on my side. But, no. Haven't seen or heard from him in a quite a while.

I was uneasy about this conversation. "But why are you searching for Boycek? The very fact that you cannot find him shows he is doing a good job of protecting the witness, does it not?"

"That is information I am unable to share with you at this time, or, for that matter, anyone outside of the bureau."

I was peeved, but didn't show it. I'm surprised he didn't say something lame like, "That's above your security clearance."

Trying to sound like I wasn't begging, I asked, "What can you tell me about Smith?

"Nothing much I can tell you. That isn't because of security clearance. It's because we really don't know much about him. He's a kind of shadowy figure who has been known to do some jobs for Gonzales Garcia. Yet he has no criminal records, not much of a résumé, only a loose connection with the Cubans. So when his name came up, we started to keep an eye on him."

I was convinced Hurlbut was authentic, that he was indeed an IBI agent, but I was cautious with my words. Tandy was a Chicago Police Officer, but he was as corrupt as the day was long. Gonzales Garcia's arm of corruption had a long reach that could extend all the way inside the Illinois Bureau of Investigation. Hurlbut could be as dirty as Tandy. I decided I didn't want to share any more info with the agent.

Early tomorrow, I would speak with Theo about Hurlbut to learn if he had any information regarding the man. I would also make a call to a friend of mine in Internal Affairs, and see if he could dig up any info on Hurlbut.

"I still have a couple of things to do this evening. Could we meet tomorrow, say eleven a.m. at my office?"

"Sure thing," said Hurlbut.

The agent sat back down on the swing that he had been sitting on before I'd interrupted him. On my walk back to the car, I realized that I needed to make a change of plans. I didn't like what I saw this evening.

Mr. Fred Smith was staying in a second floor room in the L'Auberge at the French Country Inn. Right next door, in the building called the Petite Auberge, was Theo Boycek and his prime witness.

Outside, watching Smith's comings and goings, was Agent Ron Hurlbut. I was hoping he was there only to keep tabs on Smith and had no idea that Theo and guest were tucked only yards away in another room. But I couldn't take that chance. Theo and Sophie would have to be moved once again.

I also hoped that Smith was so engrossed in playing "hide the salami" with his beautiful brunette pick up that he didn't realize he had been the topic of conversation between an IBI agent and the local chief of police just steps from the building he was staying in.

Football has often been described as a game of inches. Tonight's game at the French Country Inn could be described as one of yards.

Chapter Thirty-Eight

GENEVA, WISCONSIN

Even though I'd only had a few drinks last evening, I felt a little blurry in the mind. I swore it was the sambuca; that liqueur was like a drug to me. I didn't know why I even indulged myself with it. Or maybe it was the mixing of the drinks. If I stuck to one type of booze, I was all right, but switch from beer to wine to liqueur and I'd certainly have a restless sleep and a mind that didn't want to participate with the rest of my body the next day.

That damned liquor had affected me more this morning than it had yesterday evening, when it was newly-ingested into my system. Last night, my mind had been clear and efficient. The proof of that was, as a result of the lucid conversation with Agent Hurlbut, I'd made a calculated battlefield decision and carried out said plan with precision and stealth. Theo and Sophie had been moved from the room at the French Country Inn to a new location. Remote and impenetrable, it was a place no one would ever think of looking, because only a few were aware it existed.

First I'd loaded up my car with provisions from the local Sentry Grocery Store. Then in the wee hours of the morning, after I was satisfied Hurlbut was no longer on the premises and Smith was still in his room having the time of his life, I moved Theo and Sophie out of their room at the inn. With cover under the shadows of night, through the neighbor's yard, down the lakefront into my Jeep, the couple, over the objections of Sophie, had been whisked to a new location.

Even Theo had no idea where he was, but he'd agreed that the new location was a place he could defend and hole up in until the time he would transport his witness back to Chicago to give testimony before the grand jury.

Convinced that Theo and Sophie were safe and sound, my mind drifted instead to Annie. Dinner with her last night had been a bust. I thought about texting her to apologize for my rude behavior, but I wasn't exactly sure what I had done wrong. I didn't want to get all mushy with her, and besides, I was so inept at texting there was be a fifty-fifty chance that I would send the message to the wrong person. If it went to Nathan, he could get the wrong idea about me.

Even though it was a skillset that an officer of the law should possess, I was never one to pick up on the subtleties of others, be they male or female, expressions or gestures. Although there was no doubt about the look on Annie's face when she'd walked out on me at Kirsch's, I wasn't exactly sure what to think about last night's rendezvous with her. That practically never happened. Maybe I should consider writing a relationship book. I could title it Women are from Venus and I'm an Idiot. Even with my head filled with a fair amount of reservation, I decided to give Annie a call, but I still worried I might say something that would upset her.

"Hi Annie, it's me."

"Who?"

Even though it was only one word and she damned well knew who it was, I was sure I denoted just a minute change to her voice that indicated she wasn't as angry as she had been last night.

"Let me start out by apologizing and saying that I hate when we argue."

"Are you being honest, Chief, or are you simply telling me what I want to hear? Exactly what are you apologizing for?"

Oh my God, what now? I groped for the correct answer.

"I'm sorry for last night."

"Exactly what about last night?"

"You know, my behavior. Me always thinking about myself and my needs coming first. And I know you want our relationship to be more about us and not just me."

I could feel myself verbally stumbling down a long staircase, one with no handrail.

"And I know you want me to be more sensitive, but you know I'm just not a sensitive type of a guy. But there is one thing I know." I hesitated. "I know I love you, Annie. I have loved you from the first day I laid my bloodshot eyes upon you."

"That was nice, very nice. Sensitive too," she said.

Sensitive. Damn, I hated that word, but I knew I was in like Flynn.

"As much as I am enjoying this conversation and the sense of uneasiness in your voice, I need to go. I'm late for a meeting with the other chief in my life."

"Wait, Annie. Are you free this evening? Can you meet me at the French Country Inn at five? I have a room for the night."

"Pass up a night at the Inn? No way. Yes, of course I'm free."

"Wonderful, bring absolutely nothing to wear."

"You are a scamp. I'll see you at five-ish."

Dawg scratched at the back door and I let him in. Perry Como's mellifluous voice filled the living room with one of his old standards while I read the morning paper, drank my coffee, and mentally prepared myself for my eleven-a.m. chat with Agent Ron Hurlbut.

Besides Hurlbut, there were some other not-so-pressing items to be considered in no particular order: Navilio's missing car, the beaver problem at Martel's farm, and the lakefront burglaries. They were like a bad dream that never went away.

Then of course, I'd need to review the tickets issued in the past week by Ral Donnert, including the questionable seatbelt infraction to Lambros Pierce.

Once back in the office, I asked Dorothy for the duplicates of all traffic tickets that had been issued for the past week. Not wanting to cast suspicion on Ral Donnert, and knowing Dot's predilection for gossip and exaggeration, I requested the batch for all citations issued by all of the officers that week.

I perused the pile of tickets and I looked in disbelief at what I had seen. It was not the improper seat belt citation issued to Lambros Pierce that had caught my eye; it was the subsequent one that had stunned me.

I'd seen numerous oddities in my many years of police work in Chicago, the suburbs, and now here in Geneva. I'd heard gossip, legend, and urban folklore, tall tales, fish stories, hyperbole, and accounts that were as lame as a teenager's alibi, but never had I seen or heard what I had witnessed in the stack of citations that lay on my desk. My new officer, Ralph Donnert, the same one I'd personally interviewed, hired, and vetted, had issued a citation for the violation of "failure to come to a complete stop at a stop sign." The ticket was issued to none other than... himself.

Ral wrote himself a ticket for rolling through a stop sign.

I slapped myself across the face with an open hand because pinching myself to see if I was awake would not have been sufficient. I didn't know whether to laugh out loud or fall down laughing. What could possibly make a police officer write a ticket to himself?

This is what Bert had been alluding to when he started to say, "First, who writes himself..." before abruptly stopping and jumping to the second point.

So I wonder who else, besides Bert, knows about Ral issuing himself a ticket? Certainly Dorothy; she knew everything. It was a small town and a small stationhouse and around here gossip traveled at the speed of light rather than the speed of sound, but I really hated it when I was the last to know what was going on right under my own roof.

"Dorothy, where is Ral? Get him in here for me. Immediately," I boomed, then decided to calm down before someone asked me what was wrong.

There was a perception, an erroneous one of course, that small-town cops were dimwits who overcompensated because of their presumed inability to land a job on a police force in a larger municipality or city. The smaller the town, the greater the overcompensation must be. It was a stereotype that was promoted by movies and television sitcoms. The poster boy for this characterization was the deputy whose name had become synonymous with the bungling small town cop: Barney Fife. Here in my little "fiefdom," so to speak, I had been called Barney Fife as many times as I had been called by my real name.

In reality, nothing could be further from the truth. My staff here in small-town America, with now the possible exception of Officer Donnert, was superb. When I first hired Donnert, I believed him to be as competent and professional as those I'd served with in the precincts of Chicago. Now I had serious doubts, and it wasn't because of the words Bert Burr had lodged in my mind. If word leaked out to the public that one of my officers had issued himself a traffic citation, his actions could negatively reflect not only on himself, but the entire police force of the town of Geneva, and it could perpetuate the Barney Fife characterization for years to come.

I worried about my own reputation too, for I was the mule driver who had hired the jackass. Minutes later, there he was, standing before me as if he had a rod stuck up his ass, all five foot eight of gung-ho and glory.

"Sit down and relax, officer," I calmly requested. I had determined it best to downplay this event, perhaps almost insinuating that issuing oneself a ticket was not that unusual, but that it was a practice left for other towns and police forces. Down deep, I wanted to scream and mock the doofus, but I chose to remain calm and collected, at least on the exterior. But I had to ask him why.

"Chief, I have a high set of standards for myself and for others. If I were going to write a ticket to a resident for the same infraction, then I would have to write one to myself if I broke the same law."

"I see your point, officer." I didn't, of course. "But we can't have our staff writing tickets to themselves. It may open us up to ridicule. You see my point?"

I found myself arguing with an idiot. That was as dumb as arguing with a drunk. It was a sheer waste of time.

"Chief, I have placed myself on the honor system. If I were taking a test in high school, and the teacher left the class and put the students on the honor system, well, it would not be in me to cheat. Get my point?" He added the final comment almost as an afterthought.

Actually I did see his point, at least a little bit, but he was still an idiot.

I shook my head in agreement then told him, no, ordered him, not to write himself a ticket—never, ever. Belatedly, I added that he shouldn't write a ticket to any other officers or station or town employee. I could see Donnert issuing a speeding violation to Bert Burr for going two miles over the speed limit and starting a brouhaha in the stationhouse.

"If you have a problem with your own actions or those of anyone else around here, make a note in your journal and then come to me about it first. Don't take any actions until you talk to me. Got it?"

"Yes, Chief, definitely." He sounded like Maxwell Smart talking to the Chief of CONTROL on the old *Get Smart* sitcom. There I was, guilty as charged, comparing one of my own officers to a bungling sitcom character. This is why I didn't like to keep a gun in my office. I was afraid I might use it in a situation like the one that had just unfolded before my very eyes.

"Where is a loaf of Gonnella bread when you need one?" I whispered under my breath.

Chapter Thirty-Nine

Geneva, Wisconsin

A small grin came over Theo Boycek's face when he thought about the perfect site Chief picked for Lieza and him to hide. Much to Lieza's dismay, the duo had moved once again. Chief decided spending another night at the French Country Inn would be too dangerous, once he'd learned that Theo's room was only yards away from one occupied by the suspicious Fred Smith; Smith was under the surveillance of the IBI agent, and his proximity to the pair made Chief uncomfortable.

Chief had argued that only a more remote, unknown site would suffice, and Theo had agreed. He considered the abandoned meth-lab house with the long approaching road; the only drawback was that he had already asked one of his officers to keep tabs on the place. A better location had come to mind.

As another night approached, Theo was the most relaxed he'd been since he'd been chosen to protect Lieza Patrona from her former lover. He realized that, at this remote location, Lieza was also more comfortable, despite her initial objection. For the first time since the two had left Chicago, and for the first time since she'd heard the news of the brutal killings of Celia and Leon, she was comfortable and less afraid. The playful flirtation with her protector and the sexual games she had left behind in the hotel room in downtown Chicago had now reappeared.

That very morning the naked Lieza had bathed herself in the cool waters of Northwick Creek. The pond, she'd been told, had been

225

formed by the pooling waters in front of a beaver's dam. The still waters had been warmed by the early morning's sun, but remained cool to the touch. She stood at the edge of the pond in two feet of water and poured the water over her body and then lathered up with the perfumed soap she had taken from the French Country Inn. She splashed the water a second time over her supple body and then toweled herself dry. She lifted her face to the sun, but her body was still cool. Her delight in prancing naked outdoors in the shallow waters was evident by the glow that swelled within her.

Her only fear was that the beaver would appear and interrupt her ritual. From her position on the edge of the pond, she could not see Theo Boycek, and was unsure whether the prim and always gentlemanly police officer was watching her prance naked in the open air. But she was positive he was watching her; his eyes were never far from the young lady he had sworn to protect. She was sure he was watching, only unsure whether Theo was lusting after her the way she hoped he would.

Cooped up in this remote cabin with the older Polish Prince—as she often referred to him—without television, cellphone, or internet, had rendered the pretty Latina woman completely bored. No longer dwelling on her fear, flirtation was her only pastime.

Theo had been watching Lieza as she bathed in the pond, but he would not be beguiled by her beauty. He was more comfortable now that he was safe in this cabin in the woods, but he would not become overly comfortable with his location. Nor would he become careless or so bewildered by Lieza's sexual games that he would let down his guard. He reminded himself of the dangers of becoming too familiar with her, and the harm that could ensue if he did not remain professional at all times.

He did promise himself that afterwards, when this ordeal was over, after she'd testified against Gonzales Garcia, if the opportunity arose, he would bed the little Latina vixen who, for the past few weeks, had pushed every one of his sexual buttons.

Theo turned his gaze away from Lieza while she was still prancing naked in the sunlight. He stopped what he was doing and looked at his cell phone. Still no signal. Chief had told him he would have trouble making or receiving calls in this area. At that time he was pleased not to receive a signal, but now he wished he could call his partner in Chicago to see if there was any new information or developments.

Earlier, he'd woven together strips of twine he'd found in the cabin. Thirty yards from the cabin, he ran the twine across the pathway and then strung the cord through a window inside the cabin where it was tied to a tin can that was placed precariously on a small table. Theo had made a classic trip wire. If a vehicle or a person came down the road, they would trip the twine, that would send the tin can off the table, giving advance notice of an approaching vehicle or person. All were hidden from plain sight with twigs and branches. Primitive, but effective.

In the nearby woods, Theo had strategically placed three weapons in plastic bags along with a magazine of extra ammo. If he had to hurriedly leave the safety of the cabin without his handgun, he would be able to retrieve the weapons he had stashed in the surrounding trees. He showed Lieza the location of each, but he was positive her mind was elsewhere. His charge was tough and calculating when it was necessary, but Theo worried she had become worn down by the protracted movement from place to place. He was also concerned she may have become too comfortable in this new location. He hoped she felt safe, but that she still could retain her toughness until it was time for them to return to Chicago.

The two sat around a tiny fire that Theo had reluctantly made at Lieza's request. Before this latest move, Chief bought groceries for them. She wished he had purchased graham crackers, a chocolate bar, and marshmallows so she could make s'mores on the open flame. Although Theo agreed that it would be nice, he said nothing.

"This is the first time since we left Chicago that I feel safe. Those motels we stayed in while on the move gave me the creeps. But out here I feel free; it's refreshing. Now I know why people love to live in the country."

"Don't get too comfortable," Theo said. "We still have another night, and then it is back to Chicago."

"Why don't we run away together, Theo? We could move up to Canada where no one would ever find us. Get a little cabin in the woods just like this one." She shimmied across the log they were sitting on until she was beside him. He put his arm around her. He could feel her shudder in the cold, and he was sure it was not the cool breeze, nor the evening air that made her shake.

It was a tender moment, but his mind was elsewhere. He was determining what he would do if he and Lieza were besieged upon by a passel of Gonzales Garcia's henchman. Run through the thicket or stand their ground until help arrived? He hoped he would not have to decide between the two options. He prayed they would make it through another night. He felt her shudder once again and thought he felt a tear fall on his neck.

"We will get through this night, Lieza. I promise you."

Chapter Forty

Geneva, Wisconsin

"Depression can be very depressing." Did I say that, or once again, was it Yogi Berra? Well, whichever one of us said it first, it certainly was true. It was a harmful circle that I'd gotten myself into: I drank to ease my depression, which did help, at least while I was drinking. Then, the next day, when I was awake, I was depressed all over again. Any fool would tell you that it was because alcohol was a depressant. But it was a funny thing. My sadness was heightened when I drank alone. When I was with Annie, I was usually in such a good mood that I believed I was not fully aware of my depression.

I tried hard to think of something other than myself and my moods. The whole train of thought was making me upset. It seemed that was the way my life had always been. When there was something unpleasant, I didn't analyze why it was unpleasant or try to identify the root cause of the feeling. I simply thought about something else, something less challenging: put the TV on, pick up a magazine, or have a couple of beers or ten. Thank God I wasn't into sweets and chick flicks or I'd curl up on the couch and eat quart of Rocky Road while watching a Hugh Grant movie.

I wasn't drinking yet tonight—but I certainly planned to do so. Theo had done me a favor, one that he wasn't even aware of: He would help me get back on Annie's good side. I'd rented a room for him at the French Country Inn under a false name for a week, and now that he wasn't staying there, it was completely available.

229

With the couple now secure in a new location, I too was able to let down my own guard. Theo's appearance in Geneva had placed a fair amount of pressure on me. I wished he'd lied about the reason he was hiding up here and who Sophie really was. Theo's confidence in me was a breach of his own protocol. Only his partner and I were trustworthy enough to know the truth; we were the only ones he could rely on.

And now, with the itinerant duo tucked safely in a tiny little corner of Walworth County, and me in a deluxe room at the French Country Inn compliments of my old friend Theo, I was about to unwind. For company, I had chilled two bottles of Sonoma-Cutrer Chardonnay and a platter of jumbo shrimp large enough to sate my appetite for the evening. I thought I would get an early start before Annie arrived, so I uncorked one of the bottles and poured myself a glass of wine. Even though it was considered gauche, I added a few ice cubes to the already-chilled vino. I liked my beer and my white wine very cold—not tepid like those snooty Europeans. What the heck do they know about wines? Their excessive smoking had punished their palettes beyond repair and most wouldn't know a red from a white without looking at the color.

I downed the wine like it was a glass of grape juice and poured another while I quickly ate three shrimp that I'd dipped in the spicy cocktail sauce. I swished around some wine in my mouth to clear out the shrimp smell. I didn't want to hear Annie complain about fish breath when she arrived and planted her customary, long, I-missed-you-so-much kiss on me.

My thoughts moved to Theo and Sophie. I decided I would resist the urge to pay them a visit or give them a call; there was no reason to do so. They had enough provisions to last them until they had to return to the city. As far as a cell phone call, in that particular area, the signal—if they got one at all—was very weak, and dropped calls were frequent. I was comfortable in my belief that no one knew they were hiding up here in the Geneva Lakes area. I didn't think anyone even saw Sophie while she was at the inn. She'd never left the room during the two nights they stayed.

None of my officers knew anything about my guests, and I didn't have to worry about the two biggest gossips: Bert Burr and Dorothy. Neither was aware of Theo's visit. Even Annie was in the dark about the situation.

But what about Mr. Fred Smith? He was the only suspicious character I had seen up here in the past several days. I'd kept an eye on him, and now I wondered if he were keeping a watch on me too. I made a mental note to do a little checking on my suspicions. Tomorrow morning I would call down to the 16th district on Chicago's northwest side and talk to some of the boys to see if they knew anything about him. I'd also been remiss in my investigation of Ron Hurlbut. I would need to check with the IBI to see if they had an Agent Ron Hurlbut in the agency. Two nights ago, when I saw Smith light Hurlbut's cigar, I'd become suspicious that the two might have known each other. Was it simply a chance encounter, or was there something to it? Could they have been briefly trading info? I felt like I was starting to drift into Bert Burr's conspiracy territory.

Although I suspected that Fred Smith was an alias, I was positive that Ron Hurlbut was the fellow's real name. After all, who would choose Hurlbut as an alias? Only a guy whose real name was Leon Lippschitz.

My mental gymnastics about Mr. Smith and Hurlbut were interrupted by a knock on the door. It was Annie. Even though I'd called her this morning after my scheduled meeting with Agent Hurlbut—which he'd cancelled at the last minute—I was not entirely certain that she would show up, even though she'd said she would. It seemed of late we'd both been moody and disagreeable.

I hoped my telephone apology was sincere enough, but if need be, I would add an apology for being overly cynical, self-centered, a cad, a heel, a boor, and a lout. I opened the door.

We kissed a long kiss. When our lips parted she said, "Shrimp and Chardonnay; you started without me?"

"Just a little snack."

"I am so happy to see you. Your face looks a lot better. Does it hurt?"

"No, but I bet it's killing you. Did you really think I would fall for that old one?

We both laughed. She was still dressed in her uniform. I said, "You obviously came right from work; have a busy day?"

"Somewhat. I can't wait to get out of these clothes and into... well, nothing."

"Sounds like my type of evening wear. What's in the bag?" Annie had plopped down a nylon overnight bag on a wing-backed chair.

"Just the usual woman's equipment: lingerie, brassiere, undies, face cream, toiletries, 9mm Glock, Taser. Hey, I'd better make sure I don't shoot the Glock into your... mmm, let's see, what rhymes with Glock? Oh well, never mind."

She grinned a toothy grin, but I didn't find the remark funny.

"So how did you get this room for free? Did you let that Navilio guy out of a ticket and this is his repayment for the favor, or was it a little more sinister than that? Let me guess, better than a ticket, but larger than a breadbox. You found his Bugs Moran car?"

I shook my head no. "Drove him back to the inn instead of issuing a DUI? C'mon what was it?"

"I helped him bury the dead body of a guest who called him a Chicago greaseball."

She looked at me in disbelief. "You can do a lot better than that. Seriously, why the free room?"

"It has nothing to do with him. A friend of mine paid for the room for a week and then he left unexpectedly, so he said I could have it. Nice digs, eh?"

Annie regarded the large room with its double-sided fireplace. I thought I noticed a tinge of delight when she smiled at the two-person whirlpool tub.

"Is that the same friend who was staying here with his gumad?"

"How did you know about that? And it isn't his mistress."

"Who are they, and why did they stay here and then check out early?"

"How did you know they stayed here at the inn?"

"You just told me, doofus. Now the room is ours. Where did you friend go with his gumad?"

Ever since *The Sopranos* appeared on HBO it seemed everyone in America knew the Italian word for mistress.

"She's not his gumad. Pollacks don't have gumads."

With the knowledge that Theo and Sophie were safe and their whereabouts were known only by me, I decided to let Annie in on the whole situation, but I wouldn't tell her the location where the two were stashed. I wanted that fact known to no other, not even Annie.

When I thought about it, I was pretty sure Theo and Sophie weren't even aware of their actual location. When I took them to the safe house, I travelled side roads, back roads, and off roads, and then I doubled back to ensure I hadn't been followed. I didn't think even a skilled veteran cop like Theo Boycek could have followed the path I'd taken unless he had a GPS. Besides, after listening to the journey Theo had travelled in the past days since he left Chicago, I didn't think the combined efforts of the NSA and CIA could locate him. Now safely tucked in bed by me personally, I was positive the pair was safe.

Over glasses of Chardonnay and ice-cold shrimp, I explained the whole story to Annie, leaving out the detail about where Theo was right this moment.

Annie was raised in rural Wisconsin, and as an adult she had only lived in the town of Geneva. Burlington, Wisconsin, with a population just over ten thousand, was the largest city she had ever worked in. Her journeys to Milwaukee to shop, and her few excursions to Chicago were the only times she'd visited large cities. I think she told me once she spent a week in Fort Lauderdale—or was that Clare, Clare, who wants to marry a millionaire?

"So where do you have them tucked away now?" she asked.

"Can't say. I don't want anyone else to know."

I was going to use the line: "If I told you I would have to kill you," but that one had been worn very thin, so I simply said, "Besides, it could be too dangerous."

Even though my latest moves had made the situation less dangerous, I knew I shouldn't have said anything to Annie in the first place. Theo had taken every precaution, as had I. My fears that Fred Smith or Agent Hurlbut might be involved were unfounded; the odds remote.

"C'mon, tell me where you stashed them," she whined. She was acting like a schoolgirl who was the only eighth grader to know the question asked by the teacher. "I know, I know: It's Bert Burr's place. That's a great spot."

"Are you kidding me? I would have another homicide on my hands if I put Theo in the same room with Bert Burr for more than a couple of minutes, much less a couple of days."

"Okay. Let me think." She wrinkled her forehead as if she were deep in thought. Then she said, "Now when Bogie wanted to hide Mary Astor in *The Maltese Falcon*, he put her up with his secretary. The two are with Dorothy, right?"

"Stop it. I'm not telling you, and if I did I would have to kill you."

I let out a loud groan. I was very aware I was losing my talent for clever repartee.

"I have vays to make you talk," Annie said, in a dead-on German accent.

"It doesn't matter," I said. "I am impervious to all types of torture."

"Torture? We don't need no stinkin' torture," she said, this time in her best Mexican accent. "I'm thinking sexual favors." Then she grabbed her duffle bag and headed for the shower. After a few steps, she stopped and turned. In her best Lauren Bacall smoky voice with just the right tinge of sultriness she said, "If you need anything, just whistle. You know how to whistle don't you, Chief? You just put your lips together and… blow." She then proceeded toward the shower.

Even though I cherished the time we shared together, I was beginning to think that Annie and I were watching way too many classic movies.

"You're cute and funny too," I said.

"So are you. Now, excuse me while I take a long shower."

Chapter Forty-One

Geneva, Wisconsin

So twice in one week I'd been asked to bend my principles for the sake of sexual favors. With scofflaw Cheryl Kintrick handcuffed in the back seat of my Jeep, a probable loss of employment and possible jail time were likely consequences, and I was easily able to resist that first temptation.

The second with Annie might not be so easy.

I decided not to mention Kintrick's offer to Annie. I guessed that might not end well. I was sure she would pepper me with lots of questions about my trip, not to mention pepper me with actual pepper spray if she didn't like my answers.

Annie came out of the bathroom with her hair damp and slicked back, wearing nothing at all. "Is this a come-as-you-are party?" I asked.

In her left hand she held up a camisole. "I bought it just for tonight." She stepped into the satin garment.

"I prefer the au natural look."

"That's for later, but only if you tell me what I want to know. Now tell me where your friends are staying or else I will put on my sweatpants and robe and turn on the TV."

Turning on the TV wouldn't have bothered me at all, but not seeing Annie lounge about in the sexy lingerie would be harsh punishment.

"Tell me or I'll take a blowtorch to your cómo se llama."

"A blow torch? What's with you, you little tart?" I decided to outmaneuver her. "'Every woman should own a blowtorch.'"

"What?"

"'Every woman should own a blowtorch.' Tell me who said it, and I will tell you where I stashed Theo."

"I have a question for you first. Tell me who said this: 'You aren't getting any sex tonight, or any other night'?"

"That's easy... my ex-wife, Rita. C'mon, who said 'Every woman should own a blowtorch'?"

There was a long silence and then she asked, "Male or female?"

"Female."

"Dead or alive?"

"Dead, but she was alive at one time," I answered sarcastically. "No more questions, just guesses."

"Mata Hari?"

"No."

"Jane Fonda."

"Jane Fonda? Where did that come from? No."

"Joan Rivers, Nancy Pelosi, Barbara Walters?"

"No, no, no. I told you she's dead."

"Gloria Steinem, Lizzie Borden, the Charles Manson women?"

"No, no, no." We were both laughing so hard we could barely speak.

Then it happened.

The crash was loud and disturbing. At first I thought a car had driven into our room. Within a split second, our game of light-hearted banter had been harshly interrupted by a man who'd bolted through the front door of our room. Behind him entered a second man, shorter but wider. It happened so quickly that neither of us were able to retrieve our weapons, even though they were nearby. Before Annie and me stood two large, harsh-looking Latino men, both brandishing handguns.

It was evident that that the two were part of the Cuban cabal that Night Train Layne and Theo Boycek had warned me about: Gonzales Garcia's henchmen.

My first thought? I hope they don't have a blowtorch with them.

Chapter Forty-Two

Geneva, Wisconsin

"Where is this man?" one of the two asked as he held up the picture of Theo Boycek, Dave Tedeski, and me. His index finger was draped over the top of the photo and pointed to Theo. Both intruders were six feet tall or taller, with muscular physiques, but it was not their physical shape and proportion that scared me, it was the harshness of the look on their faces.

They were twins of the guy that Jake Tandy put a bullet into in the warehouse after I got the crap kicked out of me. They meant business. Annie's vulnerability, clad only in a revealing outfit, also had me scared, but it seemed the two were unconcerned with her femininity. I knew what they wanted, and my mind couldn't think fast enough.

I blurted out the first thing that came to my mind.

"Both of those men are dead, and I am the third."

The man closest to me punched me in the face, knocking me to the floor. "Lie to me again and you will also be dead." I was hoping he didn't have a packet of those nasty little chopsticks with him. "Where is this man? Where is Theo Boycek?"

He butchered the pronunciation of the Polish name and then screamed, "Where?"

His English was not as good as I had been described to me by Night Train. The taller of the two had a rough accent that was difficult to understand.

Abruptly and calmly the two began to converse in Spanish. They spoke so rapidly that I could not understand what they were saying, but I thought I heard the word "muerte" at least twice. The one furthest from me grabbed Annie by her hair and pulled her close to him. She resisted, but his grasp was tight and Annie could barely move without pain. Still grasping his weapon, he pulled down the front of her garment, exposing her breasts, and Annie draped her right arm over her body. The man put the barrel of his gun against her cheek. At some time in the future, I knew this man would pay for ruining Annie's garment. She didn't like what he had done, and I was sure she was already planning payback in her mind.

The man tugged harder on her hair, bending her head further back.

"The next sound you hear, señor, will be the sound of a bullet into the pretty face of your mujer." He took for granted that I understood mujer was Spanish for woman; I was sure Annie didn't hate it when I called her that half as much as when he did.

Annie did not even let out a whimper or a plea, but I knew I was defeated. They had the trump card and the full deck. I would not let them harm Annie, and they already knew that. They could surely read defeat in my eyes.

I conceded and said, "I will take you to him, but first let the girl go. She will not do anything as long as you have me. She knows nothing."

"She will come with us. If you try anything, she will be the first to die," he said.

Annie was allowed to put on the sweats she'd threatened me with just a few happy minutes ago. While driving to the safe house, I tried to plan some way to turn the table on our two angry passengers. I wished I were alone. I would stand a much better chance by myself. I couldn't stop thinking about what could happen to Annie if I tried something bold. For now I would have to rely on the wit of Theo

Boycek. He wouldn't fold as easily as I had. That was his nature, he didn't like to get pushed around, and most of all he didn't like to see the bad guys win.

I drove the most indirect way I could possibly think of without arousing suspicion from the two unwanted passengers. The one who had punched me in the face sat in the front seat with his gun pointing toward my side. The other one, who I'd labeled Back Seat Bob to myself because he looked a bit like a large and muscular Latino version of my friend Bob Di Stefano, was in the rear with Annie. He was clearly the second-in-command, as the man in the front seat did most of the talking.

I glanced in the rearview mirror. I knew Annie—given the opportunity—was ready, willing and able to rip the face off her abductor, but I worried she could become collateral damage in this situation. One she knew little about and didn't have any part in.

After driving nearly fifteen minutes, I headed to Theo and Sophie's location. Driving around the county hoping that one of my officers or a county sheriff would get suspicious after seeing my vehicle and stop us had been a hopeless plan. I drove straight toward Theo even though I had nothing to offer as a way to extricate myself and my woman from the situation. When I'd driven Theo and Sophie to this location two nights ago, I'd intentionally tried to avoid being tailed. This time I was hoping someone had gotten a glimpse of me. I looked in the rearview mirror; no one was following behind. And now, on this desolate road, I was sure I wasn't being tailed. Only minutes from the destination I wondered how this would go down. I knew Theo would not have his guard down. He would be prepared for the worst to happen.

In spite of my desire for self-preservation I didn't care so much for myself, but I prayed that the worst would bring no harm to Annie.

Chapter Forty-Three

Geneva, Wisconsin

When I turned the vehicle from Durnin Road onto the long drive that entered the Martel family farm, my Cuban passenger pushed the muzzle of his gun into my side. I guess he wanted me to know that he was serious—as if breaking into my room, threatening me with death, and abducting Annie and me wasn't serious enough. I slowed the vehicle down to just a few miles an hour as we approached the Martel home.

Jonah had told me they were leaving to visit relatives in North Dakota. That was the reason I'd taken advantage of their absence and placed Theo and Sophie into Jonah's little hideaway deep in the woods. Jonah had given me permission to be on his property while they were gone, presumably to deal with the beaver dam situation; occupying his cabin may not have been exactly what he'd had in mind. At this moment, however, I wished that Jonah had returned home, but without the missus. His fierce focus on conflict and fearlessness was exactly what I needed in our present situation. The main house appeared vacant, with just a single light burning in the foyer.

"Stop," said the Cuban in the front seat. He spoke to his amigo, Back Seat Bob, who then stuck his weapon to the back of my head.

"The cop and the girl are not here at this house," I said. "They are in a spot nearby in the woods. Down there." I made a gesture with my finger while not removing my hand from the steering wheel. The front seat man left the car, but did not close the door behind him.

Cautiously he approached the house and peered through the windows and the front door then returned to the car.

"Where are the owners?" he asked.

"They are out of town visiting friends."

"Adelante, move ahead," he said.

Now, on the rough pathway heading toward the cabin, my heart pounded harder and my mind raced. I considered, given the opportunity, I might try to push Annie into a thicket of brush and attempt to wrest the gun from whichever of the two was nearest. Or maybe I could slam the door on Back Seat Bob as he exited the rear seat.

"Stop the car, turn the lights off," said the front seat man. "If you are trying to be clever, I will shoot both of you right here, right now."

"No señor," I said. "They are in a cabin just ahead, about one hundred yards down this road and around this next curve."

"This is not a road, this is a goat path. How many people are there?"

I considered lying, but then I said two. The four of us, now on foot, proceeded forward, inching our way toward the cabin. We were only steps from the beaver-made pond that separated us from Theo and Sophie. We inched along at a snail-on-crutches pace.

"How deep is the water?" a voice whispered. Both men were now behind Annie and me, using us as shields. I stopped when the pond water ran over my loafers.

"I'm not sure; I think it is deeper in the middle." The cabin was dimly lit. I was praying Theo could see us in the light of the waxing moon, but the way this evening was going, I half expected Field Administrator Bevis to appear and write us all citations for the after-hours disturbance of a beaver's habitat.

One of the men ordered me to call out to the cabin.

"Tell them to come out with their hands in the air."

"He's not going to do that," I said. "He's a cop."

"Then tell him I will kill your woman if he doesn't come out."

I froze and contemplated what to do.

"Theo, it's me, Chief," I yelled across the pond. "They have me and my girl Annie and they say they will kill us if you don't come out with the girl."

No response came from across the water. Then I heard Back Seat Bob cock his pistol.

"Wait," I said. "Trade us for the mujer. You can have her."

"Chief, have you gone mad?" Annie said.

"Not mad, realistic. We will trade our lives for the girl a la *Rio Bravo*," I said to Annie, hoping she would remember the hostage-swapping scene in the classic John Wayne movie we'd watched last week. Back Street Bob slammed his gun against my head and ordered, "Silencio. Why did you say 'rio bravo'?"

"It means 'good luck,' like 'be brave'?" I hoped neither man was a classic movie fan. "Listen to me," I said. "I will go across the water and get the girl and trade your woman for my woman."

The men spoke rapidly in Spanish and then one asked, "How will you get the cop to give you the girl?"

"He is my friend. He trusts me. I will get close to him and then knock him out and take the girl. I will send her back across the water, and you send my woman across at the same time. You will have your pistol on her; if I try anything you will be able to shoot both of them from the shore. I will stand on the opposite side with my hands in the air, so you can see me, too."

Neither man responded, so I continued. "This is the only way. I know this cop. He will not give up the girl even if you kill both of us. We are at what you people call a Mexican standoff. Neither side can win in a Mexican standoff."

"We are Cubans, you idiot, not Mexicans."

Desperately I said, "Okay, yes, I'm an idiot. No more Mexican references. But this will work."

"This mujer, she is no ordinary woman. She will not come across the water. She will—"

I interrupted him. "If she does not go into the water, I will drown her on the shore, and you can bring her dead body back to your jefe."

They spoke in Spanish once again and then said, "When you knock out the cop, bring his body out of the cabin so we can see him. If anything goes wrong, your lady here will be the first to die."

From his back pocket, Back Seat Bob pulled out a blackjack.

"Take this," he ordered.

I hit the palm of my left hand with the heavy instrument. I would not want to get jacked by this baby, I thought. Then the Cuban unbuttoned his waist coat and removed a MAC-10 45-caliber automatic pistol, hanging from a shoulder harness. My heart stopped cold. The MAC-10 was the American version of the Israeli Uzi. Back Seat Bob's weapon had a sound suppressor attached to the muzzle. I wished I had known the Cuban had this high-powered piece before I'd hatched my plan, before I had placed Annie into even greater harm's way.

"Remember, if you mess up, your woman dies first, amigo."

Even with the added weaponry, I still had faith in my plan. I hoped Annie remembered the scene from *Rio Bravo*. If she did, when the two were about to pass each other at the halfway point across the pond, she and Sophie would dive under the water, perhaps right where the beaver had built his lodge.

I stepped in to the cold evening water up to my knees, and then I stopped and turned back to Annie. I wanted to say something that would put her at ease, but all I could think of was: "Julia Child."

"What?" she asked.

"Julia Child. 'Every woman should own a blow torch.' You know, to make crème brûlée." Then I gave her a kiss, and wondered if this was the last time our lips would ever meet.

Chapter Forty-Four

Geneva, Wisconsin

Once across the pond, I dried my face with a piece of cloth that hung on a makeshift clothesline in the side yard. I slicked my hair back and yelled toward the house.

"Theo, it's me, Chief. I'm coming in." For good measure I raised my hands above my head in a conciliatory manner.

"Stay where you are, Chief. What's on your mind?"

"Theo, let me in." I said loudly. And then softly, I added, "I need to talk to you."

The door opened and Theo ordered, "Keep your hands up and don't try anything. Sorry, but I don't trust you or anyone."

I entered the small cabin and then hurriedly explained everything to Theo and Sophie. He and I fabricated a struggle, and within a minute I'd horse-collared his prostrate body out to the front porch. Sophie screamed aloud to add to the believability of the scene. I now had Theo's 9mm safely tucked in my back waistband. Theo, likewise, had his service revolver hidden under his jacket.

I dragged Sophie, kicking and screaming, to the edge of the water. I ordered her to proceed. We were far across the pond from the Cubans. The distance and the dark, I hoped, were enough to keep the two women from getting mortally wounded. The MAC-10 sprayed bullets quickly, but it was an inaccurate weapon, and only a marksman could hit his target from this distance with a handgun. I prayed my logic on this swap was correct.

Across the pond, in the moonlight, I could see Annie in the water up to her knees. Back Seat Bob had his weapon aimed at her. Sophie would not go. I was unsure whether she was acting as planned or was so petrified with fear that she was refusing to cooperate.

Harshly, I pushed her down into the water and yelled, "Swim you, bitch." I was unsure of my own behavior. "Swim, or I will drown you right here," I yelled again.

The look of dread came over Sophie's face and I now believed she feared me as much as she feared crossing over to the other side. Without further protest, she waded into the cool water. On the other side I could hear one of the Cubans ordering Annie to slow down.

From the opposite shorelines the two women proceeded in unison to the middle of the pond. Once they met, like two synchronized swimmers, they dove below the dark water. Annie had understood my message.

I ran fast and then dove head first behind a small wheelbarrow that barely covered my full body. Theo rose like Lazarus from the dead, and ran back through the cabin door that had remained open after I'd dragged his body to the porch. We opened fire on our two adversaries across the water, but they seemed unconcerned with us. They peppered the water and the beaver dam with round after round of bullets. Back Seat Bob sprayed the pond near the beaver dam with a magazine of bullets from his MAC-10. The suppressed sound popped through the night air like ladyfinger firecrackers on the Fourth of July.

It seemed Bob was paying particular attention to the beaver's home, and I felt it safe to assume he'd given up trying to end Sophie in his boss's desired fashion. He wanted to kill her one way or another, and if Annie was collateral damage, so be it. I vowed I would personally tear that man apart if Annie were hurt in the crossfire.

My plan appeared to be failing. The two women were trapped somewhere in the pond created by the beaver dam, or perhaps in the beaver's own lodge. Theo and I were safer on the opposite side, but we had nowhere to go. If only we could get the women out of the pond and into the safety of the cabin we could hold off the Cubans for any length of time, or we could head into the woods behind the cabin until daybreak.

I knew the possibility of getting the woman out of the water and into the cabin was remote at best. Back Seat Bob continued to spray the water with his Mac-10, and then abruptly as it began, the firepower across the pond stopped. Spanish was spoken, I heard a voice: "Señor, tell your woman to give us the mujer and then we can all go home."

"You can't have the woman," I said.

"You are trapped," said the voice. "You have nowhere to go. We have more hombres coming. They will be here soon. Give us the mujer."

I did not believe him about the reinforcements. I yelled across the pond. "This is not the Alamo, señor. You are not going to get us gringos this time."

"We are still not Mexicans, señor; we are Cubans. But you are still an idiot."

I couldn't believe this Cuban henchman with his thick accent and broken English was beating me in a war of words. Note to self: No more snide remarks about nationality. When someone has a gun aimed at your head, you really shouldn't care where they come from; you only hope they are a bad shot.

"Cover me," I yelled to Theo, who immediately sprayed a volley across the water in the direction of the Cubans. They did not return fire as I ran into the cabin. I was just about to ask Theo what we should do next when I saw my Jeep drive up close to the water. Back Seat Bob had gotten a promotion to the front; in the moonlight I could see his silhouette in the driver's seat. He turned the headlights on, and then the high beams. He exited the vehicle. In the light, I could see the faces of Annie and Sophie partially hidden by the beaver's hut; they were sitting ducks in this makeshift duck pond.

Before the two Cubans could lift their guns, I heard two rifle shots ring out in the now-quiet night air. Back Seat Bob's lifeless body dropped to the ground. From out of a thicket of bushes, the second Cuban stumbled forward slouched but moving ahead. Then, a third shot burst through the night, and he too dropped to the ground. The headlights from my Jeep still illuminated the pond. I was hesitant to speak, but then yelled to the woman to stay in the water.

"What just happened?" I asked Theo. He did not answer.

For several minutes we waited in silence and then I walked through the cabin door. My best guess was that reinforcements had come.

"Bert, are you out there?" I yelled. "Geary?"

No answer. No one was stirring in the night, nor in the woods.

I motioned to Annie and Sophie to come out of the water. Miraculously, neither woman was hurt. When they reached the shore, I shielded their bodies with my own as we ran into the cabin, slamming the door behind us. Unsure of what had transpired, I still wanted to take all precautions, and protecting Annie and Sophie was my main concern.

"Did you guys shoot them, Chief?" Annie asked.

"No, I think the bullets came from behind them," I said. "I am going across to check it out."

Annie gave Sophie a blanket and she snuggled it around her cold body. When Sophie began to cry, I could see that Annie was working to keep her own composure. Both woman were cold and scared, both of us men confused.

Once on the other side, in the glow of the headlights from the Jeep, I examined the bodies. Back Seat Bob had a bullet wound in the back of his head that had taken off a piece of his skull. The other Cuban had apparently been shot two times in the back. The bullets, as Theo and I had thought, had come from the rear—behind the pond, from the direction down the road toward Martel's house.

The immediate question was: Who fired the shots that killed the two Cubans—friend or foe? I took a flashlight from the rear of the Jeep and proceeded up the road. Unsure what I might find, or who I might meet, my handgun was still in my grasp with a new clip inside. Yards up the road, I found a tire track that could possibly be over the top of the tracks of my Jeep, distinct because of the all-terrain threads on the rear wheels.

Motorcycle tracks, I thought to myself.

Chapter Forty-Five

Geneva, Wisconsin

On the drive back to Casa Blanca, I called Inspector Roger Tyrrell of the Wisconsin Bureau of Investigation. Bert Burr was going to meet him at the crime scene, along with the CSI team. I warned everyone that we needed to be discreet.

We both knew that just because these two men were dead, didn't mean that more couldn't be on their way. Gonzales Garcia and his crime syndicate were still a threat to Sophie, and the grand jury was still a day away. At the very least, the siege and the murders of the Cubans had to be kept out of the news—at least until Theo and Sophie were out of my jurisdiction and on to their next safe house.

"Safe house." It wasn't a term that even existed in Theo and Sophie's vocabulary. Especially after tonight.

We four decided we would spend the night at my place. It was a decision made by default; there was simply no other good place to go. We couldn't stay at the beaver pond, we shouldn't stay at the French Country Inn, and we wouldn't stay at the Bayside Motel; the women wouldn't allow it. I was sure the accommodations there were insufficient for their discriminating taste, even with their lives on the line.

Now that my men and the county sheriff's department were aware of the gravity of the situation, police cars would continuously patrol the area surrounding my place.

Besides, we had the added security of Dawg. He could smell a bad guy or a pizza from a mile away. The only thing we would have to worry about with him would be a bad guy delivering a pizza. In that case, he could walk right in the front door with a bazooka slung over his shoulder and Dawg wouldn't care less as long as the pizza was left behind.

Theo and I had a vodka rocks. He didn't say much; he never did.

I was sure the Cubans had not realized that, if by accident, the beaver had been wounded by their wild and random shots, the full force of the Wisconsin Department of Natural Resources would have been upon them like a bull moose in rutting season—not to mention the bureaucratic wrath of Field Administrator Harland Bevis himself.

The trying events of the evening had sapped Sophie and Annie to the brink of collapse. I tucked the two in my bed and they were soon fast asleep. Over a second vodka, Theo and I talked about different possibilities. He had little to offer. He had no idea who could have shot the two Cubans; he was only pleased they were dead. He worried that others, a whole army of Gonzales Garcia's men, had been tipped off by the two now-dead bad guys, and that they would be arriving soon and more battles would ensue.

We decided it was best for him and Sophie to be on the run once morning came. He fell asleep mid-sentence, and I was left with my own thoughts and speculation.

I had no other hypothesis than this: Fred Smith was the assassin. But why? What could be his motive? Who was he?

Chapter Forty-Six

GENEVA, WISCONSIN

I knew that it was sometimes best to let it rest when I sought the answer to a nagging question, but after the night we'd just had, that just wasn't my style. It must have been that old streak of impatience in me; I tended to move forward quickly and too rashly. I had only Fred Smith as a suspect, and I was determined to find him, and force him to give me some answers.

After I had showered and re-dressed, I went into my bedroom. Annie and Sophie were in bed, Annie barely awake, Sophie sound asleep with a pillow over her forehead.

"I'm heading out to do a little investigation," I whispered to Annie. "There is food in the fridge and I left my Beretta on the dresser." I nodded to the dresser across the room. "Theo's staying here to watch over you and Sophie; I think the danger has passed, and you are safe, but we still need to be alert. Who knows if there are more men coming up here to make a hit on Sophie."

I glanced over to the Latina to see if she'd stirred, but she appeared comfortably asleep.

"What happened last night, Chief? Who do you think killed those two?"

"I have only one suspect in mind, and I'm going out looking for him now. The two Cubans were sent up here looking for Theo and Sophie. They learned that I was connected to them and by accident, then stumbled upon my whereabouts. I've had to piecemeal all the info together bit by bit, but the story is now becoming clearer."

"I should go with you." I could see the fear in Annie's eyes. I was sure I had a similar look in my own worried eyes.

"Call in sick today if you can. I would feel better if you stayed here with Theo until I get back. My men will be nearby, checking on the area. Call me if there is any sort of concern, and I'll come flying back here like bat after a mosquito."

She smiled and gave me a kiss, one that I could sense was weak in meaning.

Why the limp kiss? I asked myself. A limp kiss is as insincere as or even worse than a limp handshake.

My first trip was to the French Country Inn, which was just a short hop from my home. It was early, and the place was quiet. I asked the innkeeper, Jocelyn, who seemed to have just arrived, if the mysterious Fred Smith had checked out; he hadn't.

"Do you know if he is in his room?" I asked.

Jocelyn looked out of the lobby door and said Smith's motorcycle was gone.

"He usually parks over near the fountain. Let me get a key and I will take you to his room."

"Just give me the key. I will go alone," I said.

Jocelyn said Smith's room was 221 in L'Auberge, the larger, newer building. She pointed to the window on the side of the building. If Fred Smith were looking out of his window, he could see me walking through the property approaching the building. More worrisome was that I knew he could get off a clean shot from that same window as I neared. I decided it was best to get into my car, drive out of the property, and then double back around to the west-side door, where I could enter room 221 unseen.

My circuitous maneuver was for naught. Smith's room, except for some empty beer bottles and a pizza box, was vacant. I smelled the odor of cigarettes and could see some butts in the bottles. If I couldn't get him on a double homicide, I thought, at least I could get him on the misdemeanor of smoking in a non-smoking room. He would also face the wrath of Jocelyn the innkeeper, who always filed charges against the guests who carelessly ignored the no-smoking directive that was posted in each room.

My next stop: Norman Bates at the Bayside Motel.

Chapter Forty-Seven

Geneva, Wisconsin

As usual, Norman saw me drive into the parking lot of the Bates Motel and immediately asked me if I wanted a Smithwick's.

"Not today, Norman. Important business. Have you seen Mr. Fred Smith yesterday or this morning?"

"Seen him, no. Sensed him, yes."

"Whadda mean?"

"Last night I did a sight check of the rooms. I don't bother the guests or check the doors to see if they are locked. I check to see who's in or out, if the TV is too loud, just makin' the rounds, so to speak. It's the last thing I do before I put in for the night. Well this morning, the door to Smith's room was ajar; when I checked last night I was pretty sure it was closed. Well, this morning I went inside and nothing had been obviously disturbed. Towels, soap, toilet seat, all were in the same order as it had been for the last couple of days."

He stroked his white beard and took a swig of his ale the way he always does. "Is that it?" I asked. "Slow down, Chief—"

I interrupted him. "Look Norm, I'm in a hurry today. I need to find Smith, and I need to find him right now. Is there anything else?"

Norman pondered for a second as I was about to prod him he said, "Well the only thing is the dust ruffle seemed to be out of place."

"Dust ruffle?" I asked.

"Yeah, you know that curtainy thingamajig that goes around the bed... at the bottom. Olga, the attendant, always straightens them out nice and neat. I'm not sure, but I sensed someone was in there last night, and Smith and I were the only two who had keys.

"And yet this morning the dust ruffle was disrupted—you know, a little out of order, as if someone had been looking under the bed."

"Or removing something that was under the bed," I speculated. Then I asked. "Did you notice anything under the bed the last few days during the time Smith had paid for his room?"

"Look at me, Chief. I try not to bend down unless it's to pick up a beer, and I certainly am not gettin' down on my hands and knees to look under a bed in a vacant room. Didn't look, didn't notice nothin' before either. Only this morning was there somethin' out of the ordinary."

"What time did you turn in last night?"

"Let's see… mmm." He was hesitant to answer and drank from his bottle.

"Norman, please."

"Okay, okay, Chief, don't get your thong all in a knot. I'm pretty sure it was early, around eight-thirty. I wasn't really sleepin', mind you. I just climbed into bed around eight or so, watchin' TV, and I dozed off. Not exactly sure what the precise time was though."

When Norman has the TV on, he has it blasting loud like he wants to annoy his neighbors. I'd witnessed that first hand. If Fred Smith had kept a bag or suitcase under the bed, he easily could have returned unnoticed, retrieved his goods, and left, without Norman being aware.

"Let's go check out Staunton's storage facility. Do you have the keys?" I asked.

"Not on me. Let me go grab them," he said.

Norman came out of the motel office with a large ring of keys in one hand and a fresh Smithwick's in the other.

"Leave the beer and get in," I said to him, opening wide the door to the Jeep so Norman could get his corpulent frame into the car.

"Chief, this a full bottle. Let me finish it off."

"Just get in, dammit," I said, giving into my impatience. Then to myself, I muttered, "This is going to look real good if I get pulled over by the Williams Bay police."

I sped up Geneva Street, and, within minutes, we were at the storage facility. I drove down the winding road to the garage spaces. I pulled my revolver from its holster, and, after Norman had unlocked the main door, I entered the large building. I looked over the area. The space was filled with vehicles and boats that were covered in blue plastic shrink wrap, but there was no sign of Smith, or anyone else.

"Anyone here?" I yelled loudly.

"There is no one here. I have the only set of keys except for Staunton, and he's down in Illinois right now. Spoke to him a couple of hours ago."

We had barely taken a step inside when Norman rubbernecked his head around and said, "Chief, Someone's been here. Nothing out of the ordinary, but someone has been here just recently. I can feel it."

"What?" I asked.

"It's the air. It's not stale like it usually is. The garage door must have been opened recently."

"Which one of these garage spaces was the one you rented to Smith, the one that has the truck in it?" I asked Norman. "They all look alike to me."

Norman led me to a garage door to our far right then said, "This is the one." There was a substantial padlock on the garage door.

"This isn't one of mine," Norman said, referring to the lock.

"I can shoot it off, or do you have bolt cutters?" I asked.

"Yeah, don't do that. I have cutters right here in the tool shed." While Norman went to get the bolt cutters, I searched the area. There was nothing of importance.

I already knew what I would find in Smith's truck in the locked garage space. Inside the truck would be Navilio's missing Bugs Moran's car and the rest of the stolen loot from the lake homes. I believed Fred Smith was responsible for last night's shooting of the Cubans out at the Martel farm, I just didn't know why. His appearance in the area had to have something to do with Theo, Sophie, and the Cubans. I also made him for the car theft and the burglaries, but those were most likely extracurricular activities, staving off boredom while he waited to take out the Cubans. I was positive my thought process was correct; doubts only surfaced when I asked myself why.

Part of me also thought Agent Hurlbut might be involved. I never verified that he worked for the Illinois Bureau, or spoke to him as I'd intended after that night at the French Country Inn; more sloppy police work on my end.

Norman was back with a pair of bolt cutters that were powerful enough to take off a man's arm with one slice. He also had a fresh Smithwick's; he must keep a refrigerated stash here at the storage facility too. I snipped off the lock with ease and I pushed Norman aside. With my gun once more in my right hand, I lifted the door with my left.

Inside I found... not what I had expected. There was no truck, no 1929 Phaeton 8 Packard Black Beauty, once owned by George "Bugs" Moran, nor was there any loot that had been stolen from lake homes. What we did find stunned us both; I looked at Norman.

"Son of a bitch," he said. He took a gulp from his bottle of Smithwick's and then repeated, "Son of a bitch."

Chapter Forty-Eight

CHICAGO, ILLINOIS

A lone Chicago police detective, armed with enough weaponry to take down an entire SWAT team, entered the front gate to the compound of Aroldis Gonzales Garcia. The men who manned the entrance knew Jacob Tandy by sight. He had often come to this location, bringing information, dropping off contraband, or merely picking up his bimonthly allowance.

The security guard who buzzed him into the front gate thought nothing of the harsh look on the man's face. He often appeared to be mad at the world. Many times, they'd seen the corrupt cop with some companion, another man who would then be introduced to their bosses. Most often these men were fellow cops or city officials who were anxious to cooperate with the Cubans, and become another entry on the cash payroll, but tonight the veteran was alone.

If all worked well, the guard would believe Tandy, like most recent visitors, was here to meet with their boss to discuss the search for Lieza Patrona. That Tandy was just another dumb cop who'd gotten himself in trouble with gambling debts and drug addiction or was in need of a political favor. Tonight though, he was here to sell his soul and extricate himself out of the deep pit he had dug for himself with his bad choices.

Tandy knew what he must do immediately after he entered the fenced-in small yard that served as the pat-down area. One guard would man the front door, while a second would search the cop for his weapon before he was allowed inside of the building.

He hoped the element of surprise would give him the edge he needed. After two steps inside the gated area, Tandy shot both men dead. The body of the guard manning the door fell backward and acted as a doorstop, allowing the cop to drag the bodies inside the building. If luck were with him this evening, no one would be watching the security cameras, or else the night would not bode well for him.

Inside, Tandy took the stairwell to the second floor, where he edged open the metal fire door of the stairwell and peeked through the crack. He approached the first door on the right in the short hallway. He could hear two men talking; the sound of a television reverberated through the closed door. He sprang into the room, and within seconds, three more guards lay dead.

His plan was to just shoot them all, and, if possible, make the chieftain squirm before eliminating him last.

Floor by floor, he moved his way up the building until he was at the top; just steps before him was the door to the Cuban's living quarters.

He could hear two men speaking Spanish and smell the aroma of cigar.

Tandy thought to himself, Most likely there will be a couple of guards with Garcia besides El Tercero. Maybe even a couple of broads. But, then again, it might be too early for women. I'll go in low and get the guards first, then El Tercero, and finally the boss.

He readied himself, placing his second gun into his left hand and then he sprang through the door like a catapulted stone.

When it was over, five men lay dead: two bodyguards, one who had managed to get off several shots before being mortally wounded; Santo Sotto, also known as El Tercero, El Hombre's misnamed second-in-command; and the Cuban crime boss himself.

Aroldis Gonzales Garcia, still seated, lay slumped in the chair. A hand-rolled cigar smoldered on the vest of his fine wool suit. The stub had been pushed from his mouth after his last surge of breath expelled it from his lips and forced it upon his chest. The blood that flowed from the wound in his right temple and from elsewhere on his body dripped onto his favorite chair. It puddled on the cushion, but it was hardly noticeable to the naked eye as it blended with the fine red leather. With little dignity, the head of Chicago's most notorious crime family had died, fittingly, in a wave of violence.

The smell of cigar smoke and gunpowder residue lingered in the now-quiet room. Silence reverberated. The final corpse in the room was that of Officer Jacob Andrew Tandy, a twenty-seven-year veteran of the Chicago Police Department. Two bullets had pierced his chest, which was unprotected by body armor of any kind.

In death, Tandy's bow-legs appeared more accentuated.

Chapter Forty-Nine

Geneva, Wisconsin

In the garage there were only three objects: the first was Fred Smith's 100cc Yamaha 1000 dirt bike, whose engine, I had been told, purred as softly as a contented fat cat, and the second was one Bushmaster XM-15 semi-automatic rifle that presumably belonged to Mr. Fred Smith, which may have been used last night to gun down the two Cuban would-be assassins. But it was the third that stunned Norman and me. Lying on the dirt floor with a bullet hole in his head was the body of Mr. Fred Smith himself.

An eternity passed. Then I said to Norman, "I'm sure glad we are in Williams Bay and not my town."

Norman grumbled loudly.

I asked him, "What was that for?"

"Sorry, Chief, but you're wrong. We are in Geneva. Don't you recall? The entrance to Staunton's property is in the bay, but these two back buildings straddle the town line. We are standing in your jurisdiction."

"Damn it!" I yelled. "One murder a year is one too many, but three in two days? That's just obscene!"

"Three murders? What are you talking about?"

"Last night, two men were killed right before my very eyes, but I didn't see the shooter, nor do I know who it is for sure. Presumably, it was our friend here, Fred Smith. That's all I can tell you right now."

After my call to the stationhouse, Dorothy sent Geary to the scene of the crime to await the County Coroner and CSI team. They

263

had been busy the last twenty-four hours: two dead bodies by gunshot, and now they would have to deal with a third. I didn't have to wait around to learn the cause or time of death for Smith. I had seen the gunshot wound in his forehead, and I figured he'd been killed sometime after the shootout at the farm.

Alone after I dropped Norman off at the Bayside, I began thinking about resigning my current post and rejoining the Chicago Police Department, where the murder rate wasn't quite so elevated.

Sometimes, I thought my officers secretly wished the crime rate in the town of Geneva was as high as Detroit or St. Louis. It would relieve their boredom, make things more exciting, and give them fodder to toss around when talking to their friends at their local hangout. The banality of a missing vintage car or burgled lakefront mansions doesn't quite give them the proper satisfaction they feel they deserve. If my musings about my men were correct, then their wishes had come true. Per capita? I was sure Geneva had now become America's murder capital.

But if Smith had killed the Cubans, then who had killed Smith—and why? I knew this: In order to tie up loose ends and ensure there were no paths leading back to the mafia dons, the mob usually took out the assassins who had been hired to rub someone out. I knew that as a fact; I saw it in The *Godfather Part II*. Did someone hire Smith to kill the Cubans, and then kill Smith in return? If that were the case and the mob was involved, then the assassin's body would end up in a trunk of an abandoned car in a parking lot at O'Hare Airport. That was the outfit's M.O. Could it have been someone in Gonzales Garcia's group, like El Tercero? Someone wanting to see him go down, so they could take command of his illegal activities?

With Smith dead, and questions and theories whirling around in my head like the blades of a Waring blender, I sped back to Casa Blanca to talk with Theo and Annie.

Chapter Fifty

Geneva, Wisconsin

Red Chimney Road is a narrow, steep road that leads from Highway 50 down a quarter mile to Lake Como. There, situated on a doglegged bend on the shore, is the French Country Inn. To get to Casa Blanca it is more direct to take the route down South Como or even Schroeder Road, but I decided I would drive past the inn, hoping I would see something new.

Smith was dead, the Cubans were dead, and Theo and the women were at my place, so I can't say what I expected to see. Nothing, I presumed, and nothing was what I found. The dirt bike was in the garage. The only thing missing was Smith's truck. I circled through the property and parked in the east lot.

I wished it were night instead of midafternoon. If it had been, I would back the Jeep into my favorite secluded spot across from the inn, reach under the front seat, and hope that by having a little vodka or brandy I would relieve the tension that was starting to accumulate in my neck and shoulders. Perhaps I would enjoy a little nap too. Even with the sun shining through the windshield, I closed my eyes for an attempt at sleep. I was unsure if I'd succeeded or not, but the stillness of the moment was interrupted by the blowing of a horn.

It was Bert Burr. His vehicle was next to mine, facing the opposite direction so that our driver's side windows were next to each other.

"Are you all right?" he asked. "I've been looking for you. I thought I might find you around here."

"I'm okay. What's going on? Why didn't you just radio me?
"I didn't want it to go out on the airways for everyone to hear. So I drove here."

"Why didn't you call me on my cell?"

"I did. Norman Bates answered it. He didn't know how it ended up in his jacket. He thought that with all the confusion he may have picked it up by accident when he got out of your car at the Bayside Motel."

"The jackass must have mistaken it for a Smithwick's."

"I picked up the phone from him and headed directly here, and then I was going over to your place."

Bert's tone and composure seemed to be smug, as if he were holding back some big news, news that only he knew. The look on my face must have been enough to get him to spill the beans, because he began to explain in earnest.

"Chief, I know you think my theories are wild and unfounded, but I'm sure it's Donnert who is behind the burglaries. When I couldn't get hold of you, I put all of our men out there looking for him. He's involved. I don't know to what extent, but he's involved."

"Good job, Bert. You may be right, but I think he is involved a lot deeper than just the burglaries. Get the description of the truck out to everyone and Donnert's car too. Have Geary and Shea take the east quadrant, you and Ovalle south. Scatter everyone else throughout the township."

"Will do, Chief. Where will you be?"

"I've got a theory of my own to pursue."

My first stop was back to Casa Blanca. The place was as solemn as funeral parlor with only three grieving attendees. Yes, there were dead bodies, but none that we cared about.

Annie was quiet and distant, barely saying a word to me, except to tell me Sophie went down for her second nap of the day. The poor thing had been so traumatized she could barely function.

Out on the porch, Theo was on his burner phone, talking to his partner in Chicago. When I stuck my head through the door, he cupped his palm over the receiver and said he was trying to dig up info on Fred Smith.

"Will you please make a pot of coffee while I freshen up?" I asked Annie. When I was finished with my five-minute shower and a change of clothes, I poured the freshly brewed java into my Thermos.

"How long has Theo been on the phone?"

"About a half hour. I thought you said he uses words sparingly." I smiled and answered, "I guess he has a lot to say about last night's events."

"Where are you going?" Annie asked. "I've got a couple of hunches and I want to see how they play out."

"Please be careful. I'm worried for you, still worried for all of us." I gave her a peck on the forehead, and said I thought the worst was over.

On my way out I motioned to Theo, putting my pinkie and thumb up to my ear and mouthing the words "call me." He nodded.

Before I could jump into the Jeep, Hurlbut pulled up in front of the house.

I asked him, "What happened to the meeting we were supposed to have the other day? Did you get lost on the way to my office?"

He didn't answer and I didn't care.

"Chief, I've got a couple of agents coming up from Chicago. We are going to escort Lieza Patrona back to the city and take over protective custody of her."

"Good luck with that," I said sternly.

"What do you mean?"

"I mean good luck trying to pry her loose from Theo Boycek, even if the danger is now diminished." I trusted Theo to sort it all out.

There was too much for me to do than to stick around and see who got the better of whom between Agent Ron Hurlbut and Detective Theo Boycek. I'd put my money on the Pole. I jumped into the Jeep before Hurlbut could say anything more.

The now-overcast sky made it appear to be later than it was. Darkness was approaching. The hunches I mentioned to Annie were in reality only singular, and I was on my way there. First, I made a quick stop at Nathan's house. I prayed he would be home so I wouldn't have to stop at the stationhouse to have Dorothy help me.

A beep of the horn brought Nathan out to the front stoop. "Probably watching reruns of *Star Trek*," I muttered to myself.

"What's up, Chief?"

"Get your iPad. I need you to find something for me."

While he went inside I sat on the stoop. He returned and sat next to me.

"Find the township for me on one of those map places."

"Geneva township?"

"No, Klingon township you…"

I stopped myself before an insult could shoot from my lips.

"Of course Geneva," I said.

He moved his fingers around the screen and the map of the township appeared.

"Okay, good," I said. "Now zoom in over here." I pointed to the screen to an area north of County Road KD, where the meth house was located.

"Can you get me closer?"

He enlarged it to thrice the size.

"Here's what I'm looking for."

Before me, on the little screen was the meth house and roads throughout the property.

"Where does this go to?" I asked Nathan.

"This is a dirt road that leads to the back end of Lake Delavan," Nathan said. "If you follow it, you will end up on a deserted service road that leads to Highway 43. I think the state highway department trucks used it at one time. It's abandoned now."

"And how do you know all of this?" I asked.

With a grin resembling the cat who'd eaten the canary, Nathan said, "Chief, ya know, I don't spend all of my time watching reruns of *Star Trek*. I have a life too."

I flew off the stoop saying, "Great, Nathan. This is really helpful. I owe you big time."

So the little nerd has a real life too. He and his buddies probably have beer parties on those remote, deserted sites. Making out with their girls, acting stupid, doing all the dumb things a red-blooded American teen was supposed to do.

The sun was beginning to set, and I sped north, then west. With the importance of moving and guarding Theo and Sophie, the surveillance of Fred Smith and the insinuation of Agent Hurlbut into our lives, the meth lab we'd nearly busted last week had fallen far off of our radar.

The property was a perfect location for a couple of guys to hide out and run a lab to produce illegal drugs. We wouldn't have even realized it was there if it had not been for the phone call that had come into the stationhouse from a disgruntled client. Once we busted the place, I'd been positive no one would return, and I was sure my crew felt the same.

But it was Donnert who'd showed interest in the place, and I played right into his hands, telling him to keep an eye on the property, but not spend too much time there.

My hunch: Donnert was indeed the perp. He had Smith's truck with the Bugs Moran car inside of it and the burgled loot inside of the car, kind of like a real-life, inanimate turducken, but more foul than fowl.

The land surrounding the meth lab was a handsome spot to hide, out of view of prying eyes and nettlesome curiosity seekers. There were copses of trees and thickets of high brush; dirt roads and paths wove throughout the property and led to who knows where. It was such a great spot to hide out that I'd briefly considered it as a safe house for Theo and Sophie.

Just off the main drive to the house, I backed the Jeep into a secluded space that seemed like it was the twin brother of the one across from the French Country Inn. Hell, the whole darn farm was a secluded spot. The angle of the parking spot afforded me a view of the long approaching road and a couple of other driveways. I was especially concerned with the secondary road, the one that Nathan showed me on his iPad that led to a service road that entered Highway 43. Highway 43 would take one south and west, eventually hooking up with Interstate 57 or 55, straight on down to Alafair, Louisiana.

I lowered the front seat to a more comfortable position, and, from the Thermos, poured myself a cup of the coffee Annie had made for me. There would be no reaching under the front seat to pull out the flask of vodka. I wanted to be alert and smart tonight. Through my binoculars I looked around the area. I should really invest in some night-vision binoculars, I thought. Hey, I'm the Chief of Police. Like a good Chicago bureaucrat, I figured the township, not I, should foot the bill.

My Remington 870 Shotgun rested at my side next to the Thermos; I knew I might be doing some big game hunting this evening.

If I were correct, I'd have my culprit. If I were wrong, the night would be a colossal waste of time, and I would have to indulge in the flask of vodka to deaden my senses.

An hour or so had passed—I'd almost fallen asleep—when I spotted a vehicle with only parking lights illuminating its approach. Damn. I was expecting Smith's truck. The car turned right down a narrow path. Through the binoculars, I could still see its taillights in the distance. Just as I was about to give pursuit, the car stopped. I left the Jeep and stepped to the side, about ten feet from my door. The tail lights went out and I couldn't determine if the car was moving or not. Then a set of headlights went on. Another vehicle, a truck with high beams, began driving in my direction.

Quickly I ran back to the Jeep and drove down the road, turning it sideways to block the approaching truck. I exited and stood next to my vehicle. When the truck neared, I fired a shot into the air, cocked the shotgun and shot a second round high above the cab of the truck. When it came to a halt, I could see Officer Ral Donnert's face behind the wheel.

I pointed the barrel of the shotgun directly at him. He exited the cab, placed his hands in the air and said, "Chief, it's me, Donnert. I found the truck with all of the lakefront loot in it. It's in the back with the Moran car, too. I'm pretty sure I know who it belongs to. It's that Smith fellow we've been watching."

I considered executing Donnert right there on the spot. No trial, no appeals, no possible governor's pardon. Then I remembered Wisconsin had no death penalty, so I thought otherwise. I could be a good guy when I wanted to be.

Chapter Fifty-One

Donnert was right: the eighty-five year old Phaeton 8 Black Beauty once owned by Chicago gangster George Bugs Moran was in the trailer of Fred Smith's truck. In the backseat and trunk of Moran's vehicle was the remaining booty from the burgled lakeside homes.

Once the vehicle was thoroughly searched, a dark blue nylon bag containing $27,000 in cash was also found. Donnert had $2,011 in his wallet. He had no good explanation for why he had so much money on him.

Funny how this had all worked out. I was so sure of my hunch that Donnert had ditched the truck in the sprawling woods behind the meth house that I hadn't even put out an all-points bulletin for Smith's missing truck. At the very least, I'd thought it would surface somewhere right here in Geneva, or elsewhere in Walworth County.

The seeds of my hunch, I must admit, came from the nuggets sowed by Bert Burr. He had been correct all along; Officer Ral Donnert was not who he appeared to be.

Now back in a holding cell at the stationhouse, I Mirandized Donnert and he hesitantly waived his right to an attorney. The glib ones often did. For most of their life, they'd been able to talk their way out of a situation. Even when faced with a capital crime, they believed they could continue that trend.

Our best efforts could not pull Donnert from his story that he was taking the truck to headquarters when I intercepted him. He swore he knew nothing of the Fred Smith murder—not even when faced with enough evidence that would have gotten him the death penalty, back in his home state of Louisiana; he still held firm. We presented all of the evidence, most of it some intersection of lies and fact: fingerprints, eyewitnesses, phone wiretaps. Bert told him we had been tailing him for weeks. I backed it all up with a few lies of my own.

When Donnert realized Bert and I were not going to buy his tale about finding the truck in the woods and then driving it to the stationhouse, he switched to another tale. He claimed that he didn't know the merchandise was the stolen loot from the lakefront homes. He said he had been paid to deliver the truck and its cargo to an antique collector and car aficionado in Memphis, Tennessee. The two-thousand and change in his wallet was payment to take the goods to Memphis. He continued to cling to his claim of not knowing anything about the murder of Fred Smith.

Donnert was clever and smart. He had enough talent to forge all the necessary documents and was clever enough to pull off grand theft auto from a guy who had pulled off a grand theft auto of his own, perpetrated a couple of high-end burglaries, and murdered a street-savvy Chicagoan with serious mob ties. His knowledge of antiques was impressive. He had known to steal the Stanford White frame while leaving behind the fake Salvador Dalí, but he had lacked the overall common sense to plan an effective exit strategy.

We wore him down minute by minute, but it was Bert who was the clever one, conning the con man.

"Are you aware, Donnert, that although Wisconsin does not have a death penalty, the law has a loophole in it? If a murder is committed by someone who is a resident of another state, a state where the death penalty remains legal, then under those circumstances, the death penalty is permissible in Wisconsin."

Bert was so convincing that I almost believed his phony assertion myself. He said he had the authority from the district attorney to waive the death penalty, but would do so only if Donnert came clean about everything, including Smith's murder.

Hoping to gain favor with the DA and avoid the phony death penalty, Donnert told us everything he knew. He cricked his neck from side to side and sat in silence. Then, all at once, the words flowed from his mouth like watered-down ketchup from a longneck bottle.

He began: "Ralph Donnert is, or I should say was, a Louisianan police officer and the half-brother of Harold "Hal" Donnert, the Chief of Police of Alafair, Louisiana, population eight-hundred and seventy-two. During a fit of drunken rage, the two half-brothers argued over stolen money and goods, and Hal stabbed his half-brother Ral to death. I helped Hal dump Ral's body deep in bayou country."

"If you're not Ralph Donnert, who are you?" I interrupted.

"Storey is my name, Carver Storey. I was a local thief, confidence man, and forger, and I'm presently wanted by the Louisiana authorities for a string of robberies."

"You mean burglaries, correct, not robberies?" Bert interjected. He looked at me with an I-told-you-so glance, reminding me that Donnert didn't know the difference between burglary and robbery.

I said nothing, except, "continue."

"It was my money and stolen loot the Donnert brothers had argued over. With a little bit of bribery and a whole lot of blackmail, I convinced Hal to allow me to assume Ral's identity. Hal agreed provided that I, his "new" brother, leave not only the state of Louisiana, but the entire South. We forged some documents and created an excellent law enforcement resume and a phony multiracial heritage that was my own true bloodline, creating a new and improved Ral Donnert, I headed north along the I-55 Corridor.

"Before leaving Alafair, under the name Ralph Donnert, I sent out twenty-two resumes to small, rural police departments throughout the Midwest, seeking employment in the field of law enforcement. My number one criteria was that the department had to be located in or near resort areas or well-heeled towns, ones that I considered, as they say in Alafair, 'Easy pickins where the pickins is easy.'

"You know, Chief, you were the only one of the twenty-two who nibbled on the bait that I cast out requesting employment."

I was embarrassed by his almost taunting words. Storey had cast out his bait and now it was me who was stuck with bits of bayou worm in my teeth. But I had a really good reason for hiring him. Acting on a directive from the US EEOC, the state of Wisconsin was to encourage minority hiring in the law enforcement community, especially in towns with populations of ten thousand residents or less. The encouragement was in the form of raw tax dollars, given to qualifying departments for the hiring of minority police officers. There were certain amount of dollars granted for the hiring of an African American, a lesser amount for Hispanics, and an even lesser amount for other minorities—you talk about discrimination, this program was rife with it.

Donnert's law enforcement resume was unimpressive, to say the least, except for the one very big item—or actually three. When I saw it I'd felt as though I'd won the Irish Sweepstakes, even though the Irish didn't qualify for the minority-hiring tax dollars. Donnert, or rather the real Carver Storey, was one-third African American, one-third Choctaw Indian and the rest French and Spanish, and he had the pedigree and the proper forged paperwork to prove his lineage. It was an easy decision for me, a three-for-the-price-of-one deal.

When I hired Donnert I felt a bit like a Cook County Democrat who had just taken a bribe from an intimidated businessman. In my greed for more tax dollars, and after making only one perfunctory inquiry to brother Hal, I'd hired Ralph Donnert on the spot. It was a case of sloppy due diligence and total laziness on my part. I did it for the money, and I wasn't particularly proud of it, especially not now.

"Go back to the beginning and tell us about Louisiana." I prompted Storey.

"Back in Alafair, I had quite the reputation. The locals called me Creole Carver, Carver the Cat, and my personal favorite, Second-Story Carver Storey. It was a name I'd earned for my predilection of entering the houses I burgled through second-floor windows. You know, Chief, you ridiculed everyone who used the term 'cat burglar,' but there is such a person as a cat burglar. It's me.

"And yet here I am, caught red handed by a small-time cop in a bum-fuck town in a truck filled with over a hundred thousand dollars in stolen goods and cold cash."

"Yep," I said to myself.

It didn't get any dumber than that, unless of course you considered my own stupidity for hiring an officer without fully checking up on his background. The worst thing about the whole situation? For the rest of my life I would have to listen to Bert Burr boast about having known all along that Ral Donnert was a fake and a charlatan.

Bert was correct, so I guess he deserved the praise, even if it had to come from himself. The perp sat in his chair, collected and smug. It was almost as if he were bragging. Like he was proud of what he had pulled off; his only remorse was in getting caught.

"How much contact did you have with Fred Smith? I asked.

"All on my own I became suspicious of Fred Smith," Storey said. "I followed his every move, much of the time while I was on duty supposedly patrolling the township. After that, things just got out of control. As clever and careful as Smith was, he apparently was unaware that I was tailing him almost every day and night. Having no respect for us easy-to-outwit local police can lead to, what's the word? Complacence, that's it. Complacence can lead to carelessness.

"It's a funny thing. It all started when I fell in love with that Yamaha 1000 with the quiet engine. It broke my heart to leave it in the garage, but there just wasn't enough space in the truck."

It "broke his heart" to leave the bike behind? I thought. How sad he offered no remorse for killing Smith.

"It's funny. I left the Bushmaster XM-15 Rifle behind because it scared me; it looked too deadly."

That was funny, if black comedy was your sense of humor. In cold blood, the bastard could take a man's life, but the appearance of a semi-automatic rifle scared him into leaving behind a thousand-dollar piece of equipment.

Carver Storey continued. "Through my surveillance of Fred Smith, I figured that the Bugs Moran car was in the back of Smith's truck. The locks at the storage facility were easy for me, a skilled professional, to pick, as were those at Smith's rooms in The French Country Inn and the Bayside Motel. Even the kryptonite locks on the rear door of the truck were no match for me.

"I planned to use the Moran car as a gift to my faux brother Hal Donnert so that I would be allowed to return to Alafair, where I could change my identity back to Carver Storey and hide out in the bayou with the crawfish, mosquitoes, and whatever friends my money could buy. There I would remain in total anonymity until the heat was off."

His words, I was surprised, were florid and descriptive, as if he had been well read or well-schooled.

"Not that it matters, Chief, but there was no premeditated intent in my killing of Fred Smith; it just happened on its own. I didn't even know about the money in the nylon bag until Smith offered to split it with me if I let him go. It was like a thirty-thousand-dollar bonus."

He spoke as if he had no part in any of this matter at all. Not the murder of Smith, the burglaries of the lake mansions, or the plotting to flee back to Alafair. The entire time he was spilling his guts, Bert and I kept looking at each other, tacitly agreeing that Storey was an intelligent psychopath.

I always suspected that Smith was more than a tourist who was simply visiting the lake region to get away from the stress of the city. I made him for the theft of the Moran car, and a little part of me thought he could be the lake home burglar too, probably because I had no other suspect.

The doubts originally planted by Bert Burr had never taken hold, however. I had no true suspicions that Ral Donnert was the culprit. I simply figured it was another one of Bert's bogus theories, like his research into the Beast. I'd told myself one of my officers could not be the notorious villain—the so-called cat burglar. But here he was before my very eyes: one Carver Storey a.k.a. Ral Donnert—burglar, thief, con man, and cold-blooded killer.

Just as Bert had suspected, Storey had hatched his plan after working security during the house walk and fundraiser. He planned and perpetrated the crime alone and stored the items in the basement of the home he'd rented right here in the Town of Geneva. He'd planted the smallest and least valuable of the loot in the meth lab house, which he'd stumbled across while driving around the township in order to familiarize himself with the area. He was the one who'd tipped off the occupants that the police were coming, then he'd planted the stolen booty and called the stationhouse about the location of the house. He was clever and innovative, right down to the detail of leaving the pot of marinara sauce on the stove.

Bert and I made a half-hearted attempt to pin the murders of the two Cubans on him too, more to scare information out of him than anything else. But Donnert genuinely had no idea what we were talking about, and had nothing to offer regarding Smith's whereabouts when the Cubans were shot dead.

"Look, Chief, I've already admitted to killing Smith. I don't know nothing about any Cubans. Last night, strictly by accident, I saw Smith on his cycle. I tailed him to the Bayside Motel then followed him to the storage garage.

"It was there that I approached Smith and then shot him with a drop revolver. I always kept one with me back home to use if I needed to drop it at a scene to incriminate someone else. Afterward, I just panicked, took the truck with Moran's car inside, packed up my belongings along with that good loot from the lakeside homes, and was planning to head south for the oncoming winter. I couldn't spend one of these Midwest winters up here. I had to get back to the South, humidity and all. I stashed the truck deep in the woods behind the meth lab. If it hadn't been for you standing there with that shotgun I may have gotten away with it all and lived a life of leisure in the bayous of Alafair, Louisiana."

I was more exhausted by listening to Storey's confession than he appeared giving it up.

Fred Smith's fingerprints were the only ones on the Bushmaster rifle. Surprisingly, it appeared the weapon had not been wiped clean, and Bert and I both believed Storey's story. Forensics was sure to match the rifle's bore to the bullets lodged in the Cubans' bodies.

The nagging question and one that was hanging out there in the wind like an old undershirt on a clothesline: Why had Fred Smith wanted to keep Lieza Patrona alive?

Chapter Fifty-Two

Geneva, Wisconsin

As it turned out, Lieza Patrona never had to enter the federal witness protection program, she never appeared before the grand jury, and she never got to testify against her former lover. The violent deaths of Celia Jaynes, Leon "the Black Pearl" Du Perles, and Gonzales Garcia's henchmen in the town of Geneva—not to mention my severe beating and impaled eardrum—were all for naught.

Aroldis Gonzales Garcia and El Tercero weren't brought down by Lieza's testimony, nor by the hard work of CPD. It all came down to the bloody work of one rogue cop.

As we split up after our foray in Chicago's mean streets, Tandy had told me he had some "wrongs to right, some sins to confess, atonement to honor." I didn't know what he meant at the time. I thought it was simply the ramblings of a delusional, dirty cop who no longer knew right from wrong, nor could tell his friends from his enemies.

His final words to me were: "I need to... make a decision. It's Yom Kippur soon. I need to atone for my sins."

Tandy's father was Jewish, so I'd thought he meant he was going to pay a visit to a synagogue to atone for his sins. Later, I remembered his mother was Irish, and as a prerequisite to marriage outside her faith, she'd insisted that all the Tandy children were to be raised Roman Catholic.

People are hard to figure out; I think the word is inscrutable. I'd known Tandy for most of my adult life, and I must honestly say I could never figure him out. I've seen him slap around a guy who looked at him the wrong way or said the wrong thing. Minutes later, he could be as kind to another as a caring nun.   Like all people, Tandy had flaws, but his flaws consumed him. They ran his life, took dominion over him and made him what he was. He existed to feed them. I could not figure him out as a person, so it was fitting that I would be unable to figure out his final deed. Unless he reached out from beyond the grave, I knew I'd just never know.

A week or so after the whole rigmarole ended, while on his way to the Upper Peninsula for a fishing trip, Theo Boycek travelled through Geneva Township one afternoon. It was another one of those fine autumn days that I loved so much. We met for a couple of beers on the deck overlooking Lake Como at the restaurant in the French Country Inn. I sat to Theo's left so that I could better hear him through my "good ear," as I now referred to the right one. I was told partial hearing might return to my left, once the scarring had settled down. The only positive side effect of the trauma was when I wanted to ignore comments, especially those made by Bert Burr and other annoying people, I could simply blame it on my hearing loss.

Theo told me the true story—as opposed to the official CPD version that had been released to the media—of what had happened on the night that instantly and infamously became known as the Battle of Bonfield Boulevard.

"It was self-preservation," Theo said. "Self-preservation was Jacob Tandy's motive for the action he was about to undertake. He knew whatever would happen in the matter of his association with the crime lord would not bode well for him. If Gonzales Garcia were indicted by the grand jury, once the case moved up the ladder from city to state to the federal level, the Cuban would certainly turn states evidence and tell all in order to curry favor with the justice department in return for naming names of judges who were on the take and the dirty cops and dirty politicians. Ironically, it would then be Gonzales Garcia who would be the one offered the witness protection program."

"During this whole ordeal, I never really thought about Gonzales Garcia getting the royal treatment while Tandy ended up the fall guy," I said to Theo.

"Me neither," he replied. "I think we were both just trying to stay alive and keep Lieza alive."

Theo continued his narration. He was not his usual taciturn self. He seemed to enjoy telling me the newly-discovered secrets he had learned.

"Tandy was aware that his corruption and collusion with the crime boss would be revealed. The many crimes he committed over the years for the syndicate, the money he accepted from Gonzales Garcia, the evidence he planted on their behalf and the evidence that went missing to protect them would all become public knowledge. Gonzales Garcia, under the scrutiny of the federal agents and most likely with a waiver for self-incrimination, would tell all. When it was finished, Tandy would certainly go to jail and at fifty-one years of age, either from old age or a jailhouse assassin, he would most certainly die in jail.

"If Lieza, like the two other witnesses, was found and murdered, Tandy might have stood a chance, or at least his odds for survival would have increased. But even then, he would have been considered a liability to the Cubans and written off like a bad bank debt. Tandy knew that only way for him to survive would be to take out Gonzales Garcia and his second-in-command, Santo Sotto, El Tercero. But there was a second reason too. Tandy would take out Gonzales Garcia and his criminal cabal because they were the bad guys and in his world, even though he was one of them, the bad guys must lose."

"I agree with you." I told Theo. "Tandy was a bad guy, but in his world, his wrong doings were justifiable. His ethics were situational.

He could do what he wanted because the others were worse than he was, and therefore, the situation allowed him to take whatever action he deemed necessary."

Theo reminded me how Tandy used to ask jokingly: "Why did Kamikaze pilots wear crash helmets?" There was no particular answer of course, it was strictly rhetorical and asked for laughs.

Boycek said, "Tandy's bulletproof Kevlar vest was found at the front entrance of Gonzales Garcia's headquarters, next to the two dead men who were guards at the gate. He had removed it after gaining entrance to the building.

We sat and drank our beers listening to the gentle waves lapping against the shore. In silence we looked out at Lake Como. Then Theo started again.

"It's conjecture, Chief. But I think Tandy had removed the vest for the sake of mobility. But yet I'm conflicted. I believe he may have been on a suicide mission. Part of me believes Tandy intended to kill Gonzales Garcia, El Tercero, and as many henchman as possible and yet still survive the bloodbath. The other part of me thinks Tandy no longer wanted to live in the world he'd created for himself.

"So, you don't really know what you are telling me is fact?" I asked.

"We will never know for sure, because Tandy and his associate are both dead. My own investigation, which included talking to both of his ex-wives, revealed his state of mind and his mood while all this was all going down.

"It's pretty easy to figure this out. If Tandy had been successful in killing the crime boss and had survived, then Smith's marching orders may have been to ensure that Lieza Patrona was eliminated, preferably by the Cuban assassins. All loose ends would have been tied up in an undecipherable Gordian knot. Conversely, if Tandy did not survive or if Gonzales Garcia did, then Smith had to keep Lieza alive.

She would have been the only one who could keep the bad guys from winning. A scenario loathed by Tandy."

I chimed in with my own little summation. "From what I know of Tandy, you may be correct, Theo. If he were to survive the ordeal, in Tandy's distorted mind, he probably thought he would deserve consideration for a bravery citation. That is the twisted logic that could only come from a corrupt cop whose conscience no longer responded to a moral compass. Since he acted alone, he would be free to concoct whatever story his warped little mind could imagine. It was that type of faulty thinking that always got him in untenable positions like his final one."

Then Theo added, "But, most likely, that crazy bastard had originally planned to have Smith kill Lieza if the Cuban assassins had failed, and he himself would gun down Gonzales Garcia and El Tercero. But who really knows for sure?"

Before Boycek could restart his narrative I interrupted him.

"It has always bothered me. Why was the second-in-command called 'El Tercero'? Doesn't that mean the third? Shouldn't he be El Segundo?"

"I once asked that very question of Tandy. He said, when he first got involved with these guys back in the early days before they were organized, there was an El Segundo. He was Gonzales Garcia's cousin and the second-in-command. The boss was El Primero, the cousin El Segundo, and Sotto was El Tercero. At that time they were more like a street gang: disorganized, crude, and dumb. Then one night, Gonzales Garcia whacked some street dealer and the cousin, El Segundo, took the rap for El Primero.

They bribed lawyers, threatened the State's Attorney's family, and corrupted the judge. The murder charges were dropped, and Segundo pled to involuntary manslaughter. He got off with a light sentence, just a couple of years or so, but in prison he was killed by a couple of insane West Side gang members. They stabbed Segundo with a shiv, then cut his throat wide open with a jail-house razor."

Theo cleared his throat as he tinkered with the label on the bottle of the Modelo beer he was drinking. His beefy thumbnail scratched the label until it was unrecognizable. He hesitated for a moment then continued.

"When Gonzales Garcia learned of his cousin's death, he went insane with rage. Not only did he order the killing of the two jailed street gang members, he went on a rampage against the whole gang. He, alone, stalked, captured, and killed eleven gang members in all, each time, personally cutting the victim's throat from ear to ear, sometimes torturing them first. The wounds were so deep on a couple of them that it was almost a decapitation. He wiped out pretty near the whole gang. They don't even exist anymore.

"After killing the gang members, slicing his enemy's throat became his signature trademark. That is why he went to such extreme measures to kill Celia Jaynes and Leon Du Perles that way. That was his intended means to eliminate Lieza too.

"Later, El Tercero asked to be called El Segundo, but his boss said no. The title of El Segundo would be retired in the manner of sports teams, when they retire the number of a favored athlete. No other person, not even the new second-in-command, would ever have the title El Segundo."

"Good story," I said. "I guess it's a real cutthroat business to be in."

Theo didn't find my comment amusing.

Chapter Fifty-Three

Geneva, Wisconsin

The buzz around town was brutal. "Crime Wave Hits Geneva Lakes Area," read the headline of the Lake Geneva Regional News. The Milwaukee Journal blasted: "Chicago Gangland Activity Sweeps Small-Town Wisconsin." It was bad enough that everyone in the state of Wisconsin knew the series of events, but at times it seemed the entire country had been made aware of the fiasco. I felt like I was standing alone in my underwear in the middle of Curly Lambeau Stadium on game day, and hadn't changed my Jockeys as my mother always warned me to do.

Fortunately, the Chicago Tribune, which headlined: "Chicago Crimes Move North," confused my town of Geneva with the larger city of Lake Geneva. Not that it mattered; everyone around here knew the murders and the events happened under my jurisdiction. But, then again, who cared what those doofuses in Illinois thought? The whole state was corrupt. If Gonzales Garcia had survived and became a government witness, he might have ended up in a federal correctional facility with one of the ex-governors of Illinois as his cellmate.

On my credenza was an unopened letter that had been given to me by Theo. Jake Tandy had mailed it to Theo with the instructions to pass it on to me in the event of his death. The letter sat unopened overnight. I was reluctant to read it, but I did not know why. Perhaps I didn't want to know more of the truth. In the past several days I had betrayed more of my adult scruples—I had none as a young man—

than I'd thought I ever could. I'd witnessed a lot of illicit events and buried them deep in my psyche over the course of the last two weeks. I didn't want to learn more details, details that I would have to keep in my brain. I could confess my sins to Father Sabatino, and that would make me square with God, but I was afraid more unwanted truths would permeate my little brain. Details that I could not reveal to anyone, and details that would torment me for years to come.

Men were at their best and at their worst when self-preservation was the goal. Self-preservation was the reason I could not reveal all of the details, and self-preservation was the reason I did not want to learn any more details. Especially concerning Tandy.

If I told Annie everything—the truth about the warehouse incident, the cover up of Jake's murder of my two tormentors, the sloppy police work, the position of jeopardy I had put her, my town, and myself in—it would be disastrous.

And this envelope, most likely Jake Tandy's valediction, would place a lot more unwanted truths in my head.

Like the fool I am, I opened it and read it aloud.

Dear Perry:

I mailed this letter to Theo, and asked him to give it to you only upon my death. It is better that I go this way and take with me the evil that surrounds me.

I have made my peace with Christ, and atoned for my sins by committing more sins. Now I want to make my peace with you. You despise me, yet I still consider you my friend. I know that it will drive you crazy if you cannot figure out what has happened, and how I am involved. What you do with the information is up to you.

Marvin Sandau, the man you know as Fred Smith, is my accomplice. We have been involved with the Cubans for many years. El Tercero sent him to Geneva to steal the Moran car. But I had my reasons for sending him up there too. I knew

*that somewhere along the way Theo would look to you for
help. You are the one person he could always count on.*

*The cartel knew Sandau to be a reliable agent, but what
they didn't know was that he was also working for me.
Depending upon my orders, he was to either protect Lieza
or eliminate her. The part I regret, and that I must confess
to you, is that I told him if either you or Theo got in the
way, you were to become collateral damage. That was how
twisted I had become.*

*But after our paths crossed in Chicago, I decided the bad
guys must not win. It was okay for me to lose, but they,
under any circumstances, must not win. If you are reading
this, then I know that Sandau succeeded in keeping you and
the witness alive. As for Sandau, he will survive—he always
does. He will fade away into the shadows of the world like he
has done before. I am sorry I have left so much destruction
in my wake, but hopefully I have been able to atone for my
past sins. Please forgive me.*

*Also—sorry about putting the GPS locator in your Jeep
when you were in Chicago.*

I ask for your forgiveness.

B'Shalom,

Jake

*P.S. Someday I hope to see you at the big Superdawg in
the sky.*

Superdawg. Now that was funny. Jake loved the hot dogs at
Superdawg, Chicagoland's most famous drive-in. Jake used to eat there
three times a week when he worked the North Side precinct. Summer
or winter he would hold court outside on a picnic bench and eat two
superdawgs with everything on them. "Run 'em through the garden,"
he would always say. I was surprised he hadn't died of a heart attack
years ago brought on by enormously high cholesterol.

"See you at the big Superdawg in the sky." I surely hoped I wasn't going to end up in the same place as my corrupt fellow cop.

Then it hit me. Fred Smith's address that had been driving me crazy: 6363 N. Milwaukee Ave. That was the address of the Superdawg Drive-In. Smith, like Tandy, must have been a fan of the establishment. I wondered if that was where they'd first met.

I reread the letter and smirked. Even in his final hours, Jake was taking no chances. He evoked the name of Christ and wished me peace in Hebrew. He always looked for an angle, a possibility of doubling his chance of success once he reached the pearly gates. I didn't think there was much doubt about where he would end up though. And he was wrong about Fred Smith. He didn't slip into the shadows as Tandy predicted. He never got the chance, thanks to Carver Storey, a.k.a. Ral Donnert. I guessed that was the way it should be. Two more of the bad guys—Tandy and Smith—lost too.

In the envelope with the letter was an old black-and-white picture of me with Jake. It was my first day on the job at the Chicago Police Department. The older Tandy had his arm around my shoulder as if to say, "I'm taking you under my wing, kid." I wondered, had I stayed with the Chicago department, would I have remained under his wing and become as corrupt as him? No one starts off bad, I suppose. They develop that way and grow incrementally into evil.

I was sad over the events of the last two weeks and stayed alone in my home, taking only a few calls and telling everyone I was ill. I wasn't lying. I was ill, sick to my stomach.

Chapter Fifty-Four

GENEVA, WISCONSIN

The French Country Inn is my favorite spot, but it has always been Annie's favorite too, so it was no surprise she asked to meet me there at 5:00 p.m. a couple of days after I received Tandy's final missive. She wanted to talk—the dreaded words that made the knees of the bravest of men shake.

I arrived early, pleased I was the only one at the bar. Rick poured me a Tito's on the rocks. I eschewed the olives; I didn't want anything to get in the way of the effects of the booze. While nursing the vodka, random thoughts travelled through my bruised brain. It had been a tough week: dead bodies strewn across the township; a cop, although a dirty one, also dead; another cop, filthy dirty and an imposter to boot, was in jail; and my reputation was as sullied and damaged as my ego.

And Annie wanted to talk.

I wondered if she wanted to discuss our future together. For the past few months, things between us had been tight. I had taken quite a liking to her. I realized I'd better not say the words "quite a liking," or the evening could end up similar to the one when I said I was "fond" of her. All thoughts of Annie aside, I must admit that I have taken quite a liking to Dawg too, but then we go back a lot more years then Annie and I do.

Annie entered the room. She looked like a different person than the one I had seen just a couple of days ago. The shades of sadness and sullenness were in her eyes. Wisely, I said nothing, and hoped the look on my face would not reveal what I was thinking.

"Hi Annie," I said.

"Hello, Perry." Her tone was equally as depressed as her appearance. Plus she always called me Chief, never my given name, so I knew something grave was on her mind. Silently I hoped the words "marriage" or "moving in together" would not be forthcoming from her lips.

She signaled Rick, who brought her a vodka rocks.

"Can we go outside? I want to have a private conversation."

Before I could say "sure" the bartender said he was going down to the liquor room to get some stock and if we needed anything to let the bus boy know. We stayed in the bar.

"What's on your mind, Annie? You look so beaten down I don't know what to say to you. I know it's been a tough week, but the worst of it is behind us."

"Us, Perry. There's no us. There is just you, and I simply tag along like the little tomboy neighborhood girl. We go where you want to go, do what you want to do, and talk about the subjects you deem interesting. But I have a life outside of you too. I have a job, I have friends. I have good days and bad days. But do you ever ask about me or how I am feeling? Do you even care about my needs?"

"Of course I do, Annie. I was worried sick when you were in harm's way last week. I don't even know how I would feel if any harm had come to you."

"I don't have to think about how I would feel if harm had come to you," Annie said. "I would be crushed, devastated, not only for now, but for the rest of my life. And that, Perry, is the reason I can no longer be with you. I don't want to be in love with someone who could crush my life. If I love an insurance agent, he could die in a car crash, and I would be crushed. If I love an accountant, he, like anyone else, could die of leukemia, or a heart attack. But with a cop, the danger is too great, even in small, peaceful town such as this."

Sarcasm dripped from her lips when she said "a small peaceful town such as this." It was ironic. I'd moved up here to rural America to get away from the violence and chaos of my hometown Chicago, but it all followed me up here. Instead of saying "You can't go home again," Thomas Wolfe should have said, "Home follows you wherever you go."

At least the dirty, nasty parts of your hometown: the evil doers and gangbangers and child beaters. You can't avoid them. They follow you around like the craven odor of a stinky can of sardines.

People often say when harm comes to someone: "They were in the wrong place at the wrong time." Now, it seemed everywhere was the wrong place at the wrong time.

"Annie, my darling, I'm stunned. I had no idea you felt this way. Is this all coming from last week? That surely was an oddity. If we lived a hundred more years, nothing like that would ever happen again. You must see that."

"It isn't only about last week. I have felt this way for a long time. You are in your own world. Everything revolves around you, and you are happy that way, but I am not. Most of all I don't want to be married to a cop. I don't mean married in the real sense, I just mean I don't want to be involved with a cop. It's too dangerous, and you get yourself in more trouble than Dick Tracy.

"Plus you're completely unemotional. It's like you have a heart of a frozen stone. It may melt for a short time, but then it freezes back up like a tray of ice cubes. Not only that, but—"

I interrupted her. "Okay Annie, you made your point."

She'd made herself clear and I understood her. I didn't want her to continue or else I would have to add her to the list of femme fatales, the roster of women who meant to do me harm.

I considered saying, "I can change," but that would be a big fat lie.

I didn't want to sound too much like Popeye the sailor man, but I thought to myself, I am who I am and what I am. Change was for salamanders and caterpillars. I was happy in my own skin. There were a lot of people who liked me, admired me, and wanted to be around me, and there were others who hated me, despised me, and tried to avoid me.

I might have been able and willing to change an annoying little habit that I had, like hanging up a towel after a shower. I could eliminate altogether a chronic peccadillo or two. But at my age, there was no way I was reinventing myself. There would be no attempt to ingratiate myself to a bunch of people who wouldn't like me no matter what I did.

But for Annie, I would try. She was worth it. I was fond of her, quite taken with her, and most likely in love with her.

"Is this the end, Annie?" I asked. "Aren't we even going to try to make it work?" My words as well as my thoughts were trite like a bad script of a soap opera. I decided to say no more.

"I need some time alone," she said.

I hoped her "time alone" was different from the last time I'd heard those words from a woman. My ex-wife Rita had said she needed "time alone." She spent her "alone time" with one of my best friends and two different pizza delivery boys. When she ordered her pizza with sausage on top, that was exactly what was delivered. I was sure there were a few others to boot, but I didn't like to think about them.

I was hoping I could put Annie behind me too. Our history wasn't nearly as long or as chaotic as mine and Rita's.

Ob-la-di, ob-la-da, life goes on.

Chapter Fifty-Five

Geneva, Wisconsin

A few days after my conversation with Annie, I finally left Casa Blanca. I was no longer feeling sick, and I decided to go out for breakfast. I was enjoying a platter of poached eggs over homemade corned beef hash at my favorite diner, Daddy Maxwell's, located in the neighboring Williams Bay. It was a great place that served homemade food and freshly-baked desserts. The building was uniquely dome-shaped, like an igloo, but the ambience inside was nothing like an ice house; it was as warm as your grandmother's parlor.

Almost two weeks had passed since I'd given Jeanette, Daddy's owner, the bundle of rhubarb given to me by Jerri Martel. Jeanette had turned the unsightly clomp of vegetable into tasty, delightful pies, sold to customers and given to friends and family; I'd indulged myself with one of those pies for several days afterward.

I swabbed up the runny yellow egg yolk with the corner edge of my buttered toast when I noticed a man seat himself at the lunch counter and order a cup of coffee. He was dressed in camouflage fatigues, and a shirt that had more pockets than a person could possibly use. His outfit was similar to the one worn by DNR Administrator Harland Bevis. I wondered if the two men had talked to each other before buying their respective outfits. I'd barely thought about the beaver situation at the Martel farm at all, but remembered Jonah and Jeri would be arriving back home soon.

Daddy Maxwell's was only a couple of hundred yards from the main entrance to the Kishwauketoe nature preserve, a 150-acre natural habitat that was situated entirely within the confines of Williams Bay. Tourists, bird watchers, and nature lovers alike visited the preserve for back-to-nature hikes. Could I possibly relocate the beaver to the preserve? Bevis wouldn't like it, I supposed. Besides, there was no large pond.

Upon leaving the diner, Jeanette handed me a brown paper bag. Inside was a pie, a thank you for the rhubarb I had given her. I hoped the pie was made with a fresher batch of rhubarb than the one I'd previously delivered to her, almost two weeks ago now. Knowing Jeanette's fondness for perfection, I was sure it was.

I placed the bag in my car. When I looked up, I was greeted by the face of a friend of mine; it was Chester Proudfoot. An idea popped into my head like a flashbulb from an old-fashioned camera. I asked Chet for some advice, which he freely gave, and then I asked if he could do me a favor. He said he was available that morning, but first he had to go home. He'd meet up with me in twenty minutes.

"I'll have to pick up my life partner," he said.

As I waited for Chester in front of the Martel house, the still-warm rhubarb pie filled the inside of my Jeep with such an enticing aroma that I could barely resist opening the bag and dipping my fingers inside for a taste. Chester and his companion were going to meet me at the Martel farm. Chet had a plan, and if it worked, the beaver situation would come to an end without controversy.

Chet's pickup drove behind me as we winded through the narrow road that led to the secluded cabin isolated by the pond created by the beaver dam. We parked our vehicles. Chet said his partner would take over from here.

Chet's partner was Fang, a full-blooded North American gray wolf, nature's own predator of the beaver. Fang's appearance was as menacing as the Beast of Bray Road, but his personality was as docile as a cocker spaniel. Chet leashed Fang and marched him around the shoreline of the beaver-made pond. Fang marked the territory with his urine, claiming the site as his own. I watched man and wolf traipse back and forth along the property. It was almost as if Fang were aware of the plan. He wasn't here to harm the beaver, only to force the unwanted intruder to move to a different location, perhaps further upstream where he could create a dam, a pond, and a lodge that didn't infringe upon someone else's rights.

Chester then stripped down to his underwear, unleashed Fang and the two swam to the opposite side of the pond, where Fang started his marking all over again. Chester got into the act too, peeing along the shoreline. He rinsed his hand in the stream and perused the cabin while Fang continued with the business at hand. Chet told me he would bring Fang over later in the afternoon, and then again in the morning. He was certain the beaver would get the idea that the wolf was here to stay.

The area was pristine and tranquil. One would never suspect that only nights ago, the secluded farm had been the scene of a violent shootout and a double homicide. I sat down on a rustic bench that had been created by the falling of a bulky tree trunk. In front of me I threw together a few dried twigs and branches, and with a pile of leaves as tinder, I started a small fire. From the car I retrieved a knife and the pie, from under the front seat I retrieved my flask. I shook the metal container. It was more than half full; I did not even remember replenishing it. I hoped it was brandy and not vodka. Brandy would complement the rhubarb much better.

I returned to my perch on the tree trunk in front of the fire. My thoughts focused on the hapless beaver, assuming he had no clue about the problem he had started.

"Stupid animal," I said, but then I realized he, like us humans, was only doing what came naturally.

Remembering an old joke about the 1950s sitcom *Leave it to Beaver* made me laugh out loud. I wondered if the joke had been first told by comedian Rodney Dangerfield, and if it was in the book I'd returned to Gus. It goes: What was the first line of dialogue ever censored on television? The answer was the words spoken by the mom, June Cleaver: "You were a little hard on the Beaver last night, Ward."

Chet swam back across the pond and sat with his legs folded on the ground in front of the fire, absorbing its warmth. I offered him a hit from the flask, which he gladly took.

He asked about my laughter. I told him the Beaver joke and we both laughed out loud. Then came Fang and the three of us, together, ate the rhubarb pie until it was gone.

ACKNOWLEDGMENTS and NOTES

Thanks to Brenda Errichiello Peregrine for developing and editing my original manuscript and for encouraging me to add more words in order to enhance characters development and their relationships.

Thanks to the entire the staff of the French Country Inn for all their help and kind hospitality. They are an eclectic, eccentric, and extraordinary group; they make the inn a wonderful place.

Thanks to Marie Hix for proofreading assistance on the novel

Thanks to Robert Lindsay for the book design and layout and not getting upset with me when there were last minute changes.

For the record, the character of Chief is an amalgam, inspired mainly by a friend who wishes to remain anonymous. All the peace officers in this book are products of my imagination. The characters bear no resemblance whatsoever to the actual law-enforcement personnel of Geneva Township or Walworth County, who are as dedicated, professional, and honorable as any I have ever encountered.

For you purists, Winston Churchill, during World War II was Prime Minister of England and Minister of Defence, (not Defense) which is Great Britain's version to the U.S. President's Commander in Chief.

There is no Illinois Bureau of Investigation, but I am told at one time there was, but has now become an arm of the Illinois State Police.

"*I'm so tired I can't hear myself drink.*" Page 178, paraphrase. I cannot find who said this first, but the line has been repeated often. I believe it is from a movie by film director and writer W.S. Van Dyke. Sounds like it something Nick Charles may have said.

"In the room the women come and go / Talking of Michelangelo." From *The Love Song of J. Alfred Prufrock*. T.S.Eliot. 1920

"Torture? We don't need no stinkin' torture," Page 235, paraphrase-from the motion picture, *The Treasure of the Sierra Madre,* 1948.

"If you need anything, just whistle. You know how to whistle don't you, Chief? You just put your lips together and...blow." Page 235, paraphrase from the motion picture, *To Have and Have Not,* 1944.

There is no Geneva Lake frontage in the Town of Geneva. The panhandle referenced herein is strictly poetic license.

The source of the beaver joke in the final chapter is unknown to the author. Like so many great jokes it may have come from the Chicago Police Department or right here in the Town of Geneva. Urban Dictionary states it was: "Quote from the the (sic) 1957 TV show "Leave it to Beaver."

ABOUT THE AUTHOR

To those who know him best, Clyde Deighton is the most uninteresting man in world. Taciturn by nature and reclusive by design, he spends most of his time pursuing the life of a novelist and poetaster. Born in the Midwest, Deighton did not stray far from his small village until he was 19. Before he tried his hand at writing, the author was a cucumber salesman, Christmas-tree grower, schoolteacher, and failed piano player. He has no hobbies or interests, but spends copious amounts of time watching 1950s Westerns on television.

Even though he claimed to lack the ambition to write a sequel to *Murder at The French Country Inn,* the author has now published *Man Inn Trouble*, a second novel in the French Country Inn Mystery series.

Deighton seldom travels beyond his home in rural Wisconsin. He does, however, make occasional forays to the Lake Geneva resort area, where he stays at the French Country Inn.